I0452833

The Collector
A Novel

Dick Berman

The Collector. Copyright © 2017 by the PelhamGrp. All rights reserved. Printed in the United States. No part of this book may be used or reproduced in any manner whatsoever without written permission except in the case of brief quotations embodied in critical articles and reviews.

First edition: March, 2017

ISBN 978-0-9987164-0-4

This is a work of fiction. Names, characters, places, and incidents either are the product of the author's imagination or are used fictitiously, and any resemblance to actual persons, living or dead, businesses, companies, events, or locales is entirely coincidental.

To the Inkbloods.

CONTENTS

Moses said, "The Lord says, 'About midnight I will go through every part of Egypt. Every oldest son in Egypt will die. The oldest son of Pharaoh, who sits on the throne, will die. The oldest son of the female slave, who works at her hand mill, will die. All of the male animals that were born first to their mothers among the cattle will also die. There will be loud crying all over Egypt. It will be worse than it's ever been before. And nothing like it will ever be heard again.

Exodus 11.6

PROLOGUE
Tel Aviv
Ten Years ago

TAMARA BURNS WASN'T supposed to be home that day. She was forced to take the day off when the babysitter informed her she would be spending the day with her family, celebrating the holiday. She should have been angry with the sitter for springing it on her at the last minute, but truth be told, she looked forward to spending the day with Saul.

It was just before noon on Monday, the fifth day of Passover, when she strapped one-year-old Saul securely in his stroller. The mother and son left their third-floor apartment, took the elevator to the lobby, and began a leisurely walk to the nearby Lewinsky Gardens.

The sun sat high in the cloudless azure sky as Tamara wove her way through the packed sidewalks, bustling with holiday shoppers. A hint of salt hung in the air from the light breeze blowing in from the Mediterranean Sea. It took her fifteen minutes to reach the park entrance, first passing the large intersection of Salomon Street and Ha-Shomron Street before continuing on Sderot Har Tsiyon.

The laughter from children home on school vacation for Passover, as they romped on the freshly mowed grass, filled the air as she entered the gardens. The park was crowded with families enjoying the holiday, and the unseasonably warm weather. Saul had fallen asleep during the walk so she found an empty spot on the corner of a bench, and sat.

When Saul woke she'd let him play in the grass. Two weeks ago, he took his first tentative steps without holding on to anything. The grass would cushion the inevitable falls as he tested his balance and tried to walk upright. Tamara gazed at her son, and thought how much he looked like his father.

She had met her future husband during their mandatory military service in the Israeli Defense Force. They shared a lot in common. Both their mothers were Israelis, their fathers Americans. They were born in the United States, he in Boston, she in Baltimore. Both believed in the State of Israel as a homeland for the Jews. They each retained their U.S. citizenship, even though both chose to move to Israel after graduating high school, and become Israeli citizens.

While Tamara chose to stay on, her husband left the IDF after his obligatory service and went to college, attending The Technion, the Israel Institute of Technology in Haifa, majoring in Computer Science.

They married before he began his freshman year. She was stationed in Rosh Hanikra, along the border with Lebanon. For the first year, she lived in the female barracks, and they could only see each other on weekends. He couldn't stay with her, so she would ride the bus for an hour and forty-five minutes to reach his apartment in Haifa.

At the end of her husband's third year in college, Tamara became pregnant. The IDF granted her a transfer to Tel Aviv. They still had an hour and forty-five minutes commute, but now they both had apartments, and alternated the weekend travel.

The Mossad, Israel's elite intelligence agency, recruited her husband immediately after graduation. By that time, she'd been assigned to the Intelligence Division of the Israeli Air Force for two years.

Saul's soft whimper brought her mind back to the present. Tamara rose from the bench and started to meander through the park, hoping the gentle rocking of the stroller would lull him back to sleep. It didn't help. After making a complete circuit of the Gardens, he continued to whimper. She checked her watch. It was 1:20. She decided to head home.

He'll nap better in his crib.

As she approached the intersection of Salomon Street and Ha-Shomron Street once again, the aroma of shawarma, the Levantine Arab meat roasting on vertical spits, permeated the air as it wafted from small restaurants along the sidewalk. Her stomach rumbled, and her mouth watered from the fragrance of the cooking meat.

She headed to a restaurant a few doors away on Salomon Street, where she and her husband ate many times, to grab a sandwich for lunch. When he kissed her goodbye that morning, her husband told her he was off on a training mission. He couldn't tell her where or when he'd be home. *I'll bring a sandwich home for him, for whenever he gets there.*

When she reached the entrance, she smiled at the guard standing next to the open door. The restaurant had recently hired him for security after a bombing occurred three months before at a café a block away. He recognized Tamara as a regular, and nodded.

When she peered past the guard into the restaurant, her heart sank. Normally only half full at this time of the day, it was crowded with people having a late Passover holiday lunch. Figuring it could take twenty minutes or more to get a sandwich to go, she decided to try a different place.

As Tamara turned to leave, she heard the guard ask a young Palestinian who just arrived to open his gym bag for inspection. She glanced at them. The young man looked to be in his late teens or early twenties, wearing jeans, sneakers, and a light blue golf shirt. He held a gym bag at his side.

She couldn't put her finger on it but something about the Palestinian put her on edge. Maybe it was because he avoided making eye contact with the guard that she felt a heightened sense of awareness. Her training as an analyst in the Intelligence Division was telling her something about him was off. She became hyper vigilant. Her grip tightened on the stroller's handlebar.

The guard repeated his request to open the bag for inspection. The young man started to open the bag, and as the guard leaned over to look inside, she heard the Palestinian yell, "Allahu Akbar."

"No!" she screamed, but it was too late. The Palestinian chose that moment to blow himself up.

The explosion was the last sound Tamara would ever hear. The bomb tore her body in half. Nails and other projectiles imbedded themselves in Saul's small body, snuffing out his barely lived life. The blast blew the restaurant's sign off the building and shattered car windshields and windows of nearby structures. Glass shards and blood covered the ground. Forty-five meters away, bits of human flesh landed on a car, smearing its windshield with blood.

ERIC BURNS STOPPED to take a sip of water. He'd struggled for the last half-hour as he worked his way toward his objective, traversing the brown, dusty topography of the Negev desert. It was hard work, as his perspiration stained shirt, hat and pants could attest. He had trudged across rocky flat lands, climbed hills and mountains and descended through dry riverbeds and deep craters. He shook the canteen. It sounded half full.

He looked skyward. Based on the position of the sun, he estimated it to be late afternoon and he'd already used half his water supply. He wasn't sure he'd have enough to carry him through.

I've got to ration it better.

He was on a survival training exercise, fifty kilometers from the historic mountain top fortification of Masada. He'd been dropped off at eleven o'clock in the morning with only the canteen of water and a knife. His task... make it back to the foot of Masada before 8:00 p.m.

The Masada location for the exercise was chosen for a reason. It was at that mountain top fortification, between 72 and 74 CE that a band of 900 Jewish Zealots, the last free people in the conquered land of Israel, held out against a Roman Army of over 10,000 soldiers for more than three years. In the end, when they were about to be overrun, they committed suicide rather than surrender and become slaves to the Romans. As a Mossad agent, Burns needed to understand the meaning of what happened there.

The Romans had either enslaved or killed the population of Israel, and after the failure of the Jews to hold off the Romans at Masada, it seemed the Jewish people would fade from history. But that never happened. In fact, the population of Jews began to grow again. Masada symbolized that the Jewish legacy cannot be erased, that Jewish fortune, even at its lowest point, is destined to revive and grow, that Jews are the people of eternity.

Burns' task as a Mossad agent would be to protect the State of Israel, to carry on the Masada legacy of survival against those who would try to erase the Jews.

The engine noise was at least two kilometers away when Burns first heard it. A few minutes later, he spotted its source, a drone, approaching at an altitude of about seventy meters. The unmanned aircraft circled him twice before sweeping down. It made three overhead passes, wagged its wings, and flew off. An hour later, he saw the dust trail of a vehicle coming across the barren desert toward him.

"Get in," his training officer said, pulling alongside Burns after making a 180 degree sharp turn, kicking up a swirl of dust.

"What's going on? Why are you breaking my training?"

"I don't know. I was told to get you and bring you back to Masada. I do as I'm told, and you do as you're told. Get in." They drove back to Masada, the trip made in silence.

They never pull someone out of the exercise unless they're injured. Why me? Why now?

When he arrived at the Mossad base camp at the foot of the mountain fortress, he was ushered to a helicopter, its blades twirling, waiting to take off. Immediately after he strapped himself in and donned a headset, the chopper began to rise.

"Where are we headed?" Burns asked over the intercom when they were no more than fifteen meters off the ground.

"Tel Aviv," replied the pilot.

"Why?"

"Don't know. Got orders to pick up a passenger, obviously you, and bring him to Sde Dov Airport."

Burns turned that over in his mind. Sde Dov. At the northern edge of Tel Aviv proper. It handled only domestic flights. If they were sending him overseas they would have gone to Ben Gurion Airport.

HE TILTED HIS head back, closed his eyes, and let his mind drift back to this morning. It was just after 7:00 a.m. when he paused next to the doorframe gazing at Tamara. She was sitting at the small table in the kitchen of their two-bedroom apartment absorbed in reading the newspaper. The aroma of fresh brewed coffee filled the air.

A bright beam of morning sun spilled through the side window, like a spotlight aimed by the angels on her face and hair. It highlighted the deep-set dimples surrounded by the tiny brown freckles scattered across her cheeks like sprinkled flecks of cinnamon. Her short brown hair glimmered in its glow. He knew it was a cliché but he swore her smile could make the coldest heart melt in seconds.

God she's beautiful.

They'd been married for four years, and Burns still marveled at how lucky he was to have her. Her physical beauty aside, beneath the uniform she wore every day for work lived a very smart woman. A Captain in the Israeli Air Force, she served in the Intelligence Division and from all accounts was a highly respected analyst.

He shifted his eyes to Saul, sitting in his highchair, slapping at a plate of scrambled eggs on the tray in front of him. Burns smiled. It looked like more eggs were on the floor under the highchair than made it into his stomach. Two weeks ago, he took his first steps without holding on to anything. He'd bet the boy would be walking on his own in another two weeks.

"Good morning," she said looking up from the newspaper. "Would you like something to eat?"

"No, thanks. I don't have time."

They usually had very different work schedules and rarely saw each other at breakfast. She had to take today off she told him last night. The babysitter canceled unexpectedly. Something about spending the day with her family.

"I've got to run," he said, bending to give her a quick peck on the lips.

THE CHOPPER BANKING sharply to the right shook him from his thoughts. They were approaching the airport, coming in from the south along the edge of the blue Mediterranean, skirting the hotels, apartment buildings, and marinas dotting the beaches of Tel Aviv. They landed in the military section of the airport, close to a formation of Israeli Air Force jet fighters. As Burns unbuckled his harness and removed his headset, a black sedan pulled up twenty meters away. The driver emerged, waving Burns to the vehicle.

"Get in back," the driver said as Burns approached the vehicle.

"I'd prefer the front."

"Suit yourself. Move it. I need to get out of the landing area."

Burns slid into the front passenger seat, and the driver peeled down the tarmac toward an exit gate.

"Where am I going?"

"The Office," the driver replied. The Office was what everyone in the Mossad called headquarters.

"Know why?" Burns asked.

"No. Mind if I put on the news?" the driver asked, reaching for the radio.

Burns shrugged.

Latest on the terror attack earlier this afternoon. As of now, there are nine confirmed dead, including three children, and thirty-five wounded. Eight of the wounded are in serious condition, doctors saying some of them might not survive.

A witness, Moussa al Zidat said he saw a young man starting to open his bag. The guard began looking in the bag, and then Zidat heard a boom. Another witness, Moses Baakov, said he saw a woman and her child in a stroller standing near the guard killed by the blast.

Officials monitoring the Arab TV network, Al Jezeera, picked up a video broadcast an hour ago from the Islamic Jihad. In it, the elusive terrorist, Hakim Adwar, said he was responsible for planning the bombing and that there will be more such operations with the will of God. The video also showed the suicide bomber, identified as Sami Salim Hammed, 21, from the West Bank village of Arakeh. He was dressed in black and wearing a headband with yellow Quran verses written on it.

Officials said police stopped a car on the highway between Tel Aviv and Jerusalem and arrested three Palestinians suspected of aiding the bomber.

We shall, of course, continue to use all means at our disposal to prevent every other attempt said the Prime Minister in a statement issued twenty minutes ago.

Now to our reporter at —"

The driver reached over and shut off the radio. "Sorry, but I really don't want to hear any more about this."

"When did it happen?" Burns asked, gesturing toward the radio.

"About 1:30 this afternoon."

"Those bastards. I hope we blast the shit out of them," Burns said.

Neither man spoke for the rest of the trip as the car made its way to the Office. When they pulled up to the building, the driver said, "This is as far as I go. You'll be met inside."

Burns entered the building. He'd never been to the headquarters before.

He approached the security desk. "I'm Eric Burns. I was told to report here."

"I.D.?" the guard asked.

"Don't have any. They just pulled me out of the field from a training mission."

"Hold on." The guard typed on his computer. He looked down at his monitor for a few seconds and glanced up at Burns.

"Okay. The elevator is through there," he said, pointing to a non-descript grey door with no markings. "Take it to the sixth floor. You'll be met there." When Burns approached the door, he heard a click, the guard releasing the lock.

He took the elevator to six and stepped out into a bland lobby. He recognized the man waiting.

"Burns. I'm Gideon Ben-Ami, Director of Operations." He held out his hand.

"Yes, sir. I recognized you." They shook hands.

"Come with me," Ben-Ami said, gesturing toward a door in the wall. Burns heard a whoosh as hydraulics opened the door. They walked down a corridor and entered Ben-Ami's office. He pointed to a seat in front of his desk. Burns took it. Ben-Ami closed the door and slipped into his chair behind the desk.

"Why am I here sir?" Burns asked as soon as Ben-Ami was seated.

"Did you hear about the bombing this afternoon?"

"On the radio driving here from the airport."

"Son, there's no easy way for me to tell you this. Your wife and baby were there. Both of them were killed."

Burns felt the scream build inside. He opened his mouth to let it escape. But nothing emerged; the scream remained deep in his chest. He wanted to scream. He needed to scream. He just couldn't get it out.

In seconds, his mind ran the gamut of shock, disbelief, and then numbness. The acid which formed in his stomach rose in his chest and burned his throat. A sense of emptiness, a hollow feeling spread through his body, overwhelming his senses. He tried to push himself from the chair, to run from this office and the man telling him this horrible thing. But his legs and arms felt like rubber, and he slumped back.

He closed his eyes and pictured Tamara this morning, lifting her lips for his kiss goodbye. Saul sitting in his highchair, the scrambled egg she made for him scattered on the floor beneath him. They'd laughed at the mess.

He needed to focus on something, an anchor to ground himself. He tried to stare at Ben-Ami, but his vision was blurred with tears, their rivulets trickling down his cheeks.

"Did ... did they suffer?" he asked, his voice cracking.

Ben-Ami rose, grabbed a handful of tissues from a box on the credenza behind him, came around his desk, and handed them to Burns.

"No. As I hear it, she was no more than two meters from the bomb. If it's any comfort, it would have been instantaneous for both of them."

"Can I see them? Their bodies?"

Ben-Ami shook his head. "You don't want to see them. They were too close to the bomb. Remember them as they were when you last saw them."

Ben-Ami placed his hand on Burns' shoulder. "I know there's nothing I can say that will make this any better for you. I can't even imagine what you're going through right now. I want you to take as much time as you need. When you're ready, come back to us. You have but to ask, I'll give you any assignment you want."

Ben-Ami walked to the door, stopped, and turned back to Burns. "I'll give you some time to yourself. Sit here. Take as long as you need. I'll be down the hall, second office from the end. Come find me when you're ready."

Burns slumped in the chair after Ben-Ami left the office, his mind trying to deal with what happened, their deaths... sudden, violent, final and incomprehensible. Tamara gone... their shared plans and dreams no longer possible. Saul, with big bright eyes, a happy child, always smiling... gone.

He didn't know how much time had passed before he rose from his seat and walked to the window. Dusk had settled on the city. On the street below, he watched people move about, couples hand in hand, parents wheeling baby carriages, women walking, their arms laden with shopping bags. Burns couldn't understand how everyone else was able to go on about their daily routine when his world had stopped...come to an end.

As he stood staring outside, he felt something else building within. Anger. No, not just anger. Rage. Rage for the people responsible for their murder. Not only the bomber, but everyone connected to him. Vengeance. He wanted vengeance. He realized at that moment, he'd lost his self. Gone was the person he used to be.

In his mind, he replayed the offer Ben-Ami made before leaving the office. He swung away from the window and marched down the hall to the second office from the end. When he pushed open the door, Ben-Ami was at his desk talking on the telephone.

"I'll have to call you back," Ben-Ami said, and disconnected the call.

Burns squared his shoulders. "You said all I have to do is ask, and you'll give me any assignment I want. Did you mean it?"

"Yes."

"Then I want to be trained as a *kidon*," he said, arms by his side, fingers curled tight into fists. "God visited plagues on the Egyptians, but it took the tenth and final one, unleashing the Angel of Death, to free the Israelites. I will become the reincarnation of the tenth plague, a Mossad assassin, a new Angel of Death."

Burns' eyes blazed with fury. "You will unleash me on every terrorist and terrorist supporter until, like the ancient Egyptians, they cry for mercy and leave Israel in peace. I will be worse than anyone has ever been before, and nothing like me will ever be again."

PART ONE

CHAPTER 1
February 15
Saturday Morning
San Salvador
The Present

"He just checked into the hotel."

The call from Miguel Sanchez, the desk clerk at the Hilton Princess Hotel, came at 3:32 in the afternoon.

"Are you sure?"

"He's not using the same name, but he looks just like the picture on the flyer I got last week."

"How long is he booked for?"

"Two days."

"Is he still there?"

"Yes. He went straight to his room after checking in, and I haven't seen him leave."

Eric Burns thanked Sanchez, and immediately sent an email through a secure server to Mossad Headquarters in Tel Aviv. *'Possible sighting of Adwar in San Salvador. Will advise.'*

Ten days ago, Israeli Intelligence learned through an intercepted phone call that Hakim Adwar, a long-sought terrorist, was on a mission to purchase weapons for Hamas in El Salvador. The Mossad sent Burns to the capital city, San Salvador. His orders were to find Adwar and kill him.

Shlomo Bar-Nathan, the local *katsa*, field agent, had circulated flyers to his *sayanim* throughout the city of San Salvador. One of functions of a *katsa* was the recruitment of *sayanim*, volunteer Jewish helpers. As Jews, no matter where they live, they felt the need to protect Israel from its enemies, to help anyway possible. Throughout Central and South American, they numbered more than three thousand. The desk clerk, Miguel Sanchez, was one of Bar-Nathan's *sayanim*.

Burns rushed to the hotel, four blocks from the office. He checked the sitting area on the right side of the entrance corridor, located twenty meters from the front desk. It contained a couch, two side chairs, an ornately carved mahogany coffee table, and two end tables. The seats were unoccupied.

The location gave him a clear view of the lobby, elevators, and the front door. There was no need for him to seek a hidden spot. He knew what Adwar looked like; Adwar didn't know him. He ordered a club soda from a passing server and waited.

For more than an hour and thirty-five minutes, a parade of hotel guests exited the elevators. Some entered the dining room or bar; some left the hotel through the front door. None were Adwar. Burns placed the magazine he used as a prop on the coffee table, stretched his arms, and rolled his neck to work out the kink that had taken hold. *Was it really Adwar Sanchez saw?*

One of the doors at the bank of elevators slid open, catching his peripheral vision, and he once again shifted his gaze in that direction. A man emerged, and Burns stiffened. They'd lifted Adwar's image from the last propaganda video he made, six years ago. The face had hardly changed. There was no doubt. It was positively Adwar. Burns snatched the magazine from the coffee table and pretended to read it as the terrorist casually strolled by him to the front door.

I gotcha, you son-of-a-bitch.

Burns' pulse rate increased, and he clenched his fists. It took every bit of will power not to leap from the chair and rip the man's throat out with his bare hands. He took deep breaths, calming himself. He couldn't attack the man in a public place. *You've waited this long, a little longer won't matter.*

THE MOSSAD HAD hunted Adwar for a long time. Over the years, he became the face of terrorism to Israelis, through his propaganda films broadcasted on the Arab TV network, Al Jezeera. He first burst on the scene boasting to be the mastermind behind an attack in Mombasa. Burns remembered that one well.

It took place when he was still in the Israeli Army Special Forces group, the *Sayeret Matkal*. They sent his unit to Kenya after terrorists launched a suicide car bomb attack on an Israeli-owned beachfront hotel. His squad's assignment was to retrieve the dead.

When he entered the tent erected as the makeshift morgue, the scene hit him like a boxer's punch to the mid-section. Among the dead lay the small uncovered frail body of twelve-year-old Noy Anter. The boy's right ear and part of the surrounding skull was missing, the hair around the wound matted with congealed blood. Shards of glass and metal were imbedded in his face and chest, a twelve-inch piece of steel pierced his throat. Burns' eyes welled. Tears trickled down his cheeks.

He'd read newspaper accounts and seen television news clips of terrorist attacks and their aftermath, but nothing could prepare him for his first personal exposure to the horrific carnage done to non-combatants.

After the Mombasa attack, Adwar made more appearances on television, boasting he was the one responsible for numerous bombings in Israel and at Jewish facilities around the world, killing innocent civilians. In each video he spewed the same verbal diarrhea used by terrorists to justify their butchery... blaming Israel and America for all the world's problems.

Burns cared about Mombasa and all the other atrocities Adwar boasted about, but one of them was personal... *very* personal. It was the day the terrorist made the video laying claim as the mastermind behind the suicide bombing that took place in Tel Aviv on the fifth day of Passover. The attack that murdered his wife and son. Burns swore on the day of their funeral he would hunt down those responsible and kill them. He didn't know how or when, but promised his dead family someday he would.

A CAR HORN blaring on the street brought Burns' mind back to the present. Adwar had a few seconds head start before Burns slipped out the lobby door to follow. Walking on the opposite side of the street, he stayed thirty paces behind the terrorist.

He reached for his cell phone, an untraceable burner he bought when he arrived in San Salvador, to tell headquarters it was positively Adwar. His pocket was empty. *Shit.* He remembered he'd run out of the office so fast, he'd left it on the desk.

Twenty minutes later, Burns pulled up short when Adwar abruptly turned through the open black wrought iron gate of a private home on Calle Poniente. Picking up his pace, he had a clear view of Adwar through the open spaces in the wrought iron fence. He saw the terrorist stroll along a paved pathway, climb a short flight of steps, and press the doorbell. Adwar shook hands with the man who appeared at the threshold seconds later and entered the dwelling.

Burns crossed the street, sauntering along the fence of the home until he reached the gate where he saw a mounted brass sign. Venezuelan Embassy. Continuing to move past the gate, his gaze shifted to the opposite side of the street where he spotted an alley between two high-rise apartment buildings. It would provide a perfect view of the embassy entrance. He crossed the street, and when he was sure he was unobserved, took refuge in the alley and settled in, prepared to pick up the tail when Adwar left.

An hour and a half passed, and Adwar remained inside. Burns became concerned. He had to tell headquarters it was Adwar but was conflicted. He could lose the man if he left his post. After debating the pros and cons with himself, he decided to take the gamble, since at worst, he knew Adwar was staying at the hotel for two more days.

To avoid drawing unnecessary attention, he emerged from the alley and walked at a moderate pace until he reached the end of the street. Once he turned the corner onto 79 Ave. Sur, well out of sight of the embassy, he tore down the sidewalks to his office. It took almost thirty minutes. While still trying to catch his breath from the exertion, he rapidly typed and sent the email to headquarters.

'Adwar sighting confirmed. More details to follow.'

Burns spun from the computer and leaped to his feet. He tucked the previously forgotten burner cell phone in his back pocket, grabbed a newspaper from the desk and a bottle of cold water from the mini refrigerator. Bolting down the stairs, he managed to empty the bottle of water in big gulps. He threw the empty bottle in a recycling bin outside of the building, slid the paper under his arm, and galloped back to the embassy.

When he reached the corner of 79 Ave. Sur and Calle Poniente, he checked his watch. *Shit. I've been gone an hour and fifteen minutes.* He eyed the embassy on the opposite side of the street, while slowing his pace once again to a casual stroll, moving with the flow of the pedestrian traffic on Calle Poniente.

As he approached his former hiding place, he pulled the newspaper from under his arm and leaned against a lamp post pretending to read it. Turning pages slowly, as if looking for something particular, he waited for a gap to open in the pedestrians flow around him. Also scanning the entrance and the windows of embassy across the street, he saw no one outside or looking through any window. When he was sure he was unnoticed, he slipped back into the alley.

For the next three hours, with no food or water, Burns remained hidden from view. He focused on the embassy, never taking his eyes off the entrance except for two quick trips to a nearby half-filled trash barrel that served his need for a urinal.

What is he doing in there this long?

The weather had been comfortable for the last week, and he'd worn jeans, sneakers, and a golf shirt when he left the office for the Princess Hotel that afternoon. Now, he wished he had a jacket. The temperature dropped from a slight chill as the afternoon wore on to cool when the sun set and darkness settled over the city. He rubbed his arms to generate some warmth.

From his hiding spot a few feet inside the alley, he had not viewed one pedestrian in the last fifteen minutes, and only two cars drove by. He looked at his watch. It was nearly 8:30. He moved up to the entrance and peered both ways. Calle Poniente was quiet. The street was not particularly well lit. The gap between lamp posts spread at least two hundred feet, and with low wattage bulbs, they barely illuminated a twenty-foot radius around each pole.

Burns was beside himself with worry and doubt.

Did I lose him? Could he have gone when I left to send the email? Could he have exited the building, unnoticed, through a side or rear door?

He'd been taught, when in doubt, act. Inaction could get you killed. Or in this case, make you wait for a man who wasn't there.

Moving out of the alley, he walked on his side of Calle Poniente until he reached the corner of 75 Avenida Norte. A stand of maple trees stood across the street from him, on the same side of the street as the embassy. He jogged across the road and slipped into the mini forest, working his way to the rear. From there, he climbed over fences separating the houses until arriving at the back of the house next to the embassy.

Peeking over the separating six-foot solid wooden fence, he checked out the embassy. Light poured from what looked like three separate rooms on the second floor. But he couldn't assume that, since he didn't have plans for the building. It could be coming from one large room with three windows.

There were no lights from inside on the ground floor. A low wattage bulb beneath a protective roof illuminated a table and three chairs on a rear porch surrounded by a low railing.

Burns climbed over the fence, made his way onto the porch, and peered in a window. A light inside from an adjacent hallway lit the room enough to show he was looking at the kitchen. There didn't appear to be any movement on the lower floor.

He moved to the end of the porch, hopped on the low railing, seizing hold of one of the upright beams supporting the protective roof. Reaching up, he grabbed the edge of the gutter and pulled to see if it would hold his weight. It seemed sturdy enough. He gripped the outer edge with both hands and pulled himself up.

Snap.

The gutter pulled loose from the corner of the roof, and a two-foot section of the wood broke off in his hands. He fell backward, twisting his body, letting his shoulder absorb the impact. He landed hard, still holding the broken piece of gutter. As he lay on the ground, catching his breath, he heard the back door open.

Shit.

He dropped the piece of gutter on the grass and rolled into the crawl space under the porch a few feet away. Something hard and metal pressed against his shoulder and hip. His hand reached out, fumbling in the dark to feel it. Metal, space, metal, space. *A ladder.*

He heard the sound of two sets of footsteps on the porch.

"I'm telling you, I heard something," a voice said in Spanish.

"You're always hearing things. See for yourself. There's nothing out here," a second voice replied.

"I'm telling you I heard something. I'm going to take a look around," the first man said.

Burns, who spoke fluent Spanish, rolled further back, over the ladder. He moved his hand to the small of his back, reached under his shirt, and pulled his Beretta from the holster. One set of footsteps moved across the porch. Within seconds, he saw a pair of legs leave the bottom step and walk across the grass, not more than five feet from where he lay. He wiggled his body until his back pressed against the concrete foundation.

"What's this?" the man belonging to the legs said, arm reaching down and picking up the piece of gutter he'd left on the grass before rolling under the porch.

The feet moved to the edge of the porch, close to his position. Burns extended his arms, aiming his pistol at the legs. He didn't want to shoot, but he had no idea if the person attached to the legs in front of him was armed. The sound would also alert Adwar.

"What is this?" legs asked the man still on the porch.

"*No sé.*" I don't know.

There was silence for a few seconds as Burns watched the legs move away from the porch. His grip tightened on the pistol when he saw the legs turn in his direction and the knees begin to bend.

Fuck. He's gonna look under the porch.

"It's from there," the man on the porch said.

The legs straightened. "Where?"

"Up there. At the corner. That's a piece of gutter you're holding. See where it pulled away from the roof?"

Legs moved away, back to the stairs.

Both men were back on the porch.

"How did this fall off?"

"I don't know. What's the difference? That's what you heard. Let's get back inside. We came down for coffee, and I want it. Leave that on the table, and we'll get someone to check the gutter tomorrow."

Burns listened to the footsteps walk across the porch, then the back door open and close. He lay in place for five minutes before rolling out. He raised his head to just above the porch floor, checking out the kitchen window. The light was still on, so he waited. It went out ten minutes later.

Reaching under the porch, he slid the ladder out onto the grass. It was a fifteen-foot metal extension ladder that could be raised to twenty-five feet. *Could have used this before.*

Burns carried it to the side of the house where he'd seen the lights on the second floor. Laying it flat on the ground, he extended the ladder slowly to limit any noise. When he felt the top would be able to rest against the building about two feet below the windows, he locked the rungs in place. He carefully lifted the ladder, placing it beside and beneath the farthest window from the corner of the building. Cautiously climbing the rungs, he stopped when his head was inches below the bottom of the window sill and slightly toward the side. He took a breath before raising his head to peer inside.

The light coming from the three windows was generated from one large room. A rectangular table, perhaps fifteen feet long, occupied the center of the room. Six high back leather chairs at one end were occupied. Adwar and five men were eating, platters of food and drinks on the table in front of them. The men were engaged in active conversation, interspersed with occasional laughter. From what Burns could tell, it looked like one of the Venezuelans was acting as an interpreter for Adwar.

A slight shiver hit him as he looked at the opposite end of the table. Displayed were weapons he recognized as Russian made. Kalashnikov AK-47 assault rifles, Vityaz -SN submachine guns with suppressors, Makarov pistols and body armor. The most ominous Burns saw was the Russian made anti-tank weapon, the RPG-30 rocket propelled grenade and launcher. It was designed to defeat tanks protected by active defenses, such as the Trophy system currently deployed on Israel's tanks.

He'd seen enough. He verified Adwar was still in the building, and now he knew what Adwar was doing in the embassy. This was the place he'd come to purchase weapons. It wasn't surprising. Ever since Hugo Chavez and his socialist government came to power, the country developed close ties to Russia, purchasing billions of dollars' worth of arms from them. Venezuela also replaced its conventional allies with more likeminded states opposed to U.S. influence—among them, fellow OPEC nations like Libya and Iran.

When Israel invaded Lebanon in 2006, the Venezuelan government, acting in solidarity with its new friends, aggressively denounced the actions of the Jewish state. Chavez publically deemed the conflict with Lebanon a "New Holocaust" against the Palestinians and Lebanese. Government billboards sprang up around Caracas showing Israeli soldiers brutalizing children. They also showed Iran's President Ahmadinejad and Chavez holding hands to denounce Israeli imperialism. The current Venezuelan leadership continued its anti-Israel rhetoric. Little wonder that Venezuela would sell arms to those that sought to annihilate Israel.

He climbed down from the ladder and slid it back under the porch. Scaling the fences once again, he worked his way through the mini forest and back to the alley, waiting for Adwar to depart. Finally, at 9:10, Adwar left the Embassy. Burns followed him back to the hotel.

He stood outside the Princess, watching through a window as Adwar boarded the elevator. Burns scampered inside, moving quickly to the bank of elevators. He watched the floor indicator stop at the second floor. He resumed his spot on the couch in the lobby hallway, making sure Adwar did not come back down in the elevator or take the stairs and emerge from the emergency exit into the lobby. After thirty minutes, he felt confident Adwar was in for the night.

Burns saw Sanchez emerge from a back office, and hand a waiting guest an envelope. When it looked like no other guests were coming to the front desk, he approached Sanchez.

"Miguel, thank you. I need you to keep your eyes open. If you see anything you think is important, call me, no matter what time."

Burns left the hotel and called Bar-Nathan at home on his cell phone. "It's Burns. Get down to the Princess as fast as you can. I've got Adwar. I need you to pick up surveillance for the night while I get some shuteye. I'm across the street from the entrance. I'll wait for you here. Oh, and do me a favor. Bring me some fruit and water. I'm starving. I haven't had a thing to eat since breakfast. "

Bar-Nathan arrived forty-five minutes later. Burns downed two bottles of water in long gulps and ate half a banana while he filled Bar-Nathan in on everything that happened. He instructed Bar-Nathan to position himself in the same chair he'd used that morning because of the overall surveillance it provided.

Burns returned to his office and sent a long email to Mossad Headquarters. He recapped the day's events, describing the weapons he'd seen and requested further instructions. Exhausted, he headed home to get some sleep.

CHAPTER 2
February 16
Sunday Morning
Local Time
San Salvador

TRILL... TRILL... TRILL. The irritating ring of the telephone woke Burns from a deep slumber. He rolled over in bed to look at the clock. 5:00 a.m. At this hour, he knew who the call was from. He got tangled in the sheets and didn't pick up the receiver until the fifth ring.

"Hello?" he answered a thick voice.

Without a greeting in return, the brusque gravelly voice of Gideon Ben-Ami, Director of the Mossad, asked. "How many people do you have to set up surveillance on Adwar?"

"There's just Bar-Nathan and me."

"Shit." *Bang.* Through the receiver Burns heard Ben-Ami slap his desk. "That's not enough. Okay, there's nothing we can do about that. A team is on a plane to you now. They left at 1:00 this morning, after we got your email confirming it was Adwar. They arrive at Comalapa Airport at 1:30 this afternoon, TACA, flight 571. Meet them. In the meantime, do you think the two of you can stay on him until they get there?"

Burns rubbed sleep from his eyes. "I'd like to tell you we can, but I don't know. Bar-Nathan is watching him now. I'm relieving him," he looked at the clock, "in three hours."

"Okay. Whatever you do... *don't lose him*. Bar-Nathan will have to watch him when you leave for the airport, but get back as fast as you can. I don't like having just one person on surveillance." Without saying goodbye, Ben-Ami hung up and the line went dead. Burns hung up the phone and shook his head. *Typical Ben-Ami.*

He'd planned to relieve Bar-Nathan at 8:00, but because of the unexpected wake-up call, he left his apartment earlier than intended. With plenty of time to meet up with Bar-Nathan, he strode leisurely to the coffee shop located a half a block from the front entrance, on the opposite side of the street.

He arrived at 7:30 and sat at a table set back from the front window, providing an excellent view of the hotel entrance. As he kept watch, he sipped coffee and pretended to read a newspaper. At 8:00, Bar-Nathan left the hotel and walked across the street to join him.

"You need to stay with me all day to watch him. I have to leave you at around 12:30," Burns said to Bar-Nathan when he sat at the table. He told him about picking up the team coming in from Israel.

Burns and Bar-Nathan rotated surveillance between the coffee shop and the hotel lobby. Adwar emerged from the hotel at 11:00. They tailed him. Adwar must have felt very confident he was in no danger. Not once did he use any basic counter-surveillance measures as he casually sauntered to his destination. Once again, Adwar went to the Venezuelan Embassy. Burns and Bar-Nathan took cover in the same alley Burns had used the day before and waited.

"Burns," Bar-Nathan said, crossing his arms on his chest. "Can I ask you a personal question?"

"Sure. I can always refuse to answer," he said, smiling.

"I always wondered. How does an American Jew, with an Irish last name, become a *kidon* for the Mossad"?

Burns laughed. "You're not the first person who's asked me that.

I know, it sounds strange. The first part of your question is easy. My father is Irish, and I was born in the United States."

"Are you kidding me?"

Burns laughed. "No. My father's name is Jack Burns. I'm not bragging when I say he's a brilliant scientist. He has a PhD in micro-biology, specializing in microbes that increase agriculture production. He was invited by the Ministry of Agriculture to work in Israel in 1974. He worked on a *kibbutz*, a farm called Beit Nir, testing a microbe he'd developed for improving productivity of fruits and vegetables on *kibbutzim*.

"While he was working there, he met my mother, Ruth Ben-Ari, a native-born Israeli, a real *sabra*. My grandparents are Holocaust survivors who immigrated to Israel in 1947. My mom was born and raised on the Beit Nir *kibbutz* and worked as an assistant lab technician to my dad. They worked together, fell in love, and in a story that sounds like a Hollywood romance movie, back in 1974, an Irish Catholic from Boston married a Jewish *sabra* from Israel.

"The next year, in '75, Princeton University offered my dad a teaching and research grant. He moved back to the U.S. with my mom, to a small bedroom community of East Brunswick, New Jersey, about twenty miles north of Princeton. One year later, in 1976, this handsome devil," Burns said, pointing to himself, "entered the world at Middlesex General Hospital in New Brunswick, New Jersey."

Burns stretched and yawned. "So that's how, by birth, I am an American citizen. My Irish last name and green eyes come from my Irish dad, and my slightly 'Jewish nose', dark hair, and dark complexion come from my Jewish mom. But, I didn't really become Jewish until I was eighteen years old."

"What do you mean you really didn't become Jewish until you were eighteen years old?" Bar-Nathan asked. "And I still don't understand how you ended up in the Israeli Mossad if you're an American citizen?"

Burns glanced at his watch. 12:30 p.m. "That's a little more personal of a story," he replied. "I might tell you about it later, but I've got to leave for the airport right now. Keep your eyes open, and don't lose him."

The team landed on time. Burns met them at baggage claim. They secured three cars from a *sayan* at the airport in the auto rental business. No paperwork had to be filled out. They drove to a safe house Bar-Nathan had set up. An empty home for sale, arranged through a real estate *sayan*.

Burns called the hotel desk from the safe house.

"Sanchez, this is Burns. Has Adwar come back to the room?"

"No."

"Good. I'll be there in about thirty minutes. Get me a master passkey. I need to check his room."

While the others got themselves settled at the safe house, Burns drove to the hotel. He spotted Sanchez standing near the elevators. Burns walked through the lobby, taking a position beside Sanchez, pretending to be a waiting guest. Sanchez slipped him a master keycard and whispered, "Two forty-five, two fifty-seven" and walked away.

Burns understood what he meant. Adwar was in room 245. But, if there was anyone in the hallway, he could go to the unoccupied room 257 and let himself in until it was safe to move to Adwar's room.

He rode the elevator to the second floor, found the hallway empty, and went straight to room 245. Burns inserted the keycard and quickly slipped inside.

"Damn," Burns said, looking at the opened, packed suitcase on the bed. *He's getting ready to leave. A day early.*

Burns searched the room. After checking the bathroom, the drawers in the dresser and night table, he found nothing useful.

Standing next to the bed, he stared at the open suitcase. *Should I go through it?*

Pondering the decision for a few seconds, he decided he better not. Anything misplaced, Adwar might notice it and know he'd been spotted. Burns didn't want to take a chance of spooking him, thinking the risk wasn't worth the possible reward.

He left, taking the elevator to the lobby to return the passkey.

Sanchez at the front desk looked around to be sure they couldn't be overheard. In a low voice he said, "Adwar called while you were upstairs. He's checking out in about twenty minutes."

"Shit," Burns said.

"He asked me to have his bill ready and reserve a room for him on May 15 for five days."

Burns said, "Okay. Thanks."

There was no time to plan his execution and no time to get the rest of the team in place. Burns rushed to his car to set himself into position to follow Adwar.

A half-hour later, waiting down the block, Burns saw Adwar enter the hotel. Bar-Nathan had followed Adwar and was across the street from the hotel entrance. Bar-Nathan hustled across the street when Burns stepped out of his car and waved to him. Less than ten minutes later, Adwar emerged with his suitcase and got into a taxi. They followed when the cab pulled away. Burns stayed at least six car lengths behind.

He'd followed the taxi for ten minutes when the low-pitched blare of a truck's horn to his right abruptly jarred his concentration. He turned and looked past Bar-Nathan's head. A small delivery truck ran a red light and was barreling at the passenger side of the car. The truck's brakes squealed in a piercing screech as the driver attempted to stop. A split second later, he felt the impact. The truck slammed into the rear passenger door and spun the car like a top.

The truck's brakes slowed its speed, and neither he nor Bar-Nathan were injured as both vehicles spun in circles. The car blocked two lanes of traffic when it came to rest seconds later.

Drivers in surrounding cars blasted their horns at the vehicles obstructing movement. Burns paid no attention to them as he swiveled his neck in all directions, scanning the roadway.

"No," he wailed, slamming his clenched fist against the steering wheel. His shoulders slumped as he lowered his head, resting it against the wheel, and let out a heavy sigh.

He lost Adwar.

CHAPTER 3
February 16
Sunday Morning,
Local Time
Be'er Sheva, Negev Desert, Israel

S EVEN YEARS OF painstaking trial and error were about to come to fruition or become another bitter pill to swallow in yet another series of failures. He'd never been closer, but as before, one wrong code, and he'd have to start all over again.

These thoughts ran over and over in Dr. Seth Shernicoff's mind as he tossed and turned in bed, desperately trying to fall asleep.

If the experiment succeeded, the ramifications would be enormous, causing upheavals in the scientific community, forever altering the concept of evolution. No more gradual evolving of a species through natural selection. Instead of thousands, or millions of years, change could occur in weeks or months.

Am I playing God? If it works, what am I unleashing?

He fretted about the other certain, nonscientific consequences. His success would most certainly trigger unprecedented seismic shifts in global power and create chaos in world financial systems. He felt knots form in his stomach.

Giving up hope of getting even a few minutes of slumber, he

dressed, penned his wife a note telling her where he was going, and left home at 5:30 in the morning.

It was dark when he pulled into his parking space in the faculty lot thirty minutes later. The sun would not rise for another forty-five minutes. The knots in his stomach had grown worse.

Sitting in his car, staring at the whitewashed building housing the laboratory, he absentmindedly twisted his wedding ring. He felt small beads of sweat on his forehead. His heart pounded in anticipation as he tried to calm himself with deep breaths.

He couldn't procrastinate any longer. He slipped from the car, jogged up the stairs to the main entrance, and took the elevator to the third floor.

The security guard lowered his newspaper and pulled his feet off the desktop in the small reception area when the elevator doors opened and Shernicoff emerged.

"Dr. Shernicoff?" The guard said looked at the clock on the wall. "Six o'clock on Sunday morning? Everything okay?"

"Good morning, Mike," Shernicoff replied, lifting a hand to his mouth to stifle a yawn. "Yes. Everything's fine. I'm running a test and couldn't sleep. I didn't want to disturb my wife, so I thought I might as well get dressed and come in."

"Ahh. Well, good luck with whatever you're doing."

The guard turned and pressed a black button on the wall behind him. The lock clicked on the door leading into the secure main corridor of the research facility. Shernicoff glanced at the mission statement of the department posted on the door. He'd read the same statement each day since beginning his project.

MISSION STATEMENT

Plant the seeds that will lead to the growth of successful biotechnology industries in Israel, particularly in the Negev, by engaging in creative and groundbreaking biotechnological research.

He walked down the corridor to his lab. While everything that occurred inside was a team effort, it was *his* lab. Only he knew how all the components fit together. He entered his security code, strode inside, and flipped on the light. As the overhead fluorescents flickered on, his eyes perused the sixty-foot long and fifty-foot wide front portion of the lab.

On the left were empty workstations once occupied by biologists. On the right, the air-conditioned room, housing banks of HP Superdome computers where the coders worked, translating DNA code into binary computer codes. Through a large window, he could see numbers scrolling across monitors churning out data.

He moved toward the rear wall and another security door. On the other side lay the functioning laboratory, where all biological experiments took place, including the current one. His heart beat faster and his palms sweated as he stepped to the door.

Okay. Here we go.

Entering his security code, he hesitated for a brief second and inhaled deeply before pushing the door open. The industrial 300-watt light fixtures, hanging over the scaled down version of the closed-tank bioreactor, illuminated the entire room like high noon in the desert. Donning a lab coat and slipping on a pair of surgical gloves, he wound his way past stainless steel workbenches crowded with test tubes and beakers, to the transmission electron microscope a few feet from the bioreactor.

The powerful microscope, purchased at a cost of 3,250,000 shekels, almost one million U.S. dollars, was one of only fifteen in the world. It allowed visualization of objects down to the size of a single atom and made experiments in DNA sequencing possible. He pressed a button, and the instrument began its warm up process.

Shernicoff turned to the bioreactor and looked at the glass grow tank. He stared in disbelief. His mouth gaped open. *That's impossible.*

He'd begun the experiment seven days ago by inserting computer generated DNA codes into five hundred microscopic cells of common pond algae. The objective was to see if the altered DNA could take over and replace the cell's natural DNA. If he was right, one result would be that every twenty-four hours the cells would multiply more rapidly than they would under natural conditions. To either succeed or fail, the experiment needed at least a week's time. He'd decided not to come back into the lab until it was time... and today was the time.

Now he was looking at a manmade miracle. It looked like the original cells had multiplied exponentially; he'd guess more than thirty times the normal rate every day. In place of the original five hundred cells, today there were billions of algae cells.

He turned a valve allowing some of the expanding mass in the grow tank to flow through an overhead tube into the harvesting tank. Grabbing a pipette, he suctioned up a small sample and placed it on a glass slide. He brought it to the electron microscope and slipped the prepared slide into the holder.

Now to see about the second, and most important, part of the experiment.

Using specialized tools, he separated a single cell from the sample and dissected it. The lipid, or oil content of the cell, was 91%. He shook his head in astonishment. *Ninety-one percent!*

Before today, the most bio-engineered strains could achieve was a 57% lipid content and could only double a cell's mass in forty-eight hours.

Shernicoff leaned back from the microscope and rubbed his forehead.

Ninety-one percent. Mass increased at least thirty times every twenty-four hours. I did it.

Now he had to extract the lipid from the mass and measure how much of the 91% the cell would actually yield.

He suctioned two ounces of algae from the harvest tank into a beaker and poured it into a centrifuge to de-water it and create a paste. He placed the paste in a high-pressure screw press to separate the lipid. The extracted lipid content remained at 91%.

Shernicoff pushed himself back from the table and contemplated the significance of what he'd done. By use of a computer, he took a life form that existed on earth for over three billion years, altered its DNA and eliminated the evolutionary process. He created a modified life form that would serve humanity in ways unimaginable fifty years ago.

He had one more critical test. Using a fresh sample, he separated a single cell and searched the cell's newly created sequenced DNA. After twenty minutes of exploration, there it was. The on/off switch, what he called the suicide switch. If he hadn't created it, he would never have found it. It was something that didn't occur in nature. A smile crossed Shernicoff's face.

I did it. That's the last piece. It's ready.

Shernicoff spent the next four hours in the lab, re-running the tests. The results were always the same.

He looked up at the sign he placed on the wall next to the bioreactor when he began the project, the quotation responsible for everything he just accomplished.

Let me tell you something that we Israelis have against Moses. He took us 40 years through the desert in order to bring us to the one spot in the Middle East that has no oil!

Golda Meir, Prime Minister of Israel - June 10, 1973

Shernicoff broke into a wide smile. He took a deep breath. "Not for much longer, my dear Golda. Not for much longer."

CHAPTER 4
Five Weeks Ago
January 14
Be'er Sheva

I N THE DARKEST circles of the criminal world, his reputation
was unparalleled. He never failed. For the right price, he would
murder, kidnap for ransom, or secure whatever the client wished.
A former client dubbed him the Collector. Only one person knew his
real name.

Potential purchasers of his services could only contact him through
an untraceable email account. The latest contact was made five weeks
ago.

*New scientific discovery near completion. When finalized, collect
formula and kill professor who created it. Willing to pay 200,000 U.S
dollars. Advise if you accept contract. Details will follow.*

The Collector replied, *I accept. Send details.*

After confirming half his fee was deposited in his Swiss account, as
dictated by the follow up email, he arrived in Be'er Sheva, the largest
city in the Negev Desert. The first order of business, the communication instructed, was to install listening devices. An email attachment
included a floor plan in the target facility and where to install them.

He rented an apartment on Yahuda Halevi Street as a base of

operation, three quarters of a mile from Ben-Gurion University of Negev.

"My doctor in Tel Aviv diagnosed that I have a chronic pulmonary disorder," he told the rental agent. "He strongly suggested I move to the desert, away from the pollution of the city. I'm not sure how long I'll be staying. Can I have a three-month short-term rental and renew if needed?"

"No problem," the agent said.

Later that afternoon, using a different identity, the Collector rented another apartment on the other side of the city. He gave the new rental agent the same medical cover story.

He began eating breakfast and dinner at a coffee shop on Derech Matsada. The coffee shop had fourteen tables. At any given time, men playing chess occupied four or five of them. Soviet immigrants had made the game of chess a major sport in Be'er Sheva, and the city became Israel's national chess center, with more chess grandmasters per capita than any other city in the world.

After the third day, the Collector began taking an active interest in the chess matches. He would sit at his table next to a game, concentrating on the players and their moves. On his fourth day at the coffee shop, the owner approached him.

"You are Russian?" the owner asked in Russian.

"Da," he replied.

"You play?" the owner asked.

"A little. I'm not so good. But I like to hear the players speak Russian, to be around fellow countrymen. I know very little Hebrew."

"I know how you feel," the owner said. "I came to Israel seven years ago and also did not speak Hebrew."

The Collector introduced himself as Boris Bobrov, who'd immigrated two years ago. The proprietor asked what he was doing in Be'er Sheva. Bobrov told him of his illness and the doctor's orders.

"You keep coming to the cafe. I make real Russia food," the owner said.

"Thank you," Bobrov said, "I look forward to it. Since arriving in Israel, I make my own meals, and I confess I'm not a very good cook." Both men smiled.

One day over dinner, Bobrov, who'd now become a fixture at the café, told the owner he was getting bored. All he did was eat breakfast and spend the day at the Neve Midbar Spa prescribed by his doctor. The 43° C water, believed to be over 10,000 years old and rich in minerals, would be good for him, the doctor said.

"I spend the day soaking in the mineral water, come back to Be'er Shiva, have dinner, and go to sleep. I needed something to do, to break the routine. Do you have any idea where I can find some work? Even something part-time would help break the dull monotony."

When the owner asked what kind of work he did before, Bobrov said he was learning the jewelry trade, but he would take anything, even manual labor, just to keep busy. The owner mentioned a good friend, also from Russia, was head of maintenance at the university. Perhaps he might have an opening. Would he be willing to do that kind of work?

"Of course," Bobrov replied. "As long as it doesn't cause breathing problems. Can you set up an appointment with your friend?"

Bobrov had done his research. He didn't start coming to the café by accident. Before he'd stepped inside, he knew the owner was an immigrant from Russia, and his good friend was head of maintenance at the university.

Two days later, over breakfast, the owner told Bobrov if he was willing to miss a day at the Spa, his friend, Ayal Markovic, would interview him the next morning at 10:30 at the University.

Bobrov arrived on time and filled out an application form. When he met with Markovic, they spoke Russian. He showed Markovic his Russian passport, confirming the application information that his name was Boris Bobrov, age 42, unmarried, place of birth, Odessa, Russia. For previous occupation, he repeated what he told the restaurant owner about his apprenticeship at a jewelry store owned by a cousin in Tel Aviv. He explained to Markovic that he wished to keep himself occupied and would even take part-time work.

Markovic said there were no openings at present. However, if anything came up, he'd keep him in mind. Bobrov thanked him and left.

As he walked out of the administration building, he knew it was up to him to make sure something came up.

For the next few days, he walked the campus. He observed the maintenance workers all wore the same navy blue uniform with the university symbol on the back. Bobrov began to formulate a plan. He followed the blue uniforms as they moved about the campus, finally selecting his prey, someone who always worked at the targeted building.

For the next week Bobrov shadowed the man, keeping a record of when he arrived at work, which buildings he worked in, how long he stayed in each, and what time he left for home. When his prey took morning and afternoon breaks in the university food court with other maintenance workers, Bobrov listened in on the conversations. He'd lied to the owner of the café when he said he didn't speak Hebrew. In fact, he knew the language well.

He learned the man was a widower, lived by himself, and was a creature of habit. It was time to act.

ON THE LAST day of his life, Abner Baum's alarm clock woke him at 7:00 a.m. He shuffled to the bathroom; relieved himself, brushed his teeth, shaved, and showered. He put on his uniform and made his usual breakfast; two scrambled eggs, toast, coffee, and orange juice. This routine had not varied in the nine years since his wife lost her three-year battle with ovarian cancer.

He stepped out on the balcony of his sixth floor apartment, a cup of coffee in hand, and looked up at the azure sky, watching a single wisp of a cloud float by. His eyes drifted to the apartment buildings lining both sides of Shlomo Skulski Street. They were all built with tan bricks. Each brick reflected a different hue of the desert sands that lay beyond the outskirt of the city.

The antique table clock his wife had bought at the flea market in Tel Aviv two years before her diagnosis, chimed eight times through the open balcony door. His shift began at 9:00 a.m. It was time to leave and catch the 8:15 bus.

The doorbell rang as he stood at the sink rinsing out the coffee cup. *Who could that be?* He placed the cup in the rack on the drain board and called out, "Coming."

A man stood framed in the open door, a large gift wrapped package in his hands. "I sorry to disturb you so early in morning, but you are Abner Baum?" Bobrov said in Hebrew.

"Yes."

"You work at Ben-Gurion University of Negev?"

"Yes, I do. Why?"

"Then this package is for you," Bobrov said. He thrust the package forward, and Baum grabbed it with both hand. His own hands now free, the delivery man whipped his left hand forward, grasped the front of Baum's shirt, and pushed him back into the apartment. Simultaneously, his right hand, which had been beneath the package, jerked up, pressed the hidden suppressed pistol against Baum's forehead, and pulled the trigger.

TWO DAYS LATER, when he walked into the café for dinner, the owner said to Bobrov, "There you are. My friend Ayal called about an hour ago. It seems one of his men hasn't shown up for work in two days, and no one can find him. If you want to fill in until he shows up, you can start tomorrow. You'll have to be there by 9:00 a.m. sharp."

"That's great. Thank you."

Bobrov arrived five minutes before nine and knocked on Markovic's door. A voice shouted, "Come in."

Markovic sat behind his desk.

"Bobrov. Good. You got my message. One of my workers is missing. No one has heard from him in days or knows where he is. I can't afford to fall behind. Can you start today? Right now?" Markovic asked.

You want to know where he is? About twenty kilometers south of here, in a shallow grave in the desert.

"Yes, I can. Thank you. I'll work for as long as you need me, but I'm sure he'll show up in a few days. Maybe he found a woman or had too much to drink."

"Well, I'm not sure his job will be waiting for him when he does. Never mind. Here is a temporary employee badge and key card. Go down to the basement in this building. You'll find a room that says 'Maintenance Employees Only.' Viktor, also from Russian, will be there. He'll show you your duties for today, and tomorrow you'll be on your own. Okay?"

"Sure." Bobrov shook hands, took the badge and key card, and left for the basement. He introduced himself to Viktor and shadowed him for the rest of the day as he went about the janitorial tasks. Bobrov paid particular attention as they worked their way through the building housing the Department of Agriculture and Biotechnology.

Over the next few days Bobrov worked on his own. It was physically demanding, something he wasn't used to, but he made sure he did his job well. He cleaned the buildings assigned and always had a friendly smile for the guards and people who worked there.

On the fourth day, he was ready. He arrived early for his shift so he could park close to the employee entrance. During his afternoon break, he slipped outside to his car. It took him three trips to get all the equipment from the car and hide it in the bottom of his cleaning cart.

He took an extra-long time cleaning at the other two buildings assigned to him. As a result, as planned, he didn't arrive at the one housing the Department of Agriculture and Biotechnology until after 6:30 p.m.

When he reached the third floor, everyone was gone for the day. He stepped from the elevator with his cleaning cart, a permanent employee badge, replacing his temporary badge, clipped to the lapel of the blue uniform. The guard stationed outside the security door gave him a cursory glance and went back to reading his newspaper.

He used his security card to enter the main hallway and made his way to the laboratory of Dr. Seth Shernicoff. The door was secured with a keypad lock, but the cleaning crew's security card was programmed to over-ride the keypad entry.

He'd cleaned the lab for the last three days and confirmed the accuracy of the floor plan he'd received, showing where to put the devices. Bobrov removed the components from the bottom of the cleaning cart. Working methodically, it took twenty minutes to install the units. He took his time, insuring he left no traces. The most difficult part was placing the transmitting booster. He had to balance the weight so it wouldn't fall through the acoustic tiles of the drop ceiling.

After finishing the installations, he cleaned the laboratory and moved on to the other rooms on the third floor. Two hours later, he said good night to the guard and left the building.

The next morning, before his shift began, he went to Markovic's office. "I'm sorry, but I can't continue working here. Last night I had trouble breathing and called my doctor. When I told him about my maintenance job at the university, he actually yelled at me. He said I have to quit immediately. The cleaning chemicals are affecting my breathing."

Markovic was not happy to lose him but said he understood. After leaving Markovic, he went to the café to tell the owner what happened. He said he had to return to Tel Aviv for a few days. His doctor wanted to run some tests.

When Bobrov didn't return in a week, the café owner became concerned. He contacted Bobrov's landlord and got contact information from the rental agreement. He called the number listed in Tel Aviv. A recording said it was not a working number.

He called information, gave the address from the agreement, and asked for Bobrov's phone number. The operator checked. "There is no listing for a Bobrov at that address," she said.

He asked her to check for any listing for a Boris Bobrov. She put him on hold. "Sorry," she said a half minute later. "There is no listing for anyone named Boris Bobrov in Tel Aviv."

CHAPTER 5
February 16
Sunday Afternoon
Present
Be'er Sheva, Israel

S HERNICOFF WAS ELATED. After seven years, this sequence worked. *I better back this up in case anything happens to the main frames.* He left the lab and moved to the computer room. He sat at a table in front of one of the linked Superdome computers and turned on the monitor. From a drawer, he pulled a stack of 3.0 terabyte digital flash drives, each the size of his palm. Connecting the first to the computer's Ethernet port, he began downloading the program containing the altered DNA sequencing of the mass growing in the lab. It took five drives and forty minutes to copy the information.

On a sixth drive, he downloaded the sequencing required to incorporate the on/off suicide switch into the new species and how to activate it.

He had to give the good news to Simon Bloom, the department chairman. He tried to reach him at home. His wife said he was playing golf and expected he'd be finished in about an hour. If her husband called home she'd be happy to relay a message. "Please tell him I'm at the lab, and I did it. He'll know what that means."

He called Bloom's cell phone. Shernicoff knew they did not permit cell phones on the course and it went to voice mail. He left a message. "Simon, it's Seth. Remember when I told you I was very close? Well, I hope you're sitting down because *I did* it! It worked! Call me back. No, better yet, come to the lab so I can show you.

AFTER HIS EMPLOYER contacted him by email the week before, the Collector was now back in the compact kitchen of his rented apartment two miles from the lab, drinking a cup of Turkish coffee, reading a book.

The email left no doubt he'd be doing what he did well, very soon.

Return to Be'er Sheva immediately and monitor listening devices. Completion of formula imminent. Secure formula. Kill professor.

He rose to pour himself a fresh cup of coffee.

The Collector turned up the volume on the MP3 player as one of his favorite Russian ballads began to play. He hated all things that had to do with the Russian government. but even after all these years, still loved its culture. Russia. His homeland. He thought back to his early life.

HE WAS BORN Yuri Elson, on October 12, 1975, in the town of Trosna, Russia, along the banks of the river Oka into a Jewish family. Trosna was not a good place to live if you were a Jew. As far back as 1904, Cossacks began pogroms against Jews living there, slaughtering the men and raping the women.

In the decades to follow, Trosna, like many outlying towns in Russia, continued to suffer official and unofficial pogroms against the Jews. The town also suffered a different type of onslaught when, after Stalin's death in 1953, the Gulag prisons released thousands of convicts, many of whom found their way to his town.

Elson grew up in a tough neighborhood where many of the former convicts lived. He saw how they prospered and became rich, while his father slaved in a state run factory, barely making enough money to feed his family. From the time he was eleven years old, Elson decided excelling as a criminal was the only way to get out of the Jewish ghetto.

He spent as much time as he could around the places where the toughest of the toughest congregated, just to be near them and pick up bits and pieces of their conversations. They spoke of jail, how to survive the Gulags, how to not pay attention to Russian laws. These men lived through the worst jails in the world, the Gulags, and survived. Elson told his friends, "I want to be like those guys. They're tough. They're not afraid of the police. They're not afraid of anything." They became his heroes.

With the oppression and injustice of the communist system, corruption was widespread. A culture of larceny and graft permeated society, creating an underground economy, a black market trade in everything from basic foods to medicine. Most people did black market business with the criminals on a daily basis and held the powerful ones in high regard. This is where Elson's heroes flourished.

The gangsters even enjoyed a reputation of Robin-Hood honesty as they meted out justice in what they called the People's Court, where the common people by-passed the corrupt government legal system to have their personal disputes solved. A special breed of criminal called *vor v zakonye*—thieves-in-law—a fraternal order of elite outlaws dating back to the time of Peter the Great, ran the People's Courts.

The *vor v zakonye* swore to follow a rigid code of ethics that included never work a legitimate job, never pay taxes, refuse to fight in the army, and never, for any reason, cooperate with the government, except to trick them. A giant eagle with razor sharp talons tattooed on their chest showed they were *vor v zakonye*. Tattoos on their kneecaps meant they would not bow to anyone. Elson would thrive among men like this.

He went to school but was always in trouble. He liked to fight. He liked to steal. Older kids would extort money from him so he extorted money from younger kids. He began doing small jobs for the *vors* and soon had run-ins with Soviet law, which became a crucial step in becoming a full fledge member of the underworld. He didn't break during police beatings, so the *vors* considered him a stand-up guy.

Before long, Elson graduated to one of the highest callings in the Eastern European criminal pecking order... a pickpocket. Skilled pickpockets received great respect from other criminals, often accorded leadership status in their gangs. But this wasn't enough, so he moved to Moscow to prove himself. He joined a gang that specialized in extortion. Years later in America, he recounted to others, "I don't want brag, but I great at this. I do it thousands of times. If victim balk, I could be nice or put gun in mouth. I no show pity or regret when kill someone. I not even think about it."

At age twenty-six, Elson made a big change in his life. His Soviet passport was stamped "Jew," so he applied for Jewish refugee status to move to Israel, the only way a Soviet Jew could leave Russia. He was a Soviet Jew, but by birth and name only. "They called me fucking kike everywhere I went," he told friends later. "If someone called me a Zhid, I fight back. But otherwise, what kind of Jew I am? I not even know any Jewish holidays. I never hear of them. I was Russian. I sang Russian songs, ate Russian food, spoke Russian language. I just no good in Russian culture. Only thing I like about being Jewish, some of Soviet Union's top crooks also Jewish."

He was shipped first to Vienna, then to one of three transit camps near Rome. In the camps, criminals from the far reaches of the Soviet empire converged, waiting for months at a time to move on. It was in these camps that global Russian organized crime grew. Criminals leaving Russia met criminals headed to diverse places such as Israel, Brussels, Holland, London, and the United States. Russian criminals, scattered around the world, could call their new friends for advice, intelligence, and contacts.

Although he wanted to get to America as fast as possible, Yuri learned something valuable in the camp. They told him to go to Israel first and become an Israeli citizen under the Law of Return. Then, if he went to America and ever found himself in trouble, he could get back to Israel fast. Under Israeli law, they never extradite one of their citizens, even to the United States.

ELSON WENT TO Israel and received citizenship four months after arrival. Two months later, he flew to New York, heading for Brighton Beach in Brooklyn. After passing through U.S. immigration, he stood outside a terminal at JFK and looked at the skyline of Manhattan. A rush of excitement rippled through him, like a nine-year-old at the circus. *I'm free. I can rob, I can steal, I can do whatever I want.*

He quickly discovered the Russians had built Brighton Beach into a closed society, inhospitable to outsiders. Modeled after Odessa, a Baltic Sea port, once considered the Marseille of Russia, the locals called it "Little Odessa." And like the real Odessa, powerful crooks preyed upon the small. Gangs made money in Medicare and Medicaid fraud, counterfeiting and drug deals. A professional murder cost as low as $1500. It was often cheaper to hire a hit man than to pay off a debt. Almost every Russian in Brighton Beach had family who was either connected to the gangs, owed them a debt, or paid them extortion.

As a newcomer to Brighton Beach, Elson found himself in a strange land and had to learn a different set of survival skills. He found that people didn't carry a lot of money on them, so he couldn't make a living as a pickpocket. They carried credit cards, so he started working credit card scams, even though he didn't speak English.

Teaming up with a distant cousin, Evsei Brokin, he embarked on a crime spree. Well known in criminal circles was the rampant corruption in the diamond district on 47th Street in Manhattan, so they identified crooked storeowners and demanded diamonds. Their victims, so deep in their own crimes, never reported the thefts to the police. They stole hundreds of thousands of dollars' worth of jewelry. Soon, storeowners in the diamond district sought out Elson and Brokin to stage fake robberies, so they could scam their insurance companies. The storeowners would give them a percentage of the insurance payments.

Although he made good money, it was still a small time operation, and Yuri wanted to make a name for himself. He turned to more violent crimes. He hired himself out as a hit man. He engaged in extortion.

One day, he got a job offer that changed his criminal life. He received a call from a man he met months before at a Manhattan bar, Bob Siegel. Siegel asked if Elson could meet him that evening at the bar in the Skyline Motor Inn on 10th Avenue in mid-town Manhattan.

They'd first met through mutual friends and Siegel spoke a little Russian with Elson. He'd learned the language from his parents growing up in the Bronx. Elson appreciated Siegel's effort to make him comfortable and took an immediate liking to him. "We like neighbors," he told Siegel when he learned Siegel's parents immigrated to America from a small village in Russia, twenty kilometers from Elson's home town of Trosna.

"I have a problem," Siegel said when they were seated in a booth in the bar. "I own a few printing plants, and a guy named Herb Cohen runs one of them. My accountant discovered he stole a lot of money from me."

"How he do this?" Elson asked.

"My account said it worked like this. A printing job would come in worth, say $10,000. Cohen tells the customer if he paid cash, the cost will be $8000. The customer agrees. Why wouldn't he? He saves $2000. Then Cohen put the job on the books for $5000, pocketing the $3000 difference. My accountant figures Cohen stole well over $200,000 from me in the last two years. Can you help me get it back?"

"I think yes," Elson replied. He asked Siegel for personal information about Cohen and made notes on the back of cocktail napkins. When Siegel finished, Elson said, "I get stolen money, I charge twenty percent of what get. Is okay?" Siegel readily agreed.

Two days later, Elson visited Cohen at the factory. "Do you have an appointment?" the receptionist asked.

"No," he said, "but this urgent family matter. I sure Mr. Cohen want see me."

"What's this about?" Cohen asked when Elson entered the office.

"For money you owe Bob Siegel."

"What are you talking about?"

"For $200,000 you steal."

Cohen pointed to the door. "Get the hell out of my office."

"Before go, I show you first something."

He reached in his pocket and took out his cell phone. He pressed some buttons. "You come look. It important," Elson said, rising to his feet.

Cohen came around his desk. Elson outstretched his arm and held the phone with the screen turned to Cohen.

"Come close," Elson urged, wagging his free hand.

On the screen, Cohen saw his twenty-two-year-old daughter, tied to a chair in the kitchen of her apartment in New Jersey. A man in a ski mask stood behind her. He wore a blue shirt with the name ABC Carpentry stenciled across the breast pocket. In his hand, the whirling tip of a portable drill hovered next to his daughter's left eye. His daughter's muffled screams penetrated the gag in her mouth. Cohen's face blanched. A chill rippled through his body as he spun and threw up in his wastepaper basket.

Elson gave Cohen a few seconds to pull himself together. "I know you have safety deposit box in bank in two blocks. I bet much of cash in box. I also check. You have $90,000 in personal check account. We go to bank now. You take cash from box. What not make $200,000, you take from check account. When I collect money, you call Mr. Siegel, tell him you quit job, and he never hear of you again. Then I call carpenter. He go from house, no repair work. I no get all money, carpenter do drilling."

Elson called Siegel that afternoon and said to meet him at the

Skyline at 7:30. The last slivers of dusk were about to morph into the dark of night when Elson stepped in the bar. Squinting from the bright indoor lights, he spotted Siegel in a booth. A bottle of vodka sat in an ice bucket on the table, two shot glasses next to it.

Elson placed a cardboard box on the table in front of Siegel. "In here, $160,000 cash. I take already my twenty percent." He poured himself a shot glass of vodka as Siegel pulled the box close, slide the cover up from one end, and peeked inside. "It all there."

Siegel smiled, poured a shot of vodka, and raised the glass. "I couldn't believe it when Cohen called this afternoon and quit. I knew it had to be you but didn't think it would happen this quick. You're certainly the collector I hoped you'd be. *Na zdorovie*—to your health." Both men gulped down the shots.

Siegel leaned forward across the table, closing the distance with Elson, and in a quiet voice said, "Can I ask you a question? Call it curiosity. I know you did this for me because we know each other. I have friends who also have trouble getting money or other things owed to them. Would you be interested in acting as their collector?"

Elson shrugged. "Sure, why not? This easiest money I make. If they as easy, I take job."

Over the next two months, Siegel gave Elson three requests from friends. Two jobs went as smoothly as Siegel's. Elson collected the money. No one got hurt.

The third did not go as smoothly. A company owed Siegel's friend money, he told Elson, and his friend sued. But their lawyer said he had proof his client would not have to pay. Siegel's friend wanted to know what it was. Elson visited the lawyer at his office and asked for the evidence. The lawyer refused to give it. On the phone, Elson showed him his wife, in their bedroom, tied to the bed, the ski-masked carpenter standing alongside. The lawyer still refused to divulge the evidence.

Elson barked out a command in Russian. The carpenter pulled a hammer from inside his jacket, grasped the wife's left leg, and smashed her tibia, four inches below the knee. She screamed so loud Elson thought secretaries outside the lawyers closed office door would hear it through the phone. The lawyer gave Elson the information.

Before he left, Elson warned, "If try use evidence later and won case, come back, rape wife many times, and when done, shatter both knee caps, make cripple for life." Siegel's friend won the case when the opposing lawyer convinced his client to settle and pay the money owed.

Elson's exploits as a collector got back to the Russian gangsters in Brighton Beach. As a result, they hired him to collect debts outside the Russian community. Sometimes he collected people to get the debts paid, holding them for ransom. The Italian Mafia, who did business with the Russians, learned about his new business. Soon he collected for them.

Two years after he began his new career collecting debts for people, Elson received a call from a Russian gangster he met in the transit camp outside of Rome. The gangster lived in London, heard about his new business, and wanted to hire him. Elson accepted the assignment and flew to England. As his plane took off from JFK Airport in New York, he couldn't help smiling to himself. He made it. He was what he always wanted to be. Tough, famous, strong. At the top of the pile, a gangster's gangster.

With his business growing, he realized so did his chances of being caught. He hired a young Russian computer hacker to set up an email address that couldn't be traced back to him. Then he put out word to the Russians. From now on he could only be contacted for an assignment through Bob Siegel.

Elson set up an agreement. Siegel would act as a middleman, confirm a client was legitimate, but not reveal the client's name to Elson. And in a reversal of the roles from when they first did business, Siegel now collected the fees for Elson, deducted a five percent commission and deposited the balance in accounts Elson set up in off-shore tax havens.

Now known as the Collector, and between assignments, Elson took his mistress to his apartment in Caesarea, Israel. He planned to spend a few weeks relaxing, but a week after arriving, a request for his services appeared in the email account. It came from an anonymous source in Arizona, offering to pay Elson $200,000 for his services. *Almost 780,000 Israeli new shekels.*

Elson called Siegel and confirmed it was not a trap. Satisfied with Siegel's okay, Elson emailed the client, accepted the assignment, and requested extensive background information on the subject.

An Israeli Professor at Ben Gurion University of the Negev, in Beer-Sheva, was about to make a break through discovery, and his client wanted it. The job required him to rent an apartment near the university for as long as needed, monitor the professor's lab, and when the breakthrough came, steal the formula and kill the professor.

Elson looked forward to the assignment. He had never been to Beer-Sheva. Waiting for the professor to make his discovery, he could soak in the curative natural hot mineral springs of the Neve Midbar Spa, outside the city. *This will be an easy job. Good money, and a better vacation than I planned. What could go wrong?*

Ding, ding, ding.

The alert tone on Elson's computer sounded whenever one of the listening devices installed throughout the lab, including the phones, relayed anything vocal. When the recorder/transmitter, placed in the ceiling of a campus bus stop a quarter of a mile from the lab picked up any talk, it sent the signal. At his leisure, the Collector could play back all conversations.

He put on headphones and listened to Shernicoff's call to the department Chairman.

So, you actually did it. My client was right.

He knew he had to act fast. From the wife's comments, he estimated he had about an hour and a half before the chairman got the message and headed over to see Shernicoff.

WAITING FOR BLOOM to call back, Shernicoff sat at the computer, elbows on the desk, his chin resting in cupped palms. Now that it was a reality, he contemplated what this breakthrough meant.

He'd read someplace that logic suggested if the most advanced species on a planet keeps making larger and larger leaps forward, at an ever-faster rate, at some point they'll make a leap so great that it completely alters life as they know it. Had he just done that?

This one would certainly cause upheavals in the scientific community. But, what about the shifts in global power and the chaos it would create in world financial systems? There could be forces who'd like to prevent his discovery from becoming a reality. Or, want it for themselves.

He worried. What would happen if the wrong people got ahold of it? He knew he always had the on/off switch. Still, he'd have to keep the discovery secure. But how?

What the hell, he thought, chastising himself. *I have a PhD in Computer Science for crying out loud. I can come up with something.* He pondered the situation for a while before he settled on a course of action.

He re-connected the drives to the computer's Ethernet slot and encrypted each one with the same password code. On the drive with the on/off switch, after encrypting it with the password, he wrote a non-password protected note, explaining what all the drives held, why he was making the copies, and why keeping them safe was a concern. He also included a cryptic message in the note, a clue to figuring out the password that protected the drives.

When he was done with the flash drives, he encrypted all the HP Superdome computers with the same password.

He placed the drives in a padded envelope and addressed it to the one person he could absolutely trust with them. And to the only one who could understand the cryptic message and figure out the password.

Telling the guard he would return shortly, he took the elevator to the lobby and walked to a mailbox located in the next building. He dropped the envelope in the mailbox, noting the next pick up was tomorrow, Monday morning, at 10:00 a.m. He strolled back to his lab to wait for Bloom to arrive.

CHAPTER 6
February 16
Sunday Afternoon
Be'er Sheva

THE COLLECTOR PULLED into the student parking lot at the side of the building. It was empty. *Not good. Can't be the only car.* He drove around until he came to a dumpster next to the freight platform at the rear of the building and pulled next to it. Unless someone drove directly up to the freight door, the dumpster blocked any view of his car. It was Sunday, so the chances of that happening were remote. He looked at his watch. *1:50 p.m. Not much time left before company arrives.*

He worked his way to the front entrance and took the elevator up to the lab. Before reaching the third floor, he slipped on a black ski mask, pulled his pistol from the small of his back, and attached a silencer. He held the weapon down behind his right leg. When the doors opened, the guard stared at him with a quizzical expression, obviously not expecting a masked person to be inside the elevator doors. The guard had no chance to react. The Collector took two quick steps into the reception area and shot him in the forehead, toppling him out of his chair. A dark red splotch formed on the wall where the bullet, blood splatter, and brain matter hit.

The Collector pressed the black button on the wall, unlocking the door leading into the corridor of the research facility. He walked to Shernicoff's lab door and tried the handle. *Locked.* He knocked on the door.

"That you, Simon?" came a voice on the other side.

Thinks I'm the chairman.

"Umhum," he mumbled.

The door opened. Jamming his hand into Shernicoff's chest, he grabbed the lab coat and pushed him back into the lab. Slamming the butt of the pistol into the side of Shernicoff's head, he knocked him unconscious and lowered him to the floor, then quickly scanned the room.

Confident they were alone, he pulled a roll of duct tape from his pocket and pressed a strip across Shernicoff's mouth. Grabbing the professor under the arm, he dragged him into the computer room and lifted him onto a chair. Securing his arms and legs to the chair with duct tape, he wound more around his chest, holding him upright. He then checked his watch to see how much time had passed since he'd entered the building. *Less than five minutes.*

He shook Shernicoff, bringing him back to consciousness. He saw Shernicoff's eyes flutter open and bulge when they locked on to his masked face. He swiveled his head rapidly from side to side before refocusing on him again, fear crossing his face.

"You make copies of program sequencing new DNA?" the Collector asked, grasping the man's shoulders. He felt Shernicoff's body tense.

"Ouch," winced Shernicoff when the duct tape was ripped from his mouth.

The Collector slapped him hard across the face. "Answer question," he demanded.

Shernicoff's head rocked back and a trickle of blood emerged at the corner of his mouth.

"Who are you? What new DNA?" Shernicoff asked, his voice barely audible.

"This wrong answer." The Collector punched Shernicoff in the mouth with a closed fist and blood spurted from a swelling lip. The Collector re-taped the oozing mouth and searched the man's clothes. He found nothing connected to the work in the lab.

He looked around the room and noticed a monitor screen glowing next to one of the computers. He moved to the table and tapped the keyboard. A pop-up screen asked for a password.

He walked back to his captive, and ripped the tape from his mouth. "What is computer password?"

Shernicoff grimaced but said nothing. The Collector hit him across the right cheek with the back of his hand. "What is password?"

Shernicoff's head snapped back from the blow, his eyes watered, but he remained silent.

The Collector knew he didn't have much time before the chairman arrived. If he showed up alone, it wouldn't be a problem. He'd kill him and keep working on Shernicoff until he gave up the password. But, what if the chairman called others to tell them the news and a bunch of people showed up? He couldn't take the chance.

He cut the tape binding his prisoner's body and arms to the chair, pulled him forward, and taped his wrists behind his back. He then cut the tape holding Shernicoff's legs to the chair, grabbed him by the hair, and hauled him to a standing position. The Collector pulled his pistol from his waistband and jammed the silencer under Shernicoff's jaw.

He snarled, "You come with me. I like keep you alive but you give me problem, I kill." In truth, his employer wanted Shernicoff dead, but that was only after he secured the formula. Since he couldn't get it from the computer, he needed to get it from the professor.

He dragged Shernicoff from the lab to the elevator. As they passed the body of the guard lying beside the reception desk, Shernicoff's gait slowed. A large pool of blood had spread out under the dead man's skull. "Give me trouble, that happen to you," the Collector said, tugging him to the elevator.

He pushed Shernicoff out of the building to his car behind the dumpster. Opening the trunk, he removed a suitcase, the size of an airline carry-on bag. He turned his prisoner's face to the open trunk. "You climb in by self or I hit again with gun and stuff you in. You smart, you climb in by self."

The Collector tensed and raised the pistol, pointing the butt toward the man's head. He relaxed when Shernicoff lowered his body and rolled himself into the trunk.

He slammed the trunk closed, knelt next to the suitcase, and withdrew a syringe and vial. He filled the syringe with the vial's clear liquid. Opening the trunk, he grabbed Shernicoff's wrists and jabbed the needle into his arm. When the man's eyes closed, he lowered the trunk. The injection would keep Shernicoff asleep for hours.

The Collector grabbed the suitcase, ran back to the building, and took the elevator once again to the third floor. He dragged the dead security guard to the elevator and laid the body half inside the cab, stopping the doors from closing, keeping the elevator available.

He re-entered the lab and moved quickly to the rear wall. After shooting the security lock several times, he kicked open the door, hustled to the bioreactor, and filled two eight-ounce specimen jars with the growing mass from the harvesting tank. From the suitcase, he removed three bricks of C-4 plastic explosive, taping one to the bioreactor's tanks and two to building support columns. He inserted the primer caps, checked his watch, and set the timer for fifteen minutes.

Placing the specimen jars in the suitcase, he dashed back to the computer room. He attached bricks of C-4 to three of the HP Superdome computers and one brick each to four building support columns. A check of his watch showed a little over five minutes had passed. He set these timers so all the explosives would go off within seconds of each other and the ones in the lab.

He jogged to the waiting elevator, pulled the body out of the way, and pressed the lobby button. It felt like an excruciatingly slow decent to the first floor before reaching the lobby. He burst out of the building to his car.

Just past the campus bus stop holding the recording/transmitting device, shock waves buffeted his car as the explosions destroyed the laboratory and all traces of Shernicoff's discovery.

The Collector didn't know who hired him and didn't care. It didn't matter. He presumed his reputation of successfully collecting and delivering targets is what led to his selection for this mission. He would fulfill it... mostly. He didn't have the formula and hadn't kill the professor.

But, his client would have everything needed to reproduce the breakthrough discovery. They'd have samples of the discovery, and Shernicoff, if they needed him, when he handed off both in Switzerland. Then they, or he, could kill him.

CHAPTER 7
February 16/17
Sunday/Monday
San Salvador/Israel

THE FULL TEAM spread out, scouring the city for Adwar. They rushed to the airport, bus terminal, and rental car lots. Adwar was gone. Dejected, they returned to the safe house after five hours of searching. Burns called Ben-Ami. When his office answered, the aide told him Ben-Ami was in a meeting with the Prime Minister and could not be disturbed.

He looked at his watch. It was 4:45 in the morning local time, 1:45 in the afternoon in Tel Aviv. Burns left a message that he'd lost Adwar and for Ben-Ami to call back as soon as possible. He stumbled to a bedroom and flopped across the bed.

Ring, ring. The telephone's ring jarred him awake. Groaning, Burns looked at the clock on the night stand. *8:17 a.m.* He'd only had four and a half hours of sleep. He fumbled for the receiver.

"Hello?"

"Burns. It's Ben-Ami—"

"I'm sorry," Burns blurted out, interrupting. "I let him get—"

"Forget that," Ben-Ami shouted. "We'll get him. This is more important. Get back here as fast as you can. There was an explosion at your Uncle Seth's laboratory today. He's missing. We don't know if he was there when it happened, but no one has seen or heard from him since."

Burns bolted upright and swung his legs off the bed. "What? What are you talking about?" he said, shaking his head, trying to clear sleep from his brain.

"That's all I know. I got the call five minutes ago. Get on the phone now and arrange to get home as fast as you can. I'll keep you updated when I learn anything new."

"Where is my Aunt Miriam?"

"She's at home. Don't waste any time. Make your travel plans, and let me know what they are."

"But, my uncle. What's—"

"I don't know anything else. Just get going."

Ben-Ami hung up.

Burns spent the next two hours on the phone with airlines and was able to change his previous travel arrangements.

He caught a 2:00 p.m. flight from San Salvador to Frankfurt, Germany. With the eight hour time difference, the overnight flight would connect the next day with a 12:30 p.m. El Al flight, getting him to Tel Aviv at 4:05 in the afternoon. He called Ben-Ami from Frankfurt during his layover for an update. There was nothing new.

He called his Aunt Miriam. The phone rang six times before she answered.

"Hello?" Her normally quiet voice sounded softer and weak.

"It's Eric."

"Oh, Eric. Where are you? Do you know about Seth? He's—"

"I know. I got a call last night. I'm in Germany, waiting for my flight home. I'll be there this afternoon."

"I'm so worried. He left me a note yesterday telling me he couldn't sleep and was going to the lab. There was an explosion. They don't know if he was in the building. I haven't heard from him. That's not like him. I'm frightened. When can you get here?"

Burns could tell how distraught she was. She wasn't thinking straight. He'd just finished telling her he'd be there that afternoon, and she didn't remember. His nerves were on edge too. He was rocking on his feet, twisting his neck as if to get soreness out. *Adwar getting away was bad; this is worse.*

"I'll be there this afternoon. I land around 4:00, and I'm going straight to the university. I'll find him. I promise. He'll be okay."

"Eric, I need you. Please hurry home."

"I will. I have to go. They're calling my flight. I'll see you soon. I love you." He hung up and boarded the plane.

AFTER THE PLANE reached cruising altitude, Eric laid his head back and closed his eyes. His thoughts were on his uncle and aunt, and his mind drifted back to the events that led to them becoming his surrogate parents in Israel.

He'd immigrated to Israel after graduating high school in New Jersey and claimed citizenship under the "Right of Return" law, which granted Israeli citizenship to anyone claiming to be a Jew. All he had to do was prove his mother was Jewish, which wasn't hard. She was a *sabra*, a native born Israeli.

While waiting for his paperwork to be processed, he lived with his grandmother on a *kibbutz* near the Golan Heights in Northern Israel. It was the same *kibbutz* where his mother was born and raised. From the time he was eight years old until high school graduation, he spent every summer school vacation there. It's where he learned to speak fluent Hebrew and Arabic.

Uncle Seth, his mother's brother, and Aunt Miriam came to the *kibbutz* every summer vacation when he was there. He immediately took a liking to them, especially his uncle, who spent a great deal of time with him. His uncle was a brilliant man, holding a PhD in Molecular Biology and Genetics, a Master's Degree in Evolutionary Biology, and a PhD in Computer Science.

Uncle Seth taught him about all of Israel, not just the area around the kibbutz. Looking back, Burns realized it was his uncle who helped him develop his mind. They spent hours each day playing games that required him to think, to analyze. His uncle taught him how to play chess and how to think not only of the next move, but three to four moves ahead. They played puzzle games, which helped him develop analytical skills, a talent that served him well in college and as a Mossad agent.

During his second year in the IDF, serving as a member of the *Sayeret Matkal*, the elite Israeli Special Forces, a group of Hamas terrorists infiltrated the Golan Heights from Lebanon. They attacked his *kibbutz*. The alarm sounded. Most of the terrorists were killed before they could break through the *kibbutz* perimeter. But not all of them.

They captured two terrorists running from the school. His grandmother worked in the school building where the children of the *kibbutz* spent the day while their parents worked in the fields.

The terrorists had not harmed any of the children, but they found his grandmother's body riddled with bullets in one of the classrooms. The children said before the terrorist burst into the room, she pushed them into a closet, locked the door, and shielded them with her body. The terrorists couldn't open the door, so they shot into it. Her body absorbed the bullets that penetrated the wood, but none struck a child.

They asked the terrorists why they only went after the school. The reply was chilling. "To kill all the children," they said. "That way we would wipe out an entire generation of Israelis."

For the captured terrorists, there was no judge, no trial, no jury. Only swift *kibbutz* justice. They led the terrorists out to a field and summarily executed them, their bodies buried with the other terrorists, deep in Israeli soil. In the spring, fresh fruits and vegetables bloomed in those same fields, feeding the generations of Israelis the terrorists sought to wipe out.

Uncle Seth and Burns made the funeral arrangements for his grandmother. After her murder, his aunt and uncle were his only family in Israel. Whenever he had leave from the IDF, vacations from college, for birthdays and the Jewish holidays, he'd be at their home in the Negev. With his real mother and father in the United States, his love for his uncle and aunt grew, and they became his surrogate parents.

He promised his aunt he'd find his uncle and everything would be okay. But would it?

CHAPTER 8
February 17
Monday Afternoon
Tel Aviv, Israel

THE FASTEN SEATBELTS announcement snapped him back to the present. He glanced out the window at the blue water of the Mediterranean. As the plane banked in its final approach into Tel Aviv, a shudder rippled through his body. *What happened to my uncle?*

Burns sat in the back of the Office vehicle Ben-Ami sent to pick him up. He'd asked to be driven straight to Be'er Sheva, but the driver said his orders were to drive him directly to Ben-Ami.

The car pulled to a stop in front of a non-descript grey commercial building. Eric stepped into the spacious lobby. He glanced at the big clock on the wall above the security desk. *4:38 p.m.* Two plainclothes security men sat behind the desk. They nodded to him.

There was no directory to indicate the building was the headquarters of The Institute for Intelligence and Special Operations, the Mossad. If you worked for it, as he had for the last eight years, you called it the Office. Burns walked to a plain grey door with no markings, located to the left of the lobby's security desk. There was an electronic pad to scan ID cards. In addition to the guards in the lobby, an overhead security camera picked up his approach.

Burns didn't have his ID card with him and had to wait until the guards clicked him in. He walked down a short corridor to a bank of three elevators. Waiting for an elevator, he reflected on how he became an agent of the Mossad.

ONE OF HIS uncle's degrees was a PhD in Computer Science from MIT. Based on a recommendation from his uncle, after Burns completed military service, he was admitted to The Technion, Israel's equivalent of M.I.T or Stanford in the United States, and majored in computer science.

A month before graduation, studying for a final exam in a computer science course in the rear of a nearly empty coffee shop, he heard a voice say, "Excuse me. You're Eric Burns, aren't you?"

He looked up. A man who appeared to be in his forties, dressed casually in khakis and a short-sleeved white shirt, the top two buttons opened at the neck, stood across the table.

"Yes, I am," he replied in a sharp tone, annoyed at the interruption.

"May I have a few minutes of your time?"

Without waiting for an answer, the man reached into his shirt pocket, removed a plastic ID card, and sat across from him. He slid the card over. "My name is Yoni, and I'm from The Institute for Intelligence and Special Operations. Do you know what that is?"

Burns inserted a bookmark in the textbook and closed it. He bit the inside of his lip. *What do they want with me?* He pushed his chair back in an awkward attempt to put more space between them.

"Of course. Everyone knows that's the official name of the Mossad. How can I help you?"

"How you can help us is precisely why I'm here," Yoni said. "I'm from the recruiting department, and you can help us by considering a career working for us.'"

Burns stammered, "The Mossad wants *me* to join *them*? Why?"

"We've been following your time in Israel, since you first applied for citizenship, through your service in the army and your studies at Technion. You speak six languages fluently, your record in the military is exemplary, and according to your professors, you have a brilliant analytical mind. We know that you are also quite a talented computer hacker."

"Am I in trouble?"

The man called Yoni smiled. "No, not at all. As far as we can tell, you've done nothing criminal in your hacking. Simply put, beside your talent for hacking, you excel in the traits we look for in an agent."

The man retrieved his ID card from the table and placed a small business card in front of Burns, printed with only 'Yoni' and a phone number. "I understand this wasn't something you imagined would happen to you today. Think about it. You can be of great service to your adopted country. Give me a call if you want to talk or have any questions."

He rose, reached across the table, and shook Burns' hand. "I hope to hear from you soon," he said and walked out of the coffee shop.

Burns sat in his chair looking down at the card. After a moment, he shook his head and began to chuckle at the absurdity of the situation. He thought, *how the hell am I supposed to study for a final exam after that conversation?*

A week later, he called Yoni and accepted the invitation. Two months after graduation, he went through an array of tests to determine if he had the psychological makeup to be a Mossad agent. He passed them easily, demonstrating an uncanny ability to detach events and compartmentalize his mind that surprised even him.

Although a fine athlete, he went through physical fitness tests that pressed levels of strength and endurance he never knew he possessed. At times, he thought his lungs would collapse as he willed his battered body over hazardous terrain he didn't think existed in Israel. Then came the specialized training: weapons, martial arts, and survival skills in a host of grueling conditions.

In the classroom, he learned how to research a target and study their background to acquire valuable intelligence. He honed his foreign languages. He learned how to lie with ease and to detect when others were doing the same. They trained him how to trail someone so stealthily that they would only know they were being followed if he walked up to them and told them. They taught him how to create new personas, even how to apply makeup. These and dozens of other skills were drilled into him to such an extent that he no longer had to think about them.

Then came April, the fifth day of Passover, the day Tamara and Saul were murdered by terrorists. Ben-Ami had offered him any assignment he wanted. Burns chose to be a *kidon*.

Ben-Ami later told him that one look in his eyes and he knew two things for sure. First, Burns had what it took to be a *kidon*, an assassin. And second... he pitied any man Burns was sent after.

BING. THE ELEVATOR chime nudged him back to the present. He glanced up at the camera that watched his every move as he entered the elevator. He fidgeted and shifted his weight from foot to foot, listening to the metallic hum of the cables and vibrations of the elevator. *Where is my uncle?* Emerging on the sixth floor, he entered a small reception area. It was devoid of any furnishings. No signs or markings indicated what the floor housed.

He approached the receptionist window located on the wall opposite the elevators. The window was two-inch thick Lexan bullet-proof plastic. The entire wall surrounding the window an impene-trable security barrier made of two and a half inches of solid tempered steel, covered by sheet rock. On his first visit here, they told him the Lexan window and barrier wall was because the Office was a prime target for terrorists.

Burns nodded at the receptionist. Her voice came through the speaker mounted above the window. "Good afternoon, Burns. He's waiting for you in the conference room."

He listened to the click of the electronic locks unlatching a door set flush to the wall and the whisper of hydraulics as they slowly swung the door open. Burns marched down the corridor to the conference room as the security door shut behind him. He knocked on the door. Ben-Ami called out, "Come in."

They shook hands and took seats. "Anything new since I spoke to you?"

"Yes and no," Ben-Ami said. "We still don't know anything more about your uncle, but here's what we do know. He was at his lab early Sunday afternoon. He left your aunt a note telling her he couldn't sleep and was going to the lab. She said that he'd been restless for the last few days. He told her he was positive he was on the verge of achieving the big breakthrough on a project he'd been working on for years.

"We know he tried to reach Simon Bloom, his department chairman, around 1:30 Sunday afternoon. He tried him at his home and got Bloom's wife. She told him he was playing golf. He left her a cryptic message to give to Bloom and told her that her husband would understand what it meant. He tried Bloom on his cell and left a voice mail message asking him to come to the lab as soon as possible. We found your uncle's car in the faculty parking lot, covered with debris from the explosion."

"Did Bloom's wife tell you anything else?" Burns asked. "Did he sound worried? Did he give her the impression there was any kind of a problem?"

"No. As a matter of fact she described his tone as sounding excited."

Burns stood, ran fingers through his hair, and began pacing behind his chair. "And no one has spoken to him since he went to the lab?"

"No. Not that I'm aware of."

"What do you know about the explosion itself? What caused it? How much damage?" Burns asked, his questions shooting out like machine gun fire.

"Take it easy. I know you have a hundred questions, but right now, I don't have a hundred answers. Please, sit down," Ben-Ami said, pointing to the chair.

Burns sat, reached for a bottle of water, and took a sip. "Sorry. It's frustrating. I'm in San Salvador and all this is happening here."

"I know. By the way, we'll get to your debrief on the Adwar operation later, when all this is done. We'll get another chance at him in May, presuming he keeps the reservation he made," Ben-Ami said. He grabbed a few grapes from a bowl and popped them into his mouth.

Ben-Ami continued. "Here's the rest of what we know. And I want you to remain calm because you're not going to like most of it. At the beginning, we thought a leaking gas line caused the explosion. When the fire was out and the investigators were able to get in to the building, or what was left of it, they found traces of C-4."

"C-4? C-4 was used in the building?" Burns shouted.

"I told you to stay calm. Don't interrupt me until I'm finished. Do you understand?" Ben-Ami said, raising his voice. Burns knew that tone. He'd heard Ben-Ami use it when he got mad, and you didn't want Gideon Ben-Ami mad at you.

"Sorry."

"All right. Moving on. When they discovered that someone used C-4, they called in *Shin Bet* because they handle domestic terrorism and us because it may be outsiders. Based on the amount of damage done to the building, we agreed that someone used a lot of C-4. The structural engineer experts determined the primary point of the explosions occurred on the third floor. Your uncle's lab was on the third floor."

"Sorry to interrupt, but are you saying you think my uncle's lab was the reason the building was blown up? Why? What was he doing that someone would want to blow up the building and destroy his lab?" Burns asked. "It doesn't make any sense. I want—"

The phone rang. Ben-Ami held up his hand to signal Burns to wait, as he picked up the receiver. Ben-Ami listened for a couple of seconds. "Send him in as soon as he gets up here."

"That was the receptionist. Simon Bloom is downstairs. When he gets upstairs, maybe he'll be able to answer some of your questions."

A few minutes later, the door to the conference room opened, and Simon Bloom entered. Burns had met him a few times at his uncle's home when he was visiting. Bloom and his wife attended some parties his uncle threw for colleagues at the University.

"Good to see you again Eric," Bloom said, shaking Burns' hand. "Although, I'm sorry it's under these circumstances."

"Thank you," Burns said. "Please take a seat."

After the three men sat, Burns said, "Can you tell me what's going on?" He gestured toward Ben-Ami. "Gideon said they found traces of C-4 explosive in the rubble. This wasn't an accident. What was my uncle working on that could be so important someone would deliberately blow up his office and laboratory and kill him?"

"Whoa!" Bloom said, holding up his hand. "Don't jump the gun. We don't know that your uncle is dead. He might not have even been in the building when the explosion happened."

Burns rubbed his forehead. "You're right. I am getting ahead of myself. Okay. Can you tell me what he was working on?"

"Of course. Your uncle came to me seven years ago with an idea. To take simple pond scum algae, translate its DNA code into computer codes, manipulate those codes, and re-insert the new DNA codes back into the algae. Through manipulation and bypassing the evolutionary process, the goal was to create a cheap, renewable source of biofuel, which would produce a never-ending supply of diesel oil and gasoline. Using just one hundred thousand acres of the three and a half million acres that form the Negev Desert, Israel could produce all the oil the world would ever need.

"He and I have been working on the project ever since, and about a week ago he told me he was very close to making it happen. He called me Sunday and left a message saying he did it"

"But why would someone blow up his laboratory?"

"To stop us from achieving success."

"Why?"

"Here is one simple explanation. You know how they say 'follow the money'? Your uncle and I were finalizing patents for the process. Ownership of the patents would make both of us enormously wealthy. I'm talking billions. That could be one reason. Maybe someone was after the process to get the patents for themselves and become rich."

"Could they do that?"

"I don't know. Possibly. But there are other more likely factors at play."

"What do you mean?" Burns asked.

"May I?" Bloom said, pointing to a bottle of water on the table. Ben-Ami nodded. He uncapped it and took a sip.

Bloom continued. "Let me ask you a question. If Israel is able to supply the world all the oil it would ever need at less than $5 a barrel instead of $30, $50, or $100 a barrel, and by the way, oil which unlike current carbon based fuels will not pollute the atmosphere, who gets hurt?"

"Certainly the major oil producing countries. OPEC for sure," Burns said.

"Precisely. Remember your Middle Eastern history? In 1938, Saudi Arabia was one of the poorest countries in the world. King Ibn Saud's income consisted of the $5 per head tax paid by pilgrims to Mecca. He had the only car in the kingdom, and there weren't even any paved roads. With this discovery and the loss of oil income, Without the obscene amount of money Middle East oil brings in through their artificial high pricing, Saudi Arabia could revert to what it was in 1938. Can you imagine their reaction to our discovery? Do you think they'd want to stop us?"

Burns slammed his palm on the table. "Those sons-of- bitches. They did this to my uncle?" he yelled.

"I don't know. But, before you go off halfcocked on them, as I said, there are other factors."

"What do you mean?"

"There are others who wouldn't like to see our process become a reality. Think about it. If the price of oil dropped, what about the large oil corporations? They'd no longer earn four or five billion dollars profit every quarter. How do you think they'd react? Or for that matter, what about the countries that consume huge amounts of oil like China, India, Japan? Would they try to get our discovery for themselves?"

Burns slumped in his chair. "Got any more good news for me?"

"Like I said," Bloom said, leaning back in his chair, "there are other players, and you have to figure out which one could have done it. For all I know, maybe it was someone else I haven't even thought of."

Burns placed his elbows on the table and cupped his head in his hands. "Damn!" he muttered.

CHAPTER 9
February 18
Tuesday Morning
Tel Aviv

B URNS ARRIVED AT his apartment late at night from the site of the excavation work at the university. They told him it wouldn't be until sometime tomorrow afternoon before they would reach the area of his uncle's lab and office. He picked up his mail in the lobby but was too tired, physically and emotionally, to go through it or do anything else. He needed sleep. He flopped on his bed, fully clothed, and within minutes, fell into a deep sleep.

A sliver of sunshine peeking through the edge of the window shade woke him. He rolled over and looked at the clock. It was 9:30 in the morning. Sitting in his apartment wondering what was happening at the university excavation site wouldn't do any good, so he planned to go there after his coffee. He rose, showered, and dressed. While the coffee brewed, he went to the kitchen table where he'd left his accumulated mail, ready to wade through it.

A large, thick, padded envelope at the bottom of the stack of mail drew his attention. He had noticed it last night but hadn't given it much thought, piling the smaller envelopes on top of it. When he saw the return address, a chill spread through his body. It was from his uncle, the return address, his university office. Burns yanked it from the table, paying no attention to the other envelopes cascading to the floor.

He looked at the postmark. It was dated Monday, the day after the explosion. *He's alive. He mailed this after the explosion.* Burns ripped open the top and looked inside. All he could see was a bunch of computer flash drives. He tipped the envelope over and the contents spilled onto the table. There were six flash drives, each one labeled with the numbers one through six. On the sixth label, a note said, "Play this one first."

Burns booted up his computer, attaching one end of a USB cable to flash drive number six and the other end into the computer. The drive showed it contained two files, one of them named "letter to Eric," the other, "on/off switch." He clicked on the "letter to Eric" file. When the document opened, a knot formed in his stomach. He saw it was dated Sunday, the day of the explosion, not Monday, the date on the postmark. He began to read.

Sunday

Dear Eric,

I've made an amazing discovery. An inexpensive, renewable source of biofuel. The cost to produce it is equivalent to producing oil at $4 to $5 US, per barrel. That's roughly 10 to 20 times below the current price of crude oil.

We can produce a never–ending quantity of biofuel, enough to supply the entire world. And best of all, we can do it here in Israel, in the Negev Desert.

Eric shook his head. It was one thing to hear this from Bloom, now his uncle confirmed everything. He looked down and continued to read.

You're receiving this envelope because I have grave concerns. This discovery will most certainly cause chaos in the world of science and religion, as well as the world's financial markets and produce shifts in global power. Who knows how OPEC or the large oil corporations will react? Or countries like China, India, and Japan? Will they try to get my discovery for themselves?

Burns thought, *That's everything Bloom told me.* He continued reading.

Eric, you're like a son to your aunt and me and the only person in the world, beside your aunt, I have complete trust in. I've password protected the flash drives in this envelope and the computer files in my lab. To insure the password doesn't fall in the wrong hands, I'm not enclosing it with this letter.

As I write this, even though you've grown, I can't help thinking of you as the bright boy your aunt and I spent the summers with at the kibbutz each year with your mother and grandmother. I remember how you made your grandmother laugh when she yelled out the window for you to come eat, calling to you in Yiddish, and you'd pretend you didn't understand.

I think about how you showed signs of persistence and remarkable intelligence even as an eight-year-old, and how those traits served you so well as you became an adult. I recall when I taught you about computers and how you became fascinated by the simple power of three words.

Maybe I'm being too paranoid about all this. But just in case, keep these drives in a safe place.

By the way, I've given you a clue to the password, one I know you'll figure out.

Love, Uncle Seth

Burns exited the letter file and clicked on the file titled "on/off switch." A pop-up screen appeared requesting a password.

Eric slouched back against the chair and pinched the bridge of his nose. *His mind whirled. It's been three days since my uncle went to his lab on Sunday. They're still excavating, and I don't know if he's alive or dead. Now, this. He sent me flash drives related to his work at the lab because he's worried, but not the password to open them. He said there is a clue to the password, but I have no damn idea what he's talking about.*

CHAPTER 10
February 20
Thursday
Five Days After Kidnapping
Phoenix, Arizona

"Shit." Elliot Johnson slammed the printed out email on his desk. It was the first communication from the Collector in four days. The last one from him, five days ago, said Shernicoff's experiment had succeeded, and he was going to Shernicoff's lab to steal both the computer program containing the altered DNA sequencing and a sample of the new species.

This new email informed him the sample taken from Shernicoff's lab died, and the Collector didn't know why. The message also said he had no choice but to blow up the Israeli's lab and computers because the computers were password protected, and he couldn't download anything from them. As a result, he'd reverted to plan B. Kidnap Shernicoff, who should have all the knowledge needed in his head to replicate the discovery, and get him out of Israel.

The email went on to say that after being repeatedly drugged with truth serum, he learned Shernicoff copied all the information necessary to repeat the discovery on digital flash drives, password protected them, and sent them to his nephew for safekeeping. The only positive in the email was the Collector had the name and address of Shernicoff's nephew. Eric Burns and he lived in Tel Aviv. He requested Johnson send instructions on what further action he should take.

"What the fuck?" Johnson muttered. His contact who recommended the Collector said the guy was the best, but this was a colossal fuck up.

The email gave no indication to the Collector's whereabouts. The routed message went through different servers across the globe, making it untraceable. The email was time stamped 11:00 a.m. He looked at the clock on his desk. 7:30 p.m. in Arizona. If the Collector were someplace in Europe, as he suspected, the time difference was eight hours. *Already nighttime.* He estimated he needed to get back to the Collector with instructions in the next five or six hours. That would give the man a full day to operate.

Johnson swiveled to his computer and logged on to a special email account set up on Hotmail. Only one other person knew the account existed and had the password to open it. Jorge Moreno Estrada. Johnson opened a new message box, copied and pasted the contents of the Collector's email, and asked Moreno's advice on how to proceed. However, he didn't click the send button. Instead, he saved the message in the draft folder.

He logged off the email account and removed a burner cell phone from his desk drawer. He called a number in the City of Culiacan, in the Mexican State of Sinaloa. Johnson let the phone ring four times and hung up. He knew no one would answer. The number was a pay phone located in the rear of a small bodega in the poorest part of the city. The owner would hear the four rings and call a number in the city. That call would go straight to voice mail, where the bodega owner would leave a message that the phone in his store rang four times. Moreno would receive the voice message, access the email account, read the message in the draft file, and delete it. Since no email message was actually sent, there was no way the authorities could intercept it.

Or that's what Johnson and Moreno thought.

LOCATED ON THE floor below the office of Energy Renewables and Elliot Johnson, FBI Agent Jack Collins called Robert Hall.

"Speak to me," Hall said.

"This is Agent Jack Collins. I think I've got something hot."

"You think or you know?"

"I know."

"Let's hear it."

"I intercepted an email message to Johnson from the man he calls the Collector. The gist of it is some Israeli guy named Shernicoff succeeded in some kind of experiment, and the Collector blew up Shernicoff's lab and computers. He also kidnapped Shernicoff and has the name and address of Shernicoff's nephew, who has password protected digital flash drives containing whatever the experiment is all about. The nephew's name is Eric Burns, and he lives in Tel Aviv. The Collector asked for instructions on what to do next. Johnson just sent the information to Moreno, in the draft folder, asking for advice on how to proceed."

"Good work. Do we know who this Shernicoff is or have any idea what this is all about?"

"No, sir."

"Okay. Send me copies of everything you have. You and Vitale stay alert tonight. This could be the break we've been looking for. I expect Moreno will be back to Johnson very soon. I don't care what time it is. When you get anything more, call me."

It was almost 11:00 p.m. in New York City. Hall put down his cell phone and let out a deep satisfying breath. *Maybe the break I've been waiting for.*

He wondered who Shernicoff was and why the Collector kidnapped him. What experiment were they talking about, and what made some Israeli so important to Johnson and Moreno? Maybe Shernicoff's nephew, Burns, who had those password protected digital flash drives, had some answers.

CHAPTER 11
February 20
Thursday Night
Arizona

J OHNSON TOOK OFF his tie and unbuttoned the top button on his shirt. He rose from his desk and paced back and forth in his office, biting his lower lip. He needed a drink. He opened the credenza and pulled out a bottle of Patron Silver tequila. He raised the bottle to his lips and took a large swallow. The liquor burned his throat going down. He felt the warmth spread through his body. Holding the bottle by the neck, he sat on the leather couch across from his desk and looked out the large window. He stared at the sliver of a moon. It looked like a sickle.

Maybe the Grim Reaper's sickle. Is this the end? Was I stupid enough to believe it could go on forever? Or at least until I achieved my dream?

It began six years ago. Johnson believed he'd be the one to find the Holy Grail. Where others failed, he would succeed. He'd be famous. King of the hill. Rich as Midas. He formed his company, Energy Renewables, in Arizona, where he would grow algae in the desert that would produce an abundant supply of low cost, renewable energy, to replace oil.

But things didn't go that way. Three years and millions of dollars of his own money later, he was nearly broke and no closer to his dream.

He had a laboratory twenty-five miles outside of town, with scientists hard at work. By the following week, he wouldn't be able to meet his payroll. The dream would be gone, blown away like dry straw in a gust of wind.

He'd called his banker to see exactly how much money he had left in his account, in order to plan how distribute the balance. It couldn't be more than a few thousand dollars. His mouth fell open, and the phone almost toppled from his hand when his banker gave him an account balance of well over $200,000.

Stammering, he told the banker he had an urgent call on the other line and would call back. *It has to be a mistake.* He waited five minutes for his nerves to calm and called the bank again. They reconfirmed the balance. Johnson asked for a recap of the week's transactions. The only activity in the account for the week was the receipt of a $220,000 wire transfer from a bank in Chicago the day before. Johnson thanked the banker and disconnected.

What the hell's going on? Money from a bank in Chicago? Who put that amount of money into his account... and why?

His secretary buzzed. FEDEX delivered a box requiring his signature. He signed for the package and brought it into his office. Shipped yesterday, the sender address said Gomez Securities, Chicago, Illinois. He had no idea who they were.

Johnson opened the package. The cover letter, dated yesterday, addressed to Johnson, informed him that the thirty-five individuals on the attached list had purchase shares in his company, and a wire transfer of $220,000 for the shares, less commissions, would be forthcoming that day. The letter was signed, Angel Gomez, President.

Holding the cover letter in his hand, Johnson leaned back in his chair. When he formed his company, in anticipation of becoming rich, he decided to become a publicly traded firm. He hired a lawyer to help him. The lawyer said the easiest and cheapest way to do it was to find a shell corporation. He explained a shell corporation was one that had already filed with the Securities and Exchange Commission and been approve to sell shares in the company.

However, for many reasons, most companies never moved forward or went out of business. The lawyer said all Johnson had to do is find and buy one of these existing companies, including its shares, and he'd have control of a company ready to sell shares of stock to the public.

There was only one problem. While Johnson moved forward and bought a shell corporation, he never offered any shares for sale... to anyone.

Johnson called the telephone number on the letterhead, identified himself, and asked for Gomez.

"This is Gomez. How can I help you?"

"This is Elliot Johnson of Energy Renewables."

"Ah, Mr. Johnson. I've been expecting your call. Nice to speak with you."

"Listen, Gomez. Let's not waste time making small talk. What the hell is going on? I just received your FEDEX package, and my bank confirmed the two hundred and twenty thousand dollar deposit. The problem is, I never authorized you, or anyone one else, to sell shares in my company."

"I see. So that means you'll be returning the money to our bank in Chicago today?"

"What?"

"I think you heard me. Since you never authorized anyone to sell shares in your company, you'll need to return the money to our bank, so I can return the money to the investors."

Johnson's mind raced. He couldn't return the money. He needed it. *Who was this guy and what was his angle?*

"Look, Gomez. I don't know what's going on, but I'm not returning the money. It's in my account, and it's staying there," Johnson said.

"I thought you'd say that. Do you think we don't know that you're on your ass financially and can't afford to send the money back? Just take the money and keep your mouth shut. Someone will come to your office tomorrow morning and explain everything. Have a nice day."

Johnson sat in his chair, phone pressed to his ear, listening to a dial tone.

THE NEXT MORNING at 10:30, Johnson's secretary announced a Mr. Santo Reyes was in the waiting room. She said Reyes told her he had an appointment, made yesterday by a Mr. Angel Gomez. Johnson told her to wait two minutes and then send him in. He opened his middle desk drawer, grabbed a bottle of antacids, popped three in his mouth, and chewed them. He was losing the battle to quell the burning in his throat and chest he had since yesterday's conversation with Gomez.

He opened the top side desk drawer, removed the revolver he kept there, and checked the cylinder. Full load. He replaced the pistol but left the drawer partially open, easy to reach the gun if needed.

His door opened, and the man named Reyes walked into the office.

"Mr. Johnson," Reyes said. "How nice to meet you." He had a slight accent. *Hispanic.* Reyes didn't offer to shake his hand.

Reyes was about six feet tall. He wore a solid blue golf shirt, jeans, and a pair of scuffed cowboy boots. The man was solidly built; a well-developed chest stretched his shirt, his biceps and forearms muscular. The face thin and angular, with high cheekbones. A full mustache curved around the edges of his mouth, and a small tuft of a goatee nestled on his chin.

It was the man's eyes that gave Johnson chills and made the hair on his neck lift. They were black in color and dead as decaying leaves, deep and cold as a grave. A wide scar at the edge of his right eyebrow made his eyes look more sinister.

"Just tell me what the hell is going on. What do you want?" Johnson said. He slipped his hands to his lap, below the level of his desktop, ready to grab the revolver.

Reyes let out a small sigh. "My, my. So blunt. Have it your way," he replied. "I work for Señor Jorge Moreno Estrada Do you know that name?"

"Never heard of him. Who is he?"

"The short version. Señor Moreno is one of the leaders of the Sinaloa Drug Cartel. It is the most powerful drug trafficking, money laundering, and organized crime syndicate in the world. And as of today, your new partner."

Johnson jumped up from his chair. "Get the fuck out of my office," he yelled.

Reyes slowly pushed himself out of his chair. He shook his head back and forth. Then, as fast as a cheetah chasing its prey, Reyes lunged across the desk, clutched Johnson's shoulders, pulled him forward, and slammed his face into the top of the desk. He clenched Johnson's hair and lifted his face from the desk. Blood spurted from the man's nose. Leaning his face down to Johnson's, Reyes glowered at him. He took a deep breath, and in a soft, calm tone said, "Don't ever raise your voice to me again." He released Johnson's head and resumed his seat.

"Sit back down in your seat," Reyes said.

Johnson sat, blood dripped from his nose.

Reyes reached in his back pocket and removed a red bandana. He used it to wipe blood that had landed on his hand from Johnson's nose. He threw the bandana across the desk. "Here. Hold this against your nose with some pressure. It'll stop the bleeding." Johnson snatched up the bandana and pressed it against his nose.

"Don't say another word. Just listen. Do you understand?"

Johnson nodded.

"We need to launder money from our drug sales in the United States and get it back to us in Mexico. And you're going to help us."

"Are you crazy?" Johnson said.

"I'm not going to tell you again. Shut your mouth and listen, or I'm really going to hurt you. Do you hear me?"

Johnson nodded meekly.

"Here is how it's going to work. We own the Gomez firm in

Chicago. Gomez had a strong craving for drugs, and we had the supply. When he couldn't pay for them anymore and owed us a lot of money, we came to an understanding. He continues to run a legitimate small brokerage business handling penny stocks, but he also handles certain opportunities for us when we need it. And he gets to have all the drugs he wants to shove up his nose. He's happy with the arrangement. By the way, how's your nose doing?"

Johnson pulled the bandana from his nose to check.

"Stopped bleeding but hurts."

"Suck it up and listen. We know about your business and financial problems. Don't ask how; we just do. Here is where you come in. Gomez's firm will continue to sell shares of stock in your company. There won't be any real buyers. Gomez will pick random names and addresses out of phone books from around the country as the buyers. He'll transfer the funds that supposedly come from the buyers to your account, as he would for any company whose stock he'd sold. He'll make it look legitimate by taking a normal broker's commission on the sales. That keeps him happy. It pays for his drugs. And you'll be above board and legitimate. You'll declare the sales of your stock and report the funds on your taxes."

"Can I ask a question?"

"What?"

"How much money are you talking about?"

"I'll get to that in a minute. Just listen. You are going to begin to build a real plant for your biofuel business here in the Arizona desert. After the shell of the building is up, you'll order the best, most expensive equipment for it. The only stipulation is you have to purchase all the equipment from companies outside of the United States. You'll tell us what you need, and we'll give you names of import/export companies in the States and Mexico to order from. You'll pay for the equipment with letters of credit from funds you'll transfer from your company's account to a bank in the Cayman Islands. When you confirm to the bank the goods have been shipped, they'll execute your letters of credit and pay the companies from your deposited funds.

"I don't get it. How does this help you?"

"Simple," Reyes said. "We need to get our drug money out of the States, and we'll get it in U.S. dollars from the account in the Cayman's."

"But what about the cost of buying and shipping the equipment?"

Reyes smiled. "There won't be any equipment. You'll just have invoices. You'll even amortize the cost of the equipment on your taxes as a business expense, so the government will believe you have it. We'll let you keep enough money to maintain your payroll. As far as the government is concerned, you're a legit company, with employees, looking to make a breakthrough in biofuels. Oh, one more thing."

Reyes paused for a second, and grinned. "You'll open a personal bank account at the Cayman Island bank. They'll have instructions to transfer fifteen percent of the value of each letter of credit into your account. We're chalking that up to the cost of laundering the money. Now, I'll answer your question from before. We're talking about letters of credit running between five and ten million dollars a year. Maybe more."

Johnson leaned back in his chair. *Fifteen percent. $750,000 to $1,500,000 a year. Tax free.* His nose didn't hurt any more.

THE KNOCK ON his door brought him back to the present. It was the cleaning lady. She told him she'd come back later.

He checked his computer and saw an email in the draft folder. Moreno had replied. Johnson read the draft.

Tell the Collector to contact the nephew Burns. Offer a trade. Shernicoff's life for the digital flash drives and the password. Make Burns come to a location of the Collector's choosing. When he has the digital flash drives and password, tell him to kill Shernicoff and Burns. Let the Collector know there is a $500,000 bonus when he completes the assignment.

Johnson deleted the draft and sent an email to the Collector with the instructions.

In the office below, Agent Jack Collins, who'd monitored the email account, forwarded copies of the draft email and the one to the Collector with the instructions to Robert Hall. He followed up with a phone call to make sure Hall knew they were on the way.

HALL READ BOTH emails and thought about what his next move should be. He weighed the information and made his decision. He would use the nephew, Burns, as bait and follow him until he met the Collector.

He'd grab the Collector and use him as leverage against Johnson. He'd threaten to charge Johnson with being an accomplice to kidnapping and extortion. Either charge carried much longer sentences than money laundering. He'd squeeze Johnson into laying out the entire money laundering scheme, seize the money, and after years of avoiding the law, the United States government would finally arrest Moreno .

JOHNSON CHECKED HIS email Friday and found one from the Collector. It informed him that he'd contacted Shernicoff's nephew and instructed him to be in Berne, Switzerland with the flash drives and password on Monday. He'd have them in his possession by Tuesday at the latest. Johnson copied the email and forwarded it to Moreno in the usual way.

An hour later, Agent Jack Collins, monitoring Johnson's email account, forwarded copies of the email from the Collector to Robert Hall. But Hall didn't get them.

Hall had brought the earlier emails to his boss, Len Gagne, first thing Friday morning. After a short discussion, he received Gagne's okay to fly to Israel to shadow Shernicoff's nephew. He boarded an

El Al flight out of Newark at 1:15 PM Friday afternoon, non-stop to Tel Aviv. The forwarded email revealing the plan to lure Burns to Switzerland arrived on Hall's cell phone email folder at 2:00 PM, well after he'd shut it down prior to take off.

But, back in Los Angeles, Santos Reyes received a copy of the same email from Moreno after it was sent, along with instructions to fly first to Spain, then to Switzerland, and get the flash drives.

CHAPTER 12
February 22
Saturday Morning
Ben Gurion Airport, Tel Aviv

E L AL FLIGHT 28 from Newark, New Jersey, arrived at 7:00 a.m. as scheduled. It took Hall almost an hour to clear Immigration and Customs. He had spoken with a Captain Dekel Mitnick of the Shin Bet yesterday, explained he was tracking an international money laundering operation and was following up a lead in Tel Aviv. He told Mitnick he was taking the overnight flight, gave him Eric Burns' name, and asked if the Shin Bet, as a courtesy to the F.B.I., would compile background information on Burns for his arrival.

Mitnick said Shin Bet would be happy to help the F.B.I., and he would personally meet Hall at the El Al King David Lounge in the main terminal when he arrived.

As Hall walked through the terminal, he was impressed. He'd been in more airports than he wanted to think about in the last few years. Compared to other airports, this was a beautiful building. He looked up at the four story high star shaped rotunda, with tilted glass walls, angled toward the center of the rotunda. Skylights and windows on the upper level flooded the entire terminal with bright sunshine.

He made his way to the front desk of the King David Lounge, and they paged Mitnick.

"You must be Robert Hall"

Hall turned and saw a man about six feet tall, thin, with an angular face. He had light brown hair and brown eyes. He wore a neatly pressed khaki uniform, shirt open at the neck, with his hat slipped under the shoulder epaulet. There was an insignia on the epaulet marking rank.

"And you must be Captain Mitnick."

"Please, call me Dekel."

"Okay, and I'm Robert."

"Shall we go? I have a car waiting outside to take us to my office," Mitnick said.

As they drove to Shin Bet Headquarters, Mitnick pointed out landmarks and points of interest to Hall. Thirty minutes later, they arrive at Shin Bet Headquarters on Yerukham Meshel Street.

Entering the building, Hall asked, "What does Shin Bet mean?"

"It's a two letter Hebrew abbreviation of the word Shabak, which is actually an acronym for our real name, General Security Service," Mitnick said. "Much like your F.B.I. stands for Federal Bureau of Investigation. Your motto is 'Fidelity, Bravery, Integrity. Ours is ' Defender that shall not be seen.' Although Shin-Bet is a security agency, it is not a part of the Israeli Ministry of Defense, and unlike your F.B.I., which answers to the Attorney General, our chief answers directly to the Prime Minister of Israel."

They took an elevator to a fifth floor conference room. The room was windowless, about forty feet long by twenty feet wide with a large oak table and padded black high-back chairs, enough to seat twenty comfortably. A man sat at the far end of the table. Although seated, Hall estimated him to be around five feet eight inches; maybe about sixty years old, He was heavy set, muscular, like a smaller version of a college linebacker. His mostly bald head, with a fringe of close cropped white hair, sat atop a full face with a wide flat nose.

Mitnick said, "Robert Hall, I'd like you to meet Gideon. Gideon, this is Robert Hall of the F.B.I."

As Hall shook Gideon's hand, he was keenly aware of the fact that Mitnick had not given the man's last name or his position.

Mitnick pointed to a chair across from Gideon. "Please, Robert, have a seat." Mitnick moved around the table and sat next to Gideon.

A file folder sat on the table in front of Gideon.

"Will you please repeat for Gideon what your trip to Israel entails?"

Hall turned his gaze to Gideon. "Sure. As I told Dekel yesterday, I work out of the F.B.I.'s New York office in the Asset Forfeiture and Money Laundering Unit, the AFMLU. But, unlike regional offices that operate only in their geographical jurisdiction, I have authority to operate anywhere, and as they say, to follow the money.

"Nine months ago, our office received a tip from a confidential informant that the Sinaloa Cartel Drug Cartel in Mexico is using a company in Arizona to launder money for them. We intercepted communications between them that led me to believe an Israeli citizen may be of use in putting a case together that will lead to the arrest of one of the leaders of the cartel."

"May I ask why you believe this?" Mitnick asked.

Hall hesitated before answering. He didn't know these people, and since some of what he'd learned was gained through questionable methods, it could bite him in the ass if the Israelis made it public. He decided to give them information but not reveal how it was obtained.

Hall shrugged. "We also intercepted communication that a man known as the Collector kidnapped an Israeli scientist. However, prior to the kidnapping, the scientist sent his nephew, a man named Eric Burns who lives here in Tel Aviv, some encrypted digital flash drives. We have strong reason to believe that the Collector was hired by the company in Arizona. If we can get the Collector, we can turn him against the Arizona company, and in turn, get the Arizona company to implicate one of the leaders of the drug cartel. We've been trying for years to get at the cartel and now, we just might be able to do it. Eric Burns could be the key."

As Hall told the story, he observed Mitnick's face, which seemed to tightened, and his eyes shifted a couple of times at Gideon. On the other hand, Gideon's facial expression was stoic, his eyes never wavered. Hall had a sense that behind Gideon's large rimless wire glasses, the man's penetrating eyes were examining him like a human X-ray machine.

"How do you think this man, Eric Burns, can be of use to you?" Mitnick asked.

"We have reason to believe the Collector will try to get in touch with Burns and offer to set his uncle free in exchange for the digital flash drives and the password to them."

"Why do you believe this?" Mitnick asked.

"I can't tell you how we know, but we know."

Until he had a better feel for the Israelis, he'd hold back the information he had from the last email communication from Moreno to Johnson, to pass on to the Collector. He thought back on the message.

Tell the Collector to contact the nephew, Burns. Offer a trade. Shernicoff's life for the digital flash drives and the password. Make Burns come to a location of the Collector's choosing. When he has the digital flash drives and password, tell him to kill Shernicoff and Burns. Let the Collector know there is a $500,000 bonus when he completes the assignment.

"Do you have any idea what the digital flash drives contain?" Mitnick asked.

"Not really. All we know is that it has something to do with an experiment the uncle was conducting. Apparently, the company in Arizona is very interested in it, at least to the extent they're willing to kidnap the scientist to get it."

Hall glanced at Gideon, who remained silent, absorbing the conversation.

"And what are you planning to do regarding Burns?" Mitnick asked.

"With your permission and help, I would like to use Burns as bait. I want to put a tail on him, and when the Collector makes contact, grab the Collector."

For the first time, Gideon moved. He reached for the file in front of him and slid it closer to his body. He opened it, thumbed through a few pages, and closed it. He took a deep breath, reached into his shirt pocket, and removed a pipe. Hall could see the stem had been chewed up from long use. Gideon reached into his back pants pocket, removed a pouch of tobacco, and methodically packed a bowlful into the pipe.

"May I call you Robert, Agent Hall?" Gideon asked.

"Sure."

"Robert, can you tell me how you acquired all this information?

"I'm sorry. I'm not at liberty to discuss it."

"Okay. I'll respect that. But you see, we have a problem. My full name is Gideon Ben-Ami, and I am the Director General of the Mossad."

Hall sat back in his chair. *What the hell? The Mossad?*

"I can see by the expression on your face you're wondering why the Mossad is interested in your situation."

"You bet."

"Like you, there are things I can't reveal, but some I can," Ben-Ami said. "The scientist who was kidnapped and the digital flash drives he sent are of vital national security to the State of Israel."

Ben-Ami pulled the file in front of him closer and opened it.

"When you made your inquiry to Mitnick yesterday, as you might imagine, it set off alarm bells. So we did some checking on you."

Ben-Ami picked up a piece of paper from the file and said, "You have an impressive resume. A graduate of the City University of New York's John Jay College of Criminal Justice, then the New York City Police Department. Made detective in five years, and two years later, assigned to the Investigation Division of the New York County District Attorney's Office dealing with white collar and organized crime."

Gideon paused. "You're apparently ambitious. While working at the D.A.'s office, you went to Fordham Law School at night, and within weeks of graduation, you accepted your current position as an investigative attorney with the F.B.I.'s New York office in the Asset Forfeiture and Money Laundering Unit. Our sources tell us you've established a remarkable record of four successful investigations leading to prosecutions and forfeiture of over twenty-nine million dollars in less than two years. "

"How the hell did you get all that information overnight?" Hall exclaimed.

Ben-Ami grinned and shrugged. "Like you said, I'm not at liberty to discuss it."

"Man, I've heard you guys are good. Now I know. But what has my background got to do with the Mossad or my using this guy Burns as bait?"

Ben-Ami pulled out an old Zippo lighter and lit his pipe. He tilted his head upward and blew out a plume of smoke. "I 'm not supposed to smoke in the building, but as they say, rank has its privileges." Hall wrinkled his nose as a cloud of pungent smoke hovered over them.

Ben-Ami took another puff. "Here is what I can tell you. As you requested, we did a background check on Eric Burns. He's the international sales manager for a computer security firm headquartered in Israel. As far as we can tell, he's just an average hard working man. Bluntly, we would find it very difficult to sanction using a civilian like him as bait, particularly when it involves the type of people in drug cartels."

"But—" Hall responded.

Ben-Ami held up his palm. "I'm not done. We do want to cooperate with you and the F.B.I. in your investigation. You've given us information we didn't have, and we need time to digest it and figure out how best to proceed. Why don't I have Dekel bring you to your hotel? It will give you a chance to catch up on some rest. I'm sure you'll be hit with a case of jet lag pretty soon. In the meanwhile, I'll get together with our people and see if we can come up with a solution that will help you with your objective, while we insure our national security problem is also addressed."

Hall couldn't think of any reason not to graciously accept Ben-Ami's offer, so they shook hands, and he and Mitnick left.

As THEY DROVE to the Dan Tel Aviv Hotel, Hall thought about this case. It was different from the ones he'd worked before. The others involved United States crime organizations using American banks to launder their dirty money. This one involved an American company laundering money for a Mexican drug cartel in a foreign country.

Hall knew why his boss, Len Gagne, assigned the case to him. As much as Gagne chastised him for playing fast and loose with department rules and procedures, sometimes even going over the line, Hall got the job done. And although he would warn him to follow the rules, Gagne would let Hall do whatever he decided needed to be done. Hall was sure Gagne figured there might be the need to do a few things outside the box, but he also knew, as far as Gagne was concerned, the results spoke for themselves.

Mitnick broke the silence when he asked Hall if he would share how the F.B.I. got their information. Hall mulled it over and decided that maybe a little forthcoming on his part would sway the Israelis to work with him.

"I went to court and received authorization for wiretaps on Energy Renewables' phones. Then I contacted the largest email companies and served each with a warrant to determine all email addresses belonging to Energy Renewables and any accounts its corporate officers had. I admit I might have stepped outside the box a little to get the warrants, claiming there was suspected terrorism involved."

He glanced at Mitnick and saw him raise his eyebrows and smile.

"I like the way you think," Mitnick said.

Based on stories Hall heard, he'd bet the *Shin Bet* or the Mossad would do the same thing if they had to.

"I hit pay dirt with Hotmail. Beside an email address in the name of Energy Renewables, the owner, Elliot Johnson, had two personal accounts. He'd opened the first one a long time ago, in 1990. However, the second one was new, opened three years ago. I was intrigued that

Johnson had a second email address and wondered why he needed two."

"But how did you get access to the emails?" Mitnick asked.

"Sorry. Can't tell you that." Hall replied.

Mitnick shrugged and went silent.

This was the area Hall couldn't tell them about because this time he had really moved outside of the box. He put his head back on the seat and reflected. A month ago, he'd contacted a talented hacker named Alex Petrovich whom he'd met during his time with the New York County District Attorney's Office. Arrested for hacking credit card information, and selling it on the Internet, Petrovich faced a long prison term. Offered a deal, Petrovich saw the light and became a sometimes consultant to the D.A.'s office on Internet crimes.

Hall used Petrovich for more than a few *off the books* jobs. He gave Petrovich Johnson's corporate and personal email addresses, and in less than a week, Petrovich supplied him the passwords to open them.

The F.B.I. soon discovered the trick of putting messages in the draft folder. Hall's team was able to read the messages in the draft folder before they were deleted. It was enough to establish there was definitely a connection between Johnson and Moreno, one of the leaders of the Sinaloa Drug Cartel. But there was nothing in them to determine how Johnson laundered money for the cartel. Then came the message about the Israeli scientist and his nephew and the real possibility for a break-through presented itself.

THE CAR CAME to a stop at the hotel. Hall thanked Mitnick for the ride and walked to the check in desk. He wondered if the fact that the Mossad was involved might have complicated his quest.

As he settled in his hotel room, Hall's stomach growled. It was almost noon, and he hadn't eaten anything for close to seven hours, not since he pushed away the barely touched food the airline tried to pass off as breakfast. He dialed room service and ordered a chicken salad sandwich with well-done french fries. *What can they do to screw up chicken salad?* he thought. He snatched a can of Coke from the mini-bar and took a big sip, hoping the carbonation would bloat his stomach and ease his hunger until the food arrived.

He kicked off his shoes, sat on the sofa, and closed his eyes as leaned his head back. In less than a minute, jet lag hit, and he drifted off to sleep. The knock on the door from room service startled him awake. It took him less than thirty seconds to wolf down half the sandwich and a handful of fries from the service cart. He sat back on the couch to check his cell phone for messages. It was the first chance he had to do it since he'd left Newark yesterday.

When he got to the third message, he bolted upright. It was the copy of the email between Elliot Johnson and the Collector. A warm flush of adrenalin coursed through his body. He had to read the message twice to make sure jet lag wasn't playing tricks with his mind. The Collector had contacted Burns and instructed him to be in Berne, Switzerland, with the flash drives and password to trade for his uncle. Burns would arrive in Switzerland tomorrow.

He called the hotel concierge and booked the first available flight to Zurich. It left at 8:00 the next morning. He presumed the *Shin Bet* and the Mossad would find out. He didn't care. He had to get to Switzerland and follow Burns.

CHAPTER 13
February 22
Saturday, Late Morning
Tel Aviv

URNS WAS IN Gideon Ben-Ami's office, waiting for him to return from a morning meeting at Shin Bet Headquarters, when the call came from the university. They'd finally cleared through the rubble, and there was no trace of his uncle. A wave of relief washed over him, but at the same time, concern. *Where is he?*

Burns left the office to go to the bathroom. A few feet away from the bathroom door, his cell phone vibrated. A text message alert. He opened it.

I have your uncle. Alive but for how long is up to you. I want flash drives and password he send you. Tell no one of this message. You speak to police, he die. I contact you again soon.

Burns felt his legs get rubbery, and he leaned against the wall for support. *It's true,* he thought. *Everything Bloom said is true. Someone wants my uncle's discovery, and they kidnapped him to get it. They already killed the guard so they won't hesitate to kill him.*

Burns walked into the bathroom, took care of business, and splashed cold water on his face. He knew he had a decision to make right now. Keep the text to himself like the message instructed, or tell Ben-Ami?

When he walked back to Ben-Ami's office, Gideon was sitting behind his desk.

"Eric, I have some news for you."

"Gideon, wait. Before you begin," Burns said, putting his palm up as he stepped into the office. "There's a problem."

He handed his cell phone to Ben-Ami, with the text message displayed. The head of the Mossad read the text, looked at Burns, and re-read the text. Ben-Ami took a deep breath. "I know about your uncle being kidnapped."

"What?" Burns exclaimed. "What do you mean you know? How? When did you find out?"

Ben-Ami told Burns about the morning meeting at Shin Bet Headquarters with the F.B.I. agent, Robert Hall, the F.B.I. investigation, the intercepted text messages, and Hall wanting to use Burns for bait.

"How do you want to handle this?" Ben-Ami said. "If you want to pursue this on your own, you have my blessing. If you want to involve the Office, you'll have our full cooperation."

"I'm not sure. If he's in Israel, it's more than the Office being involved. That makes it internal and that means involving *Shin Bet*. The more people involved, the more chances things can go wrong. I have a little time to decide. Let's see what happens when I get contacted again."

Two hours later, the next text came.

Bring digital flash drives to Berne, Switzerland, on Monday. Check in Hotel Bellevue Palace. You have reservation. I contact you there. Come alone. I be watching. I see police, uncle dies.

"Okay," Burns said, once again sitting in Ben-Ami's office. "He's not in Israel, so Shin Bet is out."

"Do you want us in?" Ben-Ami asked.

"Yes. He gave me till Monday, so I have the weekend. I'd like to have our agents in Europe placed on alert, for an 'as needed' assignment. You can tell them it's for me but nothing else. I'd like to have Dov Ackerman and Gabi Bernstein go to Berne on Sunday and check into a different hotel. I'll contact them when I arrive. I don't want them to know any specifics either, just that they'll be working with me on an assignment."

"Done. What else?" Ben-Ami said.

"Nothing right now."

"All right. But we have the other problem. What about the F.B.I. agent, Hall? He wants to follow you and use you as bait to get to the Collector. What do we do about him?"

"Tell him you learned I'm out of the country. That I left on a business trip to Europe yesterday," Burns said. "You think I might be in Italy, but I had appointments in Germany, Switzerland, and Spain, so you're not sure right now where I am. Tell him my office said that I sometimes use the weekends as mini vacation time when I'm going to be gone for a week, and you're trying to pin down my location. Tell him as soon as you find out where I am, you'll let him know."

"Okay. One more thing," Ben-Ami said. "I've been thinking about something. I don't think the person who contacted you knows who you are. Did you notice that in both texts, he reminded you not to contact the police? If he knew you were Mossad, why would he have said that?"

For the first time during the stress torn week, Burns allowed a grin to cross his lips. "Yes, I noticed. That's going to be my edge. He has no idea who I am, and he'll regret it for what little time he has left alive."

CHAPTER 14
February 23
Sunday
One Week After the Kidnapping
Switzerland

BURNS LEFT TEL Aviv at 8:00 a.m. Sunday morning on an El Al flight direct to Zurich, arrived at 11:30 a.m. and passed through immigration fifteen minutes later. With only a carry-on bag, he worked his way through the baggage claim area, descending on an escalator to the large train station located underneath the main passenger terminal. He was unaware of the man in a short leather jacket following him.

He bought a ticket that would take him directly to Berne, without having to change in downtown Zurich. According to the timetable, the trip would take just over an hour. Burns picked up a copy of *20 Minuten* before boarding. Published in German, a language he spoke fluently, it was the largest circulating German language daily newspaper in Switzerland.

He settled into the upholstered single seat beside a window, halfway down the rail car. The man in the short leather jacket sat seven rows behind him.

The train arrived on time. Burns stepped out of the train station into a beautiful sunlit afternoon. A digital clock outside a bank across the street indicated a comfortable 15°C. He walked to the hotel, a ten minute leisurely stroll away. The man in the leather jacket followed discreetly behind.

Burns admired the uncomplicated old-world charm of the Hotel Bellevue Palace. He had stayed there once before, and the building still impressed him. The traditional five star hotel, located next to the Federal Parliament, occupied an elegant art nouveau building dating from 1913.

He ambled into the spacious lobby, illuminated by a large stained glass skylight which cast beams of mid-afternoon sunshine on the red carpeted staircase leading to the second floor restaurants. The interior of the lobby was a striking contrast in modern design to the majestic early twentieth century outside facade. At the reception desk, as expected, there was a pre-paid reservation in his name for one evening. A man in a short leather jacket stood a few paces behind, waiting his turn in the check in line.

Before going to his room, Burns asked the desk clerk if the hotel had a safe a guest could keep valuables in. The clerk told him they did, but there was also a small safe in his room. Burns said he preferred the hotel safe and pulled a large manila envelope from his overnight bag. The clerk asked what the value of the contents was for insurance purposes,

In case the Collector had anyone in the lobby, Burns wanted the Collector to believe, as instructed, he'd brought the drives with him, so in a voice loud enough to be heard by any guest in the lobby who chose to eavesdrop he said, "Oh, they're just some computer flash drives."

Twenty minutes after he arrived in his room, the phone rang. *It's the Collector,* he thought. *He wasn't supposed to contact me until tomorrow. I'm not ready.* He took a deep breath and reached for the phone.

"Hello?"

"Good afternoon, Eric. It's Bruno Knecht," the voice said in German.

"Bruno, how are you?" Burns replied in German. *How did he know I was here?*

"I'm fine, thank you. Will you have time to join me for a drink?"

"Of course, "Burns said. His mind raced. How do you say no to a Chief Inspector of the Swiss Federal Police? But if the Collector was watching him, as he said he would in his text message, contact with the police now could endanger his meeting with the Collector tomorrow.

"I'll be in meetings all day tomorrow. How about sometime Tuesday? Would that be convenient for you?" Burns said.

"Actually, right now would be a better time. I'm in the lobby. Why don't you meet me downstairs in the Bellevue Bar?"

Burns was surprised but understood he had little choice in accepting. "Of course. I'll be right down." *Why is he here, and what does he want?*

In the elevator, Burns tried to figure out why Knecht wanted to meet him immediately. It couldn't have anything to do with his business with the Collector. The Swiss Federal Criminal Police conducted criminal investigations such as money laundering, organized crime, and terrorism. That's how he met Knecht. Their paths had crossed two years ago, during a money laundering and terrorism plot, when Hamas almost killed both of them.

Burns entered the bar through the blond oak archway and spotted Knecht in the far back corner at one of the small round cocktail tables. He sat with his back to the wall, which allowed him to scrutinize everyone entering the bar. Only one other person was in the room. The same middle-aged man wearing a short leather jacket who was behind him checking into the hotel, sat at the bar near the front entrance, a half filled brandy snifter in his hand.

Knecht rose to greet Burns. He looked much like Burns remembered. Late forties, tall and thin, good looking, with salt and pepper hair. He wore jeans, a denim jacket, and a pair of New Balance sneakers.

"Good to see you. It's been a while. How are you?" Knecht said in German.

They shook hands.

"Fine. And you?" Burns replied.

"I'm well. Do you mind if we speak in English? I like to keep in practice as much as I can." Knecht said.

"Of course. I must admit, this is a surprise. How did you find out I was in Switzerland and here in Berne? And what are you doing here at the hotel?" Burns said.

"Minutes after you handed over your passport, I was alerted. I was home making plans with my wife on how we would spend this delightful Sunday when I got the call you were in Switzerland, headed here. As you can see, I didn't even have time to change my clothes." Knecht smiled. "My wife doesn't know you, but she is very cross with you for ruining our day."

"I'm sorry I ruined your day, but why were you alerted, and how did you know I was at this hotel?"

"One of our agents picked you up when you passed through baggage claim, and he followed you to the hotel."

Knecht's head tilted toward the man in the short leather jacket at the bar.

Burns turned his head to look the man at the bar. "He's good. Very good. I can usually pick up a tail with no problem, but I never did with him. But why the tail? Why follow me?"

Knecht sighed. "I regret to say, it's your reputation. It seems there are many times, too many to be just coincidence, where you show up in Europe, dead bodies also tend to show up."

The conversation paused when a waiter came over to take drink orders. Burns asked for sparkling water with a lemon twist. Knecht ordered a beer.

"After your last visit to our country, I was required to put your name on a watch list, although I am the only one notified when you arrive. The Federal Police are supposed to prohibit entry into

Switzerland by known or presumed members of organizations who have violated the security or public order in Switzerland. After your visit here two years ago, some people in our government think you fit the profile perfectly. While only a handful of us are aware you are a Mossad agent, you *are* a member of an organization that did violate the public order."

Knecht took a sip of his beer. "Look, you saved my life two years ago, so I will always be indebted to you. If you tell me your purpose in coming to Switzerland is not to violate the public order, I will accept you at your word."

Burns thought back to two years ago, when they first met, and how he had indeed violated the public order.

BANK LEUMI, HEADQUARTERED in Israel, had a branch in Berne. The branch alerted the Mossad a week before that two men from Hamas were coming to Berne. Their purpose, to pick up one million Swiss francs from a bank in which Iran set up an account to fund Hamas.

The information came from a Jewish employee of the bank with the Iranian account. The employee understood he was breaking the Swiss Banking Secrecy Law and subject to criminal proceedings if he was discovered. However, he willingly took the chance when he learned the funds would be used to purchase rockets and munitions to be used against Israel.

Mossad operatives in Switzerland began monitoring the major airports. When the Hamas couriers entered Switzerland through Geneva on a flight from Egypt two days prior, the agents put them under surveillance and notified headquarters. Burns arrived the day before and took over monitoring them.

Burns followed the two men all morning. They'd entered the bank over a half hour before. Directly across from the front door of the bank was an outdoor farmers market set up in the plaza in front of the Federal Palace, where the Swiss Federal Assembly and the Federal

Council were housed. Burns kept a vigilant eye on the bank building, wandering from stall to stall, waiting for the men to leave. A nearby church bell chimed three times. He looked at his watch. 3:01 p.m. *So much for Swiss precision. It's off by a minute.*

Minutes later, the bank door opened, and the two men emerged, each holding a suitcase the size of an airline carry-on bag. Burns presumed they were packed with Swiss francs.

It appeared the couriers were headed back to their car at the underground Parking Casino on Kocher, four streets away, where Burns had followed them from that morning. He slipped onto the sidewalk through a gap next to the fresh fruit stall to follow the couriers but pulled to a quick stop.

A man he hadn't seen before fell in step behind the couriers. It looked to Burns trained eye like he was tailing them. The man was tall, with salt and pepper hair, wearing corduroy pants and a short, black leather jacket. He was obviously European, not Middle Eastern. The couriers were carrying a lot of money, so maybe he was a mercenary, back-up, hired to provide protection.

Burns dropped in behind the tall man as they walked on Kocher, following the two men toward the garage. Burns reasoned they were unaware of who he was, so he picked up his pace and passed the tall man and the two with the suitcases. He made it to the Parking Casino before them, retrieved his car, and pulled out of the underground space. He parked at the curb a few meters beyond the exit ramp.

The couriers emerged in their beige Opel, followed by the tall man in a black VW Passat. Burns shadowed them. He was sure they were headed to their safe house, where they had stayed for the last two days, but he needed to keep tabs on them in case they changed destination.

The Opel, tracked by the tall man, drove on Nordring to Standstrasse and fifteen minutes later pulled in front of their single-family safe house on Berne, just off of Morgartenstrasse.

The tall man continued beyond the home and pulled to the curb a block away. Burns drove two blocks past the tall man's car, made a U-turn, and pulled to the curb facing him. He had a clear view of the tall man, whose eyes seemed focused in his rear view mirror at the two men who'd emerged from the Opel, carrying the suitcases to the house. Burns glanced at his watch. Almost 4:00 p.m.

Burns kept a watchful eye on the courier's safe house and the tall man sitting in his car, with his eyes locked on his rear view mirror. Burns turned the situation over in his head. *The tall man wasn't going into the house so maybe he isn't with them. If that's the case, who is he, and what's his interest in the couriers? Maybe he worked for the Iranians, and they hired him to keep tabs on their money?*

More than three hours passed, and sunset had slipped into a dark night. Burns stiffened upright when the dome light in the tall man's car came on, and the occupant slid out. Burns waited until the man began walking toward the safe house before slipping out of his car to follow.

He was puzzled when the tall man moved beyond the safe house to the one next door. The house was dark; apparently, no one was home. Burns hid in the shadows behind a large fir tree and watched. The tall man glanced up and down the street, then darted into the side yard.

Burns scampered up the street, then slowed down as he approached the side yard to be sure he didn't run into him. Peering around a hedge, he caught sight of the man scaling a low stone wall separating the two homes then vanishing into the back yard of the courier's house.

Burns crept to the wall and peeked over. The lower level of the house was all glass, with two sliding doors. Burns saw the tall man peek inside through gaps in the drapes drawn across all the windows. The man walked to one of the sliding glass doors, pulled something from his pants pocket, and began fumbling with the door. *He's picking the lock.*

In less than fifteen seconds, the tall man put his pick tools back in his pocket, drew a gun from under his short leather jacket, slide the door open enough to squeeze through, and entered the house.

I don't believe it, Burns thought. *The guys nothing but a thief. He's going to steal their money. Maybe I should let him. Wouldn't that be a great twist?*

Burns scurried over the wall to the same door the thief entered and looked through the big gap in the drapes the man created sneaking into the house. No more than thirty seconds passed from the time the man entered the house and Burns arrived at the door, but it was more than enough time to change the thief's plans.

The intruder lay face down on the tile floor in the dining area across from the kitchen, blood oozing from the back of his head. One of the Hamas couriers stood over him. It looked to Burns like the thief only concentrated on what was in front of him and failed to notice the small pantry behind him. One of the couriers must have been in the pantry, grabbed a rolling pin, snuck up behind, and whacked the man on the head.

The courier, his back to Burns, held the rolling pin in one hand, the thief's gun in the other. He shouted in Arabic, a language Burns spoke fluently, for the other courier to hurry to the kitchen, that someone had broken into the house. Within seconds, the other Hamas agent flew into the kitchen, arm outstretched, pistol in hand. He was the one with a drooping mustache who Burns referred to as Mustache in his reports to Mossad Headquarters.

Both couriers stood over the body, guns trained on the inert figure, Mustache querying his partner about what had happened. After a brief conversation, Mustache kneeled next to the intruder and began to shake him, yelling in Arabic, asking who he was.

The intruder moaned, slowly awakening, his hand creeping to the back of his head where he'd been struck. Burns watched him bring his bloodstained fingers in front of his eyes, rubbing them together. He tried to rise, got as far as pushing his upper body off the floor with outstretched arms, before Mustache jammed his hand down on the man's back. The intruder collapsed, his face landing solidly against the floor.

Mustache searched the man's pockets. When he got to the rear, right pants pocket, he pulled out a leather wallet. Only it wasn't one that held money. It was an identification wallet.

Mustache rolled the man over "Who are you? What does this mean?" he screamed in Arabic, waving the identification wallet. When the thief didn't respond, Mustache slapped him. The man moved his head, opened his eyes, and tried to focus. When he looked at the wallet, he mumbled something Burns couldn't hear. Mustache yelled again, waving the wallet.

The intruder, his voice weak but firm, said in German, "I'm a Federal Police Officer and you're under arrest."

Oh, shit, Burns thought. *That complicates things.*

Mustache kept screaming in Arabic, asking the man who he was, and the man kept repeating, his voice growing stronger and more authoritarian each time, that he was a Federal Police Officer and they were under arrest. Speaking different languages, neither understood what the other was saying.

Mustache must have decided the same thing because the Hamas agent slammed the butt of his revolver against the back of the intruders head, knocking him unconscious. "Let's get him upstairs," he said to his partner. They lifted the man off the floor, each grabbing him under an arm, and dragged him out of the kitchen.

BURNS STEPPED BACK into the darkness of the patio and looked up. A series of steel girders rose vertically from the ground to the top of the structure. They supported a tilted glass roof which ran the length of the house and overhung balconies on the upper level. Twelve foot horizontal girders bolted to the vertical girders supported the bottom of the second floor balconies. The closest vertical girder to him had a vine, almost an inch in diameter, curling up and around it stretching beyond the second floor balconies.

Burns climbed, using the vine for foot and hand support, until he reached the horizontal girder. He tightrope walked across the girder until he reached the balcony. Crouching, he peered over the railing. The blinds were not closed in the bedroom in front of him. It was empty. He leapt over the railing onto the balcony, found the door unlocked, and slipped inside.

His eyes immediately locked on the bed, staring in disbelief. Piled on the beige bedcover were stacks of purple 1000 Swiss franc banknotes. He then turned to the boxes stacked next to the bed, some already sealed, most empty. They were printed with the name of a well-known brand of Swiss chocolate. *So this is how they're planning to move the currency.* He figured the tall man's intrusion interrupted the packing process.

Burns heard the Hamas men talking as they dragged the tall man upstairs. He hid in the bathroom, holding his gun against his chest, ready to start shooting if needed.

"What are we going to do now?" Burns heard one of the couriers ask.

"We'll finish packing the money, load it in the car, and kill this one before we leave," the other said.

That sounds like Mustache.

The money was on the bed in this room, so they were headed to him. He pulled the bathroom door closed, leaving just a small gap between the door and the frame so he could see the bed covered with the money and part of the room.

Pushing himself flat against the bathroom wall behind the door, Burns heard them bring the man claiming to be a Federal Police Officer into the bedroom. Through the gap, he saw the Hamas agents dump the tall man face down on the floor at the foot of the bed. They resumed packing the money. He could see they hadn't bound their captive's hands or feet.

That's stupid.

He weighed his options and decided to wait the couriers out and let events dictate what he'd do. Perhaps twenty minutes passed, and it looked as if the men were close to finishing packing the boxes. He counted about thirty already sealed, stacked near the bed.

The tall man stirred, on and off, for a while. Burns got the impression the man was shifting his body with purpose. He sensed the man may be hurt and groggy but was faking how badly. If he really was a Federal Police Officer, maybe he was gathering his strength before trying anything. Of course, if he was a thief with a stolen or fake ID, he'd be dead pretty soon.

Mustache told the other man he had to go to the bathroom. Burns tensed, gripped his gun firmly, and crouched slightly, ready to spring off the wall when the time came. Mustache's foot had just crossed the bathroom door threshold when Burns heard the scream.

He snapped his head toward the gap in the door. The intruder had pushed himself from the floor and was charging at the other Hamas courier with a screech, the fury of which Burns had seldom heard. As they made contact, the momentum propelled the intruder and the courier to the edge of the bedroom doorway.

Mustache swiveled in the bathroom doorframe, grabbed his gun from his waistband, and aimed it at the man attacking his partner. He pulled the trigger just as Burns pushed himself off the wall and slammed the door into him. The pistol erupted, the thundering sound echoing through the room.

Burns grabbed the doorknob and flung the partially closed door fully open. Mustache was on his knees frantically looking for his gun. The door's impact had hammered it out of his hand and knocked him down.

When Burns leaped into the room, Mustache jumped to his feet and grabbed Burns' gun hand with both of his. He twisted Burns' wrist, trying to force him to drop the weapon. They bounced off the wall, locked together in a furious dance of death. Burns used his free hand to dig his fingernails deep into the backs of Mustache's hands, trying to pry them away. Mustache didn't seem to feel a thing, holding onto the gun hand like a man possessed.

From the corner of his eye, Burns caught a glimpse of the tall man. He had one hand wrapped around the other courier's throat, the other grasping the wrist holding a pistol.

Burns and Mustache continued to grapple for control of his gun, swinging each other against the walls and furniture. Mustache put so much pressure on Burns' wrist, his finger reflexively pulled the trigger. The bullet punched into the tall man's side, spun him sideways, and propelled both men out of the room onto the hallway landing.

Using every bit of his close combat training, Burns head butted Mustache and shattered his nose. The man screamed and snorted blood. He pulled hard on the pistol, then suddenly let go. Burns lost his balance, falling back hard against the edge of bathroom door before slipping to the floor. A searing pain radiated between his shoulder blades as he rolled on his side. He saw Mustache dash toward the stacked boxes. Burns' eyes shifted. He spotted Mustache's gun lying on top of one of the sealed boxes. Mustache reached the box, grabbed the pistol, and wheeled toward Burns. All this happened in milliseconds.

Before Mustache could aim, Burns fired from the floor, hitting him twice in the chest. Screaming in Arabic, Mustache fired wildly into the ceiling. Burns fired again, blowing out the right side of his head.

He jumped to his feet and ran into the hall. The intruder and the other Hamas courier were still locked in a battle over the pistol. Before Burns could do anything, the courier twisted the pistol against the man's shoulder and pulled the trigger. The man screamed. The pain must have been intense, but he still had the strength to butt the courier's cheek, hard enough to make the courier's eyes tear. The intruder slumped to the floor, still grappling for control of the pistol.

Burns rushed to them and grabbed for the gun. The three of them struggled for control of the weapon. Burns was able to turn the pistol, jam the barrel against the courier's chest, and yanked on the man's finger curled around the trigger. The gun exploded. The Hamas agent's eyes opened wide in shock. He let out a long sigh, then his eyes lost focus, and he slid to the floor, dead.

Burns turned to the intruder and asked in German, "How are you?"

Responding with a weak smile, he said, "I don't think I'll be throwing darts for a while, but if you get me to a hospital fast, I'm sure I'll be all right." A nanosecond later, he said," Who the hell are you?"

Burns ignored the question. Instead, he went to the bathroom, grabbed towels, and brought them to the wounded man. "Here," he said, "hold this tight against your shoulder."

Burns pulled up the man's shirt. The bullet wound in his side looked like it was a through and through. Blood wasn't pumping out, meaning no vital organs had been hit. He pressed a towel against the wound. "Can you use your bad arm to hold this tight against you?"

"Yes," the tall man said through clenched teeth. As he moved his hand to hold it, he winced.

Burns slumped against the wall. The adrenalin in his body made his hand shake as he pulled his cell phone to call for help and then hesitated.

"Are you really a Federal Police Officer or a thief who came to rob them?"

The man laughed, then grimaced in pain. "I'm really a Federal Police Officer. My name is Inspector Bruno Knecht." He scrunched up his face, fighting again against the pain. "I've been investigating money laundering by terrorist groups using Swiss banks and got a tip about these men. I've been watching them ever since they landed in Switzerland."

"Okay. Listen, I can't really make the call for help," Burns said. Holding his palm up before Hecht could say anything, he said, "I need to get out of here before more police show up."

"Why?"

"I can't get into it."

"Look, you saved my life. Tell me who you are. I'll make sure you're not in any trouble."

Burns hesitated before replying. As much as he wanted to, he couldn't break cover.

"Look, I'm sorry. I can't give you my name, but I'll give you some information. The money in that room was meant to be used to buy armaments to be used against Israel, and my job was to insure it didn't happen."

"You're Mossad?"

"Sorry," Burns shrugged. "I can't comment."

He got Knecht to promise that the money would find its way into the Swiss Federal Treasury, and not back into the Iranian account it came from. Burns' phone was a burner that couldn't be traced back to him, so he left it with Knecht to call for help. Although in severe pain, Knecht said he owed him for saving his life, and he'd wait ten minutes to give him a head start before calling.

Two days later, Burns stood at the departure gate in Geneva, waiting to catch his flight back to Tel Aviv.

"I hope you have a safe flight home, Herr Burns," the voice behind him said in German.

Burns spun around to see Inspector Knecht, his arm in a sling, smiling at him.

"How did you..."

Knecht shrugged. "As you may remember, your last words to me were, 'I can't comment.' Well, I can't comment on how I found out, but we Swiss are pretty resourceful when we need to be."

"Excuse me, sir. Would you like me to refresh your drink?" the waiter asked, snapping Burns' musing back to the present.

"Eric, what do you say? Can you tell me your purpose in coming to Switzerland is not to violate the public order? If so, I will accept your word and go back to my wife and salvage what remains of my Sunday off," Knecht repeated.

"Bruno, I give you my word. I am not here on Mossad business. This is a personal trip."

Knecht scowled. "But you didn't answer my question. Are you going to violate the public order? Will there be bodies left behind for us to deal with when you leave?"

Burns didn't want to lie to the man, so he decided to play with the truth. "I'm here strictly on a matter dealing with my family. No Mossad business. I give you my word."

Knecht rose from his seat. "All right then. In that case, I will go home and make peace with my wife and salvage what's left of the day. Perhaps if you are free while you're here, you'll join my wife and me for dinner one evening?"

"If I can, I'd like to."

Knecht left the bar, followed by the man in the short leather jacket. Burns felt a momentary twinge of guilt for misleading Knecht because he knew, before his trip to Switzerland was over, the Chief Inspector would most likely have a serious 'violation of the public order ' on his hands.

CHAPTER 15
February 23
Sunday Afternoon
Switzerland

HALL CLEARED ZURICH customs and took the train to Berne. During the flight he'd come up with a plan. To follow Burns and get the Collector, he'd need help in Switzerland and his best chance would be from Chief Inspector Bruno Knecht of the Swiss Federal Police Office. They'd worked together a few times on joint United States /Swiss money laundering task force investigations and had developed a relationship.

Being Sunday, he called Knecht at home. His wife said he wasn't there and didn't know when he'd return. Hall told her he was staying at the Hotel Innere Enge, left his room number, and asked for Knecht to please return his call as soon as he came home. "Yes," he had told her, "it was extremely urgent."

Two hours later, his phone rang.

"Hello."

"Hall? This is Knecht here. What are you doing in Switzerland? I wasn't aware of any new investigation," he said, speaking in English.

"I'm here on a money laundering investigation, but it doesn't directly involve Switzerland. I called you because I could really use your help. Can we meet?"

"Hold on for a second."

Hall listened to Knecht speak in German to someone, he presumed his wife, and a minute later Knecht came back on the line. "Yes. I can meet you, although I am in a lot of trouble with my wife. This is the second time today I had to disappoint her and ruin her Sunday."

Knecht asked if Hall had eaten lunch. Hall said no, so Knecht suggested they meet in forty-five minutes at the A Familia Portuguesa restaurant. Hall remembered the place. Knecht had taken him there three years ago on his first trip to Switzerland. The food and service were outstanding, as good as any five star restaurant in New York City. It was also convenient, only ten minutes from his hotel.

Hall arrived before Knecht, selected a table, and sat facing the door. A few minutes later, Knecht arrived and spotted Hall. Seconds after Knecht and Hall exchanged greetings, the waiter arrived and took their drink order.

"What's going on?" Knecht asked after the waiter left.

Hall told him everything about his investigation, beginning with the tip about Renewable Energy involvement in cartel money laundering, the intercepted email about the kidnapping, his meeting yesterday in Israel, and learning his quarry, the nephew, was now in Switzerland.

"I think this will be the big break in nailing not only one of the leaders of the cartel, but destroying one of the cartel's major money laundering operation," Hall said.

The waiter appeared with the drinks and took their lunch order.

"So, you need my help in following the kidnapped scientist's nephew when he meets with the man called the Collector?" Knecht said after the waiter departed.

"That's about it. I know it's a big request, and it will take manpower to cover him twenty-four hours a day. But I have no assets of my own to help me, and the man I want to follow is here in Switzerland."

Knecht waved a dismissive hand. "Don't worry. We both work to prevent money laundering, particularly when it comes to criminal and terrorist organizations. My men and I are at your disposal. It's an expenditure easily justified to my superiors."

Hall let out a soft breath, the tightness in his shoulders relaxed. He hadn't been sure Knecht would be able to help him. "Thank you," he said.

"So, what can you tell me about the nephew you want us to follow, and do you know where he is staying in Berne?"

Hall held his reply as the waiter appeared at the table with their appetizers. He waited patiently until the waiter left.

"According to an intercepted email two days ago, the Collector instructed the nephew to arrive in Berne today. It said a room was reserved for him at the Hotel Bellevue Palace and he'd be contacted tomorrow. The Shin Bet and the Mossad told me yesterday they did a background check on the nephew. He is a computer security sales manager for an Israeli company and currently traveling in Europe. His name is Eric Burns."

As a New York City detective and F.B.I. investigator for many years, Hall saw 'the deer in the headlights' reactions when someone being interrogated was confronted with surprising, unexpected news. Eyes widened, a breath that catches, a sudden stiffening of posture.

All of them just occurred with Knecht, but Hall had to admire the man. While the reactions were there, they were fleeting and Knecht quickly recovered. He reached for his glass of beer and took a slow sip. Hall presumed it was Knecht's ploy to compose himself before speaking.

"You say the nephew's name is Eric Burns, and he's a sales manager?"

Something's going on.

"Yes," Hall replied.

"All right. I'll make a call and get some people over to his hotel right away."

Knecht spoke with someone in German on his cell phone for a few minutes. Hall didn't understand what he said but heard him say the name Eric Burns twice. When he disconnected, Knecht said to

Hall, "Two of my agents are on their way to Hotel Bellevue Palace. They will stay with Burns until more of my people can pick up the surveillance."

"That's great. Look, I really appreciate your help and don't want to antagonize you, but what's going on?" Hall said.

"What do you mean?"

"Come on, Bruno. I've been a cop too long. I could tell when I mentioned the nephew's name, it wasn't the first time you'd heard it. You know something about this guy, don't you?"

Knecht leaned back in his chair, lips pressed together in a slight grimace, a pensive expression on his face. It looked to Hall like he wanted to say something and struggled to find the right words.

Finally, he said, "You really don't know anything about Eric Burns?"

Hall became wary. "No, should I?"

"No, I suppose not," Knecht said. He pinched the bridge of the nose. "Look, this is a little tricky. You must give me your word that what I am going to tell you, stays with you. I mean only you. Not your boss, not your agency, nobody but you. Can you promise me that?"

Hall hesitated before answering. If he made the promise to Knecht, he'd have to keep it, no matter what. Could he do it? How bad did he want to nail Moreno and the cartel and put a major dent in their money laundering operation? Bad enough to jeopardize his job if it came out that he withheld vital information from his boss and the F.B.I.?

Hall made his decision. "Yes, you have my word."

Hall sensed Knecht still fought an internal struggle, reluctant to continue. Finally, he bent forward and crooked his finger, signaling he wanted Hall to come close to him. Hall leaned in.

"It's true. Eric Burns *is* a computer security sales manager," Knecht said, his voice hovered above a whisper, even though there was nobody within earshot. He took a deep breath and released it slowly. "He's also Mossad, what they call a *kidon*, an assassin. You should also know he saved my life two years ago. I owe him a debt I'll never be able to repay. You can count on me to do whatever it takes to protect him."

Hall sat up, clenched his teeth, and pounded his fist on the table. "Those miserable sons of bitches. That fucking Mitnick and Ben-Ami. They played me yesterday."

Knecht said, "You're not the only one who was played. I met with Burns a few hours ago. Knowing what he does for the Mossad, I asked him directly if there would be any bodies left behind for me to deal with when he left Switzerland. He gave me his word he was only here on a matter dealing with his family and not Mossad business. Strictly speaking, he told me the truth, but never answered my question directly about leaving any bodies behind. Based on what you told me, and knowing Burns, I wouldn't bet my pension there won't be".

CHAPTER 16
February 24
Monday
Switzerland

Burns returned to his hotel room after his meeting with Inspector Knecht. He didn't like the fact that Knecht knew he was in Switzerland. It might complicate matters. He called Ackerman to let him know he'd arrived and would contact him when he needed him. Now, all Burns could do was wait to hear from the Collector.

At 4:00 p.m., his cell phone announced an incoming text message. *10:30 tomorrow morning. Go to McDonald's across tower in Zytglogge plaza. Buy two cups coffee, walk to fountain with Swiss soldier on top. Hold one cup in each hand to identify you. We watch. Come alone or uncle dies.*

The "we" will be watching meant the Collector had others working with him. Things just got more complicated.

About a half hour after he received the text message his cell phone rang.

"Hello?"

"Simon Bloom's in my office," Ben-Ami said, without any preamble. "He came to find out if we had any new news he can give your aunt about your uncle. Is there? He's been going to her house every day, and he says she's sick with worry."

Burns filled Ben-Ami in on his meeting with Knecht and the text message. "Tell Simon I appreciate his visiting my aunt but to hold off telling her about any of this for now. I have no idea what will happen tomorrow."

"Okay. Have you been in contact with Ackerman and Bernstein?"

"Yes. I spoke to Ackerman a little while ago, before I received the text. They can watch my back now that I have a time and place. I'll have them get to the plaza at 10:00 tomorrow morning and play the part of a tourist couple taking in the sights."

He ended the conversation with Ben-Ami. Tomorrow morning, he'd go to the meeting and wait for the Collector to contact him. There was nothing else for him to do now but wait.

What he still hadn't figured out yet is how to handle the fact he didn't bring the real digital flash drives and had no clue to the password. *What am I going to trade tomorrow for my uncle's life?*

BURNS SPENT THE night in disjointed bouts of deep slumber punctuated by periods of being wide awake, staring at the tiny red light in the overhead smoke detector. At 6:30 a.m., he got out of bed, showered, dressed, and finished a room service breakfast well before his eight o'clock wake up call.

He did deep breathing exercises to relax while he waited until it was time to leave for the plaza. He kept telling himself to approach this like any other mission. Except it wasn't. His uncle's life hung in the balance.

He looked at the bedside clock. 10:15. Time to go.

He stepped out of the hotel entrance into a beautiful Swiss day. The air was crisp, the sun bright in a clear blue sky. He reached the sidewalk just as an attractive woman with long dark hair, wearing a tan leather coat with a white fur collar, walked by. She carried two shopping bags. *Pretty,* he thought. His eyes followed her as she crossed the street.

He had time and took a leisurely stroll to the Zytglogge Clock Plaza, only five minutes away. He didn't want to arrive too early. As he passed the Hertz rental office on Kocherg, a young man with a swarthy complexion, sporting a few days' worth of facial hair and wearing faded jeans and a black sweater, stood in the doorway. The man glanced at him and turned his head away quickly. Too quickly. Burns' instincts kicked in. That glance and the quick body movement was all it took. Ripples of wariness percolated within. He was being watched.

Burns guessed the man worked for the Collector. What he needed to determine now is how many people watched him and what they looked like. To do that, he began to stroll at a slow pace and with more purpose. He didn't think they were very skilled. Otherwise, they would never make direct eye contact with him, like that guy at Hertz.

He continued along Kocherg to Casinopl. He paid close attention to the people around him and the cars driving by. Under normal circumstances, if he were being watched, he'd try to lose them by taking counter surveillance measures, like ducking into stores or changing direction. But he didn't want to lose them. He wanted to identify them.

He knew what to watch for. They'd probably use the basic box team approach. There'd be one person behind who'd have him under direct line of sight. That person would have a backup, ready to leap frog into place if Burns did anything that might compromise the first watcher.

Burns put his hand in his pants pocket, and when he pulled it out, he purposely dropped a few coins on the sidewalk. When he kneeled to pick them up he glanced across the street. If he were running this, he'd have a third watcher across the street, moving in the same direction as him. His eyes scanned the people who were level with him right now, trying to fix faces in his mind, to see if any of them showed up later. He figured he had at least two, possibly three, people tailing him.

Burns knew somewhere out there, somebody was in control. The controller would maneuver the other members of the team to keep him covered. He'd switch followers around, sometimes as a single person following, sometimes as a pair, mixing and matching but always keeping an eye on him. Adding a controller would make it a team of at least three, maybe four, people.

Burns knew from experience nobody would wear clothing that stood out. No reds, no blues, no flashy jewelry. Drab grays and browns would be the colors of choice. They would spend so much time walking; they would wear comfortable shoes—sneakers or hiking boots. They'd also carry bags and wear coats and hats they could take off to alter their appearance.

He'd hone in on the ones dressed like that. No civilian would detect them, but Burns wasn't a civilian. He'd know. He was trained well enough to spot the person who just didn't seem to fit. They'd have tells, even the best of them. If they had ear pieces or microphones to communicate through, they'd touch their ears or wrists. Some would try too hard to look casual.

Burns looked for all these indicators as he walked slowly toward the clock tower. He kept his breathing steady and calm and his adrenaline under control while he checked and assessed his surroundings. He looked at faces through any reflective surface he passed, stopping now and then, as if uncertain where he was going. He was attuned to any changes in the rhythm of the pedestrian traffic around him.

As Burns passed the university bookstore on Munsterg, he confirmed he was being followed. He spotted a couple next to the entrance, holding hands. He recognized the girl as the same attractive woman with long dark hair carrying two shopping bags he'd seen on the sidewalk in front of the hotel earlier. A bulky grey sweater replaced the tan coat with the white fur collar, and she didn't have any shopping bags, but it was her. He didn't recognize the man. He would make either the fourth or fifth member of the team.

Now Burns was sure they were not a skilled team. If they were, the girl would never have dressed so flashy in front of the hotel. *Okay. I'm being watched for sure, and I know at least three of them. Might as well head over to the plaza.*

Burns strolled into the large plaza, covered with cobblestones, in front of the clock tower. Built in 1191 as the western gate to the then small city, Berne's clock tower, or Zytglogge, was as old as Berne itself. At five minutes before each hour, visitors gathered before the clock to watch its nearly 500-year-old workings perform. Even at this early hour, the plaza was packed with tourists.

If the legend was to be believed, this venerable clock inspired a revolution in our concept of time itself. Albert Einstein, who lived not far from the Zytglogge, was allegedly led to his theory of relativity when he looked at the buses coming around the tower and wondered what would happen to them if they moved at the speed of light.

Streets spread out from the plaza like spokes of a wheel, forming pedestrian malls. Shops selling watches, jewelry, cosmetics, and food were situated on the ground floor of four storied buildings, with apartments and balconies above. *They can watch me from any one of those apartments,* Burns thought.

He spotted the McDonald's.

The Golden Arches across from a thousand-year old clock tower. Absurd.

He bought the two cups of coffee in cardboard containers with the McDonald's logo as instructed and walked to the fountain with the Swiss soldier on top, located in the middle of the street across from the Eastern clock face. He sat on the low wall surrounding the fountain and waited. He scanned the crowds for Ackerman and Bernstein. He knew they were out there some place but didn't see them.

He looked at the Zytglogge. 10:35. *Where's the Collector?* 10:50. Still no contact. 10:56. The crowds began to fill the streets to watch the clock chime at 11:00.

Where is he? Could he have seen me with Knecht yesterday and thought I brought the police in?

Out of the crowd of people heading to the center plaza, a boy of about ten appeared next to him.

"Mister," he said, pulling on Burns' sleeve, "this is for you."

He held out an envelope. Burns threw one of the coffees into the fountain and snatched it from the boy's hand. "Who gave this to you?"

"I don't know him. I was playing with my friends, and he asked if I wanted to earn 20 francs. He gave me the envelope and told me all I had to do was give it to the man at this fountain who would be holding two cups of McDonald's coffee. Like you are, mister. He told me to wait until just before the Zytglogge chimed at 11:00 to give it to you. Look, here's the money he gave me." The boy pulled a red 20 franc note from his pocket.

"Okay, I believe you. When did he give you the envelope?"

The boy stuffed the money back in his pocket.

"I'm not sure. Maybe twenty minutes ago. I came right here and waited next to that door," he said, pointing to the jewelry store across the street. "I saw you with the cups of coffee but waited until I saw people heading to the Zytglogge. I knew it was almost 11:00, and I did just what he told me, mister. Did I do something wrong?" The boy's lip began to quiver, and his eyes watered.

"No. You did just fine. Do you remember what he looked like? The man who gave you the envelope."

"No, I just remember he was big. Maybe bigger than you."

"What color was his hair?"

"I don't know, mister."

"Try and think about it," Burns said, grasping the boys shoulders.

"I don't remember," he said, trying to wiggle away from Burns. The boy began to whimper and passersby stopped and stared.

Burns let go of the boys shoulders and said, "That's okay." He reached in his pocket and pulled out a 10 Swiss franc note. "Here you go."

The boy grabbed the money and ran away. The people who stopped to see what was going on between Burns and the little boy lingered for a few seconds longer, then continued to the Zytglogge to watch the show.

Burns tore open the envelope.

Take 12:04 train to Interlaken. Walk to Grand Hotel Beau Rivage. You have room reserved in your name. Bring digital flash drives and password. I contact you in your room at 4:00. We watch. No forget. No police or uncle dies.

Burns crumpled the letter, squeezing his fist around the paper. *Enough,* he thought. *This guy's run me in circles. No more. Starting now, I'm going on offense.*

CHAPTER 17
February 24
Monday
Interlaken, Switzerland

BURNS HEADED BACK to his hotel, retrieved the manila envelope from the hotel safe, and checked out. He sat on a bench waiting for the 12:04 train to Interlaken and watched the ebb and flow of passengers as he pretended to read a newspaper. He'd already spotted the girl and the two men who'd followed him that morning move about the station. He tried to detect anyone else who might be part of their team.

Two men caught his attention. A tall, dark complexioned man with a full mustache that curved around the edges of his mouth with a small tuft of a goatee nestled on his chin. *Looks Hispanic.* The other man was the complete opposite in looks. Under six feet, dirty blond hair, light complexion, ruddy cheeks. *Looks Irish.*

The two men didn't do anything conspicuous that made him single them out in the crowd. It was more his sixth sense; a feeling he got in the pit of his stomach, the hair on his arms tingling when he glanced at them. There may not be scientific proof of a sixth sense, but whatever the feelings were that alerted him, he trusted them. They'd saved his life on more than one occasion.

A loudspeaker announced the boarding of the train to Interlaken on track three. Burns strolled from the station lobby, ultra-alert to his surroundings. He spotted the girl and the two men from that morning walking to track three. He didn't see the two men who caught his attention before. *Guess I was wrong. So much for my sixth sense.*

Burns settled into a window seat. The train lurched as it began to pull away from the station. Out of the corner of his eye, he caught movement on the platform. The two men who gleaned his attention sprinted to catch the train. The Hispanic looking one hopped on to the passenger car in front of his, the Irish looking one climbed aboard his car. Irish, as he decided to call him, settled in a seat two rows in front. Burns grinned. *Sixth sense still working well.*

The trip from Berne to Interlaken took forty-five minutes. Burns disembarked and stretched a six-minute walk to the Grand Hotel Beau Rivage, to over fifteen minute. He dawdled from store window to store window, checking on how many tails he could pick up. So far, it looked like he had only five, the three from that morning and the two he picked up at the station.

After he checked into the hotel, once again making a public display of depositing a manila envelope with some flash drives, he went to his room. He stood next to the door and cracked it open to give him a clear view of the elevator. A few minutes later, Irish stepped out and entered a room, three doors away. *Time to go on offense.*

He unpacked his Beretta and slipped it into his jacket pocket. He checked the hallway. It was clear. He edged his way to the room Irish had entered, knocked, and called out it was room service with a complimentary fruit basket. He placed a hand over the peephole. The other clenched the Beretta in his pocket.

Irish yelled out something Burns couldn't make out, and a few seconds later, he heard the latch unlock. The door swung inward and Irish stood in the middle of the opening. Burns pulled his gun, pointed it at Irish's face, and used his other hand to push the man back into the room.

"Don't open your mouth. Don't say a word," Burns yelled in German.

Irish raised his hands. "Ich spreche kein Deutsch," he shouted, shaking his head. "English, English. Only English."

"Who are you, and why are you following me?" Burns responded, switching languages.

"I don't know what your talking about. I'm not following you."

Burns punched Irish in the stomach. The man doubled over and fell to his knees, gasping for breath. Burns pressed the muzzle of the Beretta against his forehead.

"One last chance. Tell me who you are and why you're following me, or I'll put a bullet in your brain."

Irish raised his hands above his head and waved them. Taking shallow breaths, he said, "Okay. Okay. My name is Robert Hall. I'm from the United States. I'm an F.B.I. agent."

"Prove it,"

"My I.D. It's in my jacket." He pointed across the room. "Over there. Can I get it?"

"Stay where you are. I'll get it."

Burns walked backward toward the jacket hung across the back of the chair next to the desk. He never took his eyes, or gun, off Irish. He picked up the jacket with his free hand and patted it down, looking for weapons. He didn't find any. He felt a lump in an inside pocket. He pulled out an F.B.I. credentials wallet with Irish's picture. The name on it said Robert Hall. Not real proof of anything. He had used counterfit credentials many times himself, even passed himself off as a member of local law enforcement.

"This doesn't prove anything. How do I know this is real?" Burns asked, waving the I.D. wallet.

"Check with Inspector Bruno Knecht of the Swiss Federal Police. He'll confirm who I am. I know you know him."

Burns stepped back a pace. His eyes widened. "Knecht? How do you know Knecht?"

"Can I put my hands down and get off the floor?"

"Yes. But sit on the bed. And don't make any sudden moves."

"Okay." He slowly rose to his feet and sat on the bed. "I suppose I should start at the beginning."

"That's always a good idea," Burns said.

Burns listened as Hall told his story, from the first tip about Renewable Energy through his meeting with Knecht the day before. Burns interrupted a few times to clarify some points but mostly stayed silent and listened to Hall's story.

"So, I'm bait? You're following me to get to the Collector?" Burns asked.

Hall shrugged. "Yes."

"How did you know to follow me to Interlaken?"

"I got a call from Knecht around 11:30 this morning telling me you checked out of your hotel and were at the train station. He sent me a text picture of you and said if I wanted to follow you, I had to move right away. He said he would check me out of my hotel and get my luggage to me. I saw you buy your ticket, found out from the clerk where you were headed, and followed you."

"And those other four? They're part of a team Knecht supplied to help you?"

"What other four?"

"The girl and the two guys from this morning and the Hispanic looking guy from the train station just now," Burns said.

"I don't know what you're talking about," Hall said. "If Knecht assigned people to help me follow you, he never said a word to me about it."

CHAPTER 18
February 24
Monday
Switzerland

"Si, jefe," Santos Reyes said." I'm in Switzerland now, at the same hotel as Burns. I will call you when I have the digital flash drives."

Seconds ticked away as his boss on the other end of the line gave him instructions.

"Yes, as soon as I have them I will eliminate the Collector, the Israeli scientist, and the nephew."

Reyes disconnected the call. He grabbed a cold beer from the mini bar and gulped a quarter of the can's contents. He sat on the couch and laid his head back. His mind wandered to the maid who brought fresh towels to the room a while ago. She reminded him of his mother, who also worked as a maid in a hotel, one of two jobs she held. Back then, life was hard.

WHEN HE WAS fifteen, his mother, Rosita, told him of her past. She was sixteen the day the Mexican Federal Police, in a botched raid, killed her parents. They'd stormed the wrong house, guns blazing. She ran away to the United States three months later.

She lived on the streets in South Central, Los Angeles, met a handsome gang member named Miguel Reyes, and at age seventeen, gave birth to Santos. A year after his birth, a rival gang member killed his father.

Rosita and Reyes moved back to Mexico, where they lived with her aunt Carmen and her cousins, including twenty-year-old Jorge Moreno Estrada. Already deeply involved with the Sinaloa Drug Cartel, Moreno became protective of her and her young son. He didn't want the boy to become a gang member like him or his father. Three years after her return to Mexico, Moreno smuggled her and Santos over the border, back to Los Angeles.

Her cousin arranged a job for her and set them up in an apartment away from South Central and the barrio. He sent her money to supplement her income. His only demand... make sure her son remained out of trouble and away from the gangs. She told him that was why she pushed him to study and maintain high grades. Yes, life was hard for them, but he had no doubt things would soon be better. He'd get a good job and pitch in so his mother could work only one job.

He recalled when that all changed and squeezed the can so tight, it crushed, and beer flowed over his hand and lap.

It was May 6th. He was eighteen. His mother called from work in the afternoon to tell him she was going to the mall and would be home late. "Finish the leftovers in the refrigerator," she'd said.

He'd graduated from high school, was accepted to UCLA, and needed a part time job to help pay for tuition. That night he was in the kitchen at 10:30 reading the newspaper, checking the help wanted section, when the front door bell rang. He opened the door a crack and peered out. Two uniformed police officers stood in the hallway.

"Are you Santos Reyes?" the older one asked.

Reyes frowned. "Yes?"

"May we step inside?"

He hesitated then stepped aside, opened the door fully, and waved them in.

He eyed them warily. "What do you want? Why are you here?"

The older officer removed his hat and took a deep breath. "There's no easy way to say this. I'm sorry. They found your mother's body earlier this evening behind the mall. It appears she'd been raped first."

Something snapped inside Reyes. He felt a pounding in his ears, his breathing became rapid. He wanted to hurt someone, lash out, to see blood spilled. In a fraction of a second, the boy who did everything right, who could be a poster child for every immigrant's American dream, died.

His was in a daze when the police officer offered condolences on his loss, handed him a business card, and said something about coming to the morgue to identify her body.

Reyes mumbled his thanks, closed the door, and stumbled to a chair. Tears trickled down his cheeks. He sat in the dark for hours. At some point, he fell asleep. The sound of rain pounding against the windows woke him. The clock on the credenza showed 6:30 in the morning. He heard the distant rumble of thunder. He took a deep breath. It was time. He called his cousin Moreno to tell him.

Moreno asked Reyes to come to Mexico and stay with him. Reyes declined. He said he needed to stay in California to make funeral arrangements for his mother. Moreno said he understood and apologized that he couldn't come to the funeral. It would be too public, and between his enemies and the police, it would be too dangerous. Reyes told him he understood and it was okay. Moreno said he'd put out word to the Mexican gangs in Los Angeles to use their contacts and find the person who raped and murdered Reyes' mother. "We'll find the son-of-a-bitch," Moreno declared.

Three weeks later, Moreno called. "I've got him," he said. "The guy's name is Joe Hemstead. They released him from San Quentin Prison five months before, after serving two years of a ten-year sentence for raping a fourteen-year-old girl. You sit tight. I'll be in Los Angeles in three days to take care of things."

REYES WOULD NOT wait. He checked the phone book, found Hemstead's address, and went to the man's apartment building. He rang the bell and shouted through the closed door he had a package delivery for Mrs. Hemstead. When Hemstead opened the door, he told Reyes there wasn't any Mrs. Hemstead. Reyes apologized for the apparent mistake and left. Now he knew what the man looked like.

The following morning at six o'clock, Reyes sat in his car outside Hemstead's building. Three and a half hours later, the man came out. Reyes followed him all day, patiently waiting for his opportunity to attack. It never came. He followed Hemstead back to his apartment. Night had fallen. It was 8:45. Reyes sat in his car, deciding what to do next, when Hemstead emerged from the building and walked toward the corner of the street.

Reyes followed in his car. Hemstead's destination was a mini mart on Van Nyes Boulevard. Reyes parked on the side of the market, toward the rear. The lot was dark. The security light to illuminate it was not working. Before he exited the car, Reyes reached under the driver's seat and grabbed the short metal pipe he had put there that morning. He crept to the edge of the building, peered around the corner, and waited.

Hemstead emerged a few minutes later. Steam rose from the hot cup of coffee he held in one hand, a bag of groceries in the other. He walked to the newspaper dispenser at the corner of the mini mart, near where Reyes stood.

He put his coffee and bag of groceries on the metal newspaper stand and began fishing in his pocket for coins to feed the newspaper dispenser. Reyes lunged around the corner and struck Hemstead on the side of the head with the pipe. He dragged the unconscious man back to the car; duct taped his mouth, secured his hands and feet with the tape, and threw him in the trunk.

Reyes took Van Nyes Boulevard to Valley Vista Blvd. and worked his way into the seclusion of Deervale-Stone Canyon Park. He dragged Hemstead from the trunk and pulled him deep into the woods. He wound more duct tape securely around Hemstead's mouth and then shook him until he woke up. He remained in the woods with Hemstead for over an hour. Only he could hear the man's muffled screams.

The next day, Reyes found the story on page nine in the *L.A. Times.*

Body Found Behind Mall

Sherman Oaks: Local police reported finding the mutilated body of a man in a dumpster behind the Fashion Square Mall. The victim was identified as Joe Hemstead, a convicted rapist recently released from prison. A source from the police department, not authorized to publicly discuss the case and speaking on condition of anonymity, said the man had been tortured. Someone poured battery acid on the victim's genitals after they cut off his penis. Over one hundred slashes covered the body, deep enough to cause severe pain, but not death. The unnamed source said the victim suffered a slow death. Police have not identified any suspects or possible motives at this time.

Reyes read the account and felt nothing. He'd tortured and squashed the cockroach that killed his mother. He took pleasure in what he'd done to the man while he was doing it, but now it was over, and he wouldn't waste any more time thinking about him.

THE FOLLOWING DAY, Moreno arrived from Mexico, and Reyes told him what he'd done. Moreno said, "Okay. It's done. You've avenged your mother. Now this is what will happen. You will do what your mother wanted. You will go to college. When you finish, you'll work for me. People who only know how to use brute force, not their heads, surround me. You will learn to use your head."

Reyes did as Moreno instructed. After college, he went to work for Moreno. He eventually became the sole person in the United States and Europe representing the cartel in all deals made with the gangs importing their drugs. He was perfect for the job. An American citizen by birth, he could travel the world without scrutiny. He had never been arrested or fingerprinted. No pictures of him existed in any law enforcement files. He was a shrewd businessman when negotiating with the gangs and a dispenser of savage brutality when the cartel needed to make a point.

Now, HERE HE was in Switzerland on orders from Moreno. He needed help to follow Burns, so he flew first to Spain after reaching out to his contacts in the Charlin Clan of the Galencia crime families. Moreno was the prime source of marijuana, oxycodone, and heroin to the Clan. Reyes served as the point of contact between the two organizations for years. He visited Spain three to four times a year, arranged drug shipments, and oversaw the money laundering operation.

The head of the Charlin Clan gave him three people to help—a woman and two men. Reyes supplied them with communication equipment and drove with them from Spain to Switzerland. They knew where Burns would stay in Switzerland and shadowed him from his arrival to here in Interlaken.

None of them had seen Burns contacted by the Collector, but Reyes suspected that would change soon. And when it did, he'd be ready.

CHAPTER 19
February 24
Monday
Interlaken, Switzerland

BURNS CHECKED HIS watch. 3:45. He'd been with Hall almost two hours. The Collector's note said he'd be in contact at 4:00. *Can't be late.* He hustled back to his room. He worried about the four people who'd followed him. Hall said if they were Inspector Knecht's people, he knew nothing about it. *If that's true, they must be the Collector's.*

Burns thought how he'd play this if he were the Collector. He'd have at least one of the four tucked away in a room on this floor, watching him. He'd also have one in the lobby, one outside watching the front entrance, the other watching the rear. He looked for shadows moving under doorsills or changes in the light patterns from the door peepholes as he passed each room. He didn't see any movement.

Approaching his room, Burns felt a tingle at the back of his neck. His sixth sense kicked in again. He eased his pace before reaching the door. *Something's not right.* He inched his way close to the door and scanned around the edges. He slid his fingers along the frame next to the lock. He felt a small gap. The lock was not engaged. He was sure he'd pulled it tight when he left.

He yanked the Beretta from his jacket pocket, flattened his body against the wall next to the door handle, and slid into a crouched position. Taking a deep breath, he shoved the door open, staying low as he sprang through the doorway. Arm extended, he swept his weapon side to side, covering the room. *Empty.* He crept forward to check the closet and bathroom. *Empty.*

Burns closed the door and latched the safety chain. His heart was pounding, his mouth dry. He grabbed a bottle of spring water from the desk and drained half the contents. When he put the bottle down, he noticed the envelope propped against the phone, **ERIC BURNS** hand printed in bold block letters on the envelope, sporting the Grand Hotel Beau Rivage logo. *So, someone was in my room.* He tore open the envelope and pulled out a folded sheet of stationary.

Murphy's Irish Pub on Hauptstrasse. 7:30. Last booth on right facing bar. Don't be late. We almost done. I warn you once more. Come alone or uncle dies.

He put the note in his pocket and went to the lobby.

"Excuse me," Burns said to the desk clerk. "Do you have a business center with a computer I can use to access the Internet?"

"Yes, sir. Right over there," the clerk replied, pointing to a room across the lobby. "There is a fee of 10 Swiss Francs for each half-hour. Printed next to each computer are directions to get on the Internet. All you need to do is swipe your credit card."

The business center was vacant. Burns sat at a computer, followed the directions, and quickly accessed the Internet. He logged onto Google Maps and entered the information for Murphy's Irish Pub on Hauptstrasse. The map indicated about a ten-minute walk from the hotel. He clicked the satellite view, and from there, the street view. He could clearly see the pub and the surrounding streets and buildings.

Next, he did a Google search of the pub and found their website. It was located on the ground floor of a small boutique hotel. It had a striped awning with a half meter stone wall in front. Between the stone wall and the building, the site showed eight tables for outdoor dining and drinks. A small parking area, able to hold no more than three cars, sat to the right of the entrance. He went back to the street view on Google Maps and scanned the surrounding area. He found what he was looking for. *Good spot for surveillance.*

Burns looked at his watch. 4:30. He used his cell phone and called Dov Ackerman.

"It's Burns. Where are you and Bernstein?"

"In the lobby of your hotel. We lost you at the clock tower. What happened?"

"Too long a story to get into now. But I'm not in Berne. I'm in Interlaken. I'm meeting the Collector at 7:30 at a place called Murphy's Irish Pub. It's on Hauptstrasse. Try to catch the 5:05 train, but if you miss it, there's a train every hour. Even if you take the 6:05, it'll get you here a little before 7:00. Rent a car. Diagonally across the street from the pub is a hotel with a restaurant on the ground floor and a public parking lot next to the restaurant. I need you and Bernstein to cover me from there."

"Okay, we're on our way. Shalom."

Next, Burns called Ben-Ami.

"Ben-Ami," Gideon said, answering his phone.

"It's me," Burns said.

"Where have you been? Ackerman called before. He's frantic. He said he lost you in Berne."

"It's okay. I'm okay. I spoke to Ackerman a few minutes ago. I'm in Interlaken. I'm meeting the Collector at a place called Murphy's Irish Pub at 7:30."

"Tell me what's going on."

Burns spent the next ten minutes filling Ben-Ami in on everything that had happened in Berne and Interlaken.

"I'm sorry Hall found you in Switzerland. We tried to delay him here," Ben-Ami said.

"Yes. I know. And he knows. He's really pissed off at you because if he hadn't received the intercepted email from the Collector, he'd still be in Israel."

"He'll have to get over it. Let's not worry about him now. I'm more concerned about Knecht. Are you sure he's all right with you being in Switzerland?"

"I'm pretty sure. I gave him my word I wasn't here on Mossad business, that it's strictly a family matter. Which is technically true. I'm confident he accepted my word."

"Good. The main thing is to get your uncle back safely. I've been in touch with Simon Bloom. He said he's going through the ruins of your uncle's office and laboratory trying to find anything helpful. But so far, nothing. He asked me if you had any luck figuring out the clue to the password."

"No. Nothing."

"Okay. Well, as I told you, Bloom's been stopping by your aunt's house a lot and I've given him updates on your activities to pass on to her. He said she's grateful to know what's going on. He had a suggestion which I think is worthwhile pursuing. He thought that since your uncle wrote it, maybe your aunt could be helpful in figuring out what the password clue is. If nothing else, he felt it would keep her mind occupied from dwelling on her missing husband."

"I understand. It's not a bad suggestion. Tell him I'll think it over, okay?"

"Sure. I told him I'd keep him updated when I spoke to you. I'll pass along your message."

"Let's hope this is all over tonight," Burns said. He disconnected the call.

Burns went back to his room and lay on the bed. He'd have a major problem when he met the Collector tonight. He had an envelope with blank digital flash drives, each one programmed to need a password to open it. But what if the Collector brought a laptop and demanded he open one of the digital flash drives to prove it held his uncle's discovery and prove he could provide the correct password to open it? What would he do when the Collector saw the disk was blank? What would happen to his uncle?

HE OPENED HIS eyes and saw the red numbers on the bedside clock. 6:45. *Fell asleep.* He sat up, swung his legs off the bed and rubbed his eyes. He felt groggy. *I need a cold shower.*

After the shower, he dressed and made his way to the lobby to retrieve the envelope with the blank drives from the hotel safe. Following the directions from Google Maps, he walked along Hoheweg to Klostergrasse, around a traffic circle to Parkstrasse, and turned left onto Hauptstrasse. He spotted the red and white awnings of the Irish pub halfway down the block. Along the way, he checked to see if anyone followed him. He saw no one. *Strange. They follow me from Berne but not from the hotel.*

It took him a fraction of a second to recognize them. He was about ten paces from the pub's entrance and slowed his gait a half step. The girl and the man from the bookstore in Berne sat inside the stone wall in front of the pub, beer steins on their table. His mind raced as he walked past them, not giving any indication of recognition. *They're the Collector's people,* he reasoned. *That's why I wasn't followed. They didn't have to. They knew where I'd be.*

He strolled into the pub. As instructed, he headed to the last booth on the right facing the bar. His eyes scanned the room. He spotted the man from the rental car doorway at the bar, sipping a drink. He shifted his eyes to the booth where he was supposed to meet the Collector and saw the back of his head. *Strange,* he thought. *If I were him, I'd be facing the front, watching for me to come in.* Burns moved past the man, and stood next to the booth.

What the hell? It was the man from the train station, the Hispanic looking one. *This was the Collector?*

"You're the Collector?" Burns said in German. "You were in Berne and followed me here. So where's my uncle? Berne or Interlaken?"

The man's eyes squinted, his forehead furrowed. "English?" he asked.

Burns repeated what he said in English.

"I have no idea where your uncle is. I'm just here to get the digital flash drives and the password," the man said. He pointed at the bench seat across from him. "Please. Have a seat."

Burns slid into the booth and placed the envelope with the digital flash drives on the seat beside him. "Not until I see my uncle and know he's okay."

"I don't think you're in a position to negotiate. I'm not alone. Just give me the envelope and the password. Let's not make a scene."

"Not until I see my uncle."

"I'm afraid that's impossible. I really don't know where he is."

"What do you mean you don't know where he is? You kidnapped him."

"There seems to be some confusion on your part. I'm not the man you call the Collector. My name is Santos, and I didn't kidnap anyone. But, I do have a gun under the table, pointed at your stomach. Give me the envelope and password, or I'll shoot you and just take it."

Burns' posture deflated. He put his elbows on the table and buried his face in his hands. His mind raced as he tried to process what had just happened. This was supposed to end it. He was going to trade the digital flash drives and a made up password for his uncle and spirit them both out of Switzerland back to Israel. *Now this. This guy isn't the Collector. He said he doesn't know where my uncle is. But he knew I'd be here at 7:30 as instructed, and knows about the digital flash drives and password. He's just a messenger for the Collector.*

Burns made a decision. He straightened up and leaned forward. "I'm not giving you anything. You're just a messenger, and I don't deal with messengers, only their boss. When he's ready to meet with me and make the swap, he knows how to get in touch."

Burns started to slide out of the booth when the man named Santos grabbed his arm. "Not so fast. Did you forget I have a gun under the table?"

"No, I didn't forget. But you're not going to use it. You're sitting in the back of a busy bar. What are you going to do? Shoot me here with all these witnesses? Then try to make it all the way to the front door? And, if you shoot me, you'll get the digital flash drives but not the password. And, besides, what makes you think *I'm* dumb enough to come here alone?"

"You're bluffing."

"Maybe. Maybe not. Let's see how stupid you are." Burns slid out of the booth. "Tell the Collector to be in touch." He glared at the man and walked to the front door. In his peripheral vision he saw the man from the rental car doorway get off his stool. His instinct told him the man named Santos would now be a few paces behind him.

Burns put his right hand in his jacket pocket and grasped his cell phone. His fingers located the talk button, already pre-programmed to call Ackerman's cell. When Ackerman first arrived in Interlaken, he'd contacted Burns from the car rental office. They set up a distress signal. Burns told Ackerman if he called but didn't speak immediately, there was trouble, and he and Bernstein should be prepared to help.

Burns exited the pub. The envelope containing the false drives hung down in his left hand. It was the bait, the lure that would make sure they followed. The girl and the man from the bookstore rose from their table outside the pub and moved to the opening in the stone wall.

Instead of turning in the direction of his hotel, as they might expect, Burns turned left. He walked diagonally across the street toward the restaurant and public parking lot. Ackerman and Bernstein were in the lot, waiting.

He heard the sound of shoes clicking on the sidewalk. *Clearly not trying to be discreet.* Maybe they thought to intimidate him, make it obvious they were behind him. Perhaps this guy Santos decided Burns was bluffing after all, since no one came out of the pub after him. Burns smiled. *Four of them and only three of us. Hardly a fair fight. But that's their problem.*

Burns paused after he stepped a few paces into the entrance of the parking lot. Timing was important. He pushed the cell's call button. He heard the footsteps behind him stop as well. They had no idea the reason he stopped was to give Ackerman and Bernstein a chance to see how many they were and get into a position to strike when needed.

THE COLLECTOR ARRIVED at the pub an hour and a half before the meeting time with Burns. He strolled to the back of the pub but slowed his pace when he spotted a man in the booth where he had told Burns to meet him. Sliding onto a stool at the bar and ordering a glass of vodka, he waited for the occupant to leave. The man was by himself, and there was plenty of time for him to leave before Burns was due to show up. The Collector stared at the mirror behind the bottles of liquor and moved his gaze back and forth across the pub. He had a clear view from the front door to the booth.

For the fifth time since he arrived, he glanced at his watch. If Burns was punctual, he'd be at the pub in five minutes, and the lone occupant still sat in the booth. *There's nothing I can do about it. Let's see how Burns handles it.*

Five minutes later, with eyes locked on the mirror, the Collector followed a man as he walked purposefully from the front door to the last booth. The man stood for a few seconds, said something to the occupant, then sat down. *That must be Burns. He knows the guy in the booth. I'm being set up.*

The Collector sipped his vodka, eyes focused on the bar mirror, clearly reflecting the booth. He couldn't hear what they were saying, but based on Burns' facial expressions, the conversation didn't seem friendly. He watched Burns lean back in his seat, hesitate for a couple of seconds, then tilt forward toward the other man, a glower on his face. Burns said something and began to slide out of the booth when the man grabbed his arm. They exchanged a few more words, and this time Burns slid out of the booth. He looked down at the man, gave him an icy stare, said something, and walked toward the front entrance. In his hand, he casually swung an envelope. The Collector presumed if Burns came to deal for his uncle, the envelope held the digital flash drives. *What the hell is going on?*

The other man quickly slid out of the booth. He nodded to someone at the bar. The Collector shifted his eyes. In the mirror, he saw a man seated at the other end of the bar nod back and slip off his stool. He looked like he was going to follow Burns. The Collector threw some Euros on the bar to cover his bill and followed the man from the booth, and the one from the bar, as they exited the pub. Through the open door, he saw a man and a woman leave their outside table and fall in with the two from inside.

The Collector wasn't sure what was happening. From what he could see and the way Burns reacted, maybe he'd been wrong. The man in the booth was not with Burns. So, maybe Burns wasn't trying to set him up. But the man in the booth knew about the meeting. He knew the time and the place. How? It was obvious from the way Burns acted he wasn't the one who told him. And if the man in the booth knew about the meeting, he must know about the digital flash drives and the password. But how? Would the four people following Burns grab him and the digital flash drives and force him to give up the password?

The Collector shadowed the people stalking Burns. He stayed in the obscurity of the darkness and left plenty of space between them. Burns headed to a parking area, hesitated, and then walked into the murkiness of the lot. The four people followed him as he moved into the dim bowels of the lot.

The Collector, behind a tree, well hidden from sight, had a clear view of the entrance to the parking lot. He heard the man from the booth, standing at the entrance with his companions, shout something to Burns, but was too far away to hear what he said. He couldn't hear if Burns responded, but the man from the booth spoke to the people with him, as if giving instructions. The two men and the woman began to walk into the depths of the lot. The man from the booth stayed at the entrance.

The Collector felt a chill. *Think man. Burns is in trouble. He's got the discs and password, and they're going to take the discs. But if they kill him doing it, no password, and the discs are useless. I've got to do something, now. But what?*

CHAPTER 20
February 24
Monday
Interlaken, Switzerland

B URNS WALKED TOWARD the back of the parking lot. The quarter moon slid from behind clouds, throwing thin slices of light, casting deep shadows. He scanned the lot for a glimpse of Ackerman and Bernstein. He saw nothing.

Halfway toward the rear of the lot, a voice from behind called out. "That's far enough, Burns. Just give me the flash drives and the password. Make this easy for everyone."

Burns turned toward the voice. The four people stood thirty paces away at the entrance to the lot.

"I told you. I don't deal with the hired help."

The man who called himself Santos turned to the three people with him, *"Obtener el sobre. No lo mates. Necesito vivo."*

Burns spoke fluent Spanish. The man just instructed his people to get the envelope from Burns but not kill him because he needed Burns alive. *Interesting. He spoke to them in Spanish.* When he spoke to Santos at the pub, his English was perfect. Now he spoke Spanish with a Latin American accent, not Castilian from Spain.

Three of them began to walk toward him, the two men spread out to the sides, the girl in the middle. As they approached, they talked to each other in Spanish, but their dialect was different. It was Castilian, not Latin American. That confused Burns.

Fifteen paces from him, each assailant pulled a knife. He wasn't worried. They'd been told not to kill him, so the knives were for intimidation. He could handle himself. Maybe not four to one but certainly three to one.

His concern was for Ackerman and Bernstein. Could they handle themselves? This guy Santos didn't give orders about not killing anyone else. *Where the hell were they? Things are starting to get tight.* Burns had a decision to make. He could pull his Beretta and just shoot them. But, he was trained to be an executioner, not a murderer. And these fools were bringing the proverbial knife to a gun fight.

The three attackers drew closer. *Where were Ackerman and Bernstein?* He was actually more worried about where they were than the people coming toward him. *Looks like I have to handle this by myself.*

He took a deep breath and rapidly assessed the situation just as he'd practiced in his Krav Maga training, the form of self-defense developed for the Israeli military. Every Mossad agent took a general security course which lasted three months. Instruction was six days a week, twelve hours a day broken down into six hours of shooting and six hours of Krav Maga. As a *kidon*, Burns spent at least one week each month taking refresher and advanced self-defense instruction.

Krav Maga is extremely efficient and brutal, derived from street fighting skills. They had taught him how to defend against all varieties of situations and to either attack preemptively or counter attack as soon as possible, targeting the body's most vulnerable points, such as the eyes, throat, and groin. The objective always being to win, and to win quickly, not to fight fair.

Santos told the three coming at him not to kill him, so they would not come at him with their knives in a stabbing attack. More likely they would slash at him, trying to cut him, make him bleed. Weaken him enough to get the discs, drag him somewhere, and force him to reveal the password.

Burns leaned to the side and slid the envelope under the back of a Volkswagen to his left. Then his training kicked in, and his movements became automatic. He set his feet firmly and pulled his arm up in front, protecting his throat, chest, and the vital areas of his body. He only exposed the external part of his forearms because a slash to the internal forearms could slice through a vein or tendon and kill him.

The man on his left side made the first move. He came at Burns with his knife in his right hand and swung the blade in a right to left slash. Burns took a half-step back, and as the first strike passed his body, he stepped in and to his left, anticipating the man would slash the knife back in a left to right second attack. Burns used his forearms to block the man's arm as it swept back as anticipated, striking the assailant's arm on either side of the elbow.

From this position, Burns slid his right hand down and grabbed the man's wrist, as he smashed his left elbow up into the man's throat. The man's grip on the knife loosened as he grasped his throat with his free hand. Burns pulled the knife loose and tossed it away. Swiveling, Burns kneed him hard in the groin. The man fell to his knees, grasped his groin, and writhing in pain, he threw up. Burns kicked him in the head, and he keeled over on the pavement.

Burns spun in a half circle and faced the girl in the middle. Before she had a chance to raise her knife, Burns drove his right fist into her sternum, and a fraction of a second later smashed the heel of his open left hand upward into her nose. Down she went.

He wondered if the strike killed her, driving the bones in her nose into her brain. He didn't have time to dwell on it. The third man bellowed and attacked. Instead of backing away, Burns moved in toward the man's body, inside the sweep of the knife slashing at him, and used his left forearm to block the momentum. Sliding his hand down, he grasped the wrist holding the knife. Simultaneously, using the heel of his right hand, he initiated a counter attack with a vicious chop to the throat, followed with a knee to the groin.

Burns whipped his right hand to join his left, bending the wrist and the knife inward. The attacker tried to free his knife hand by pulling it toward his body. Instead of fighting the pull, Burns went with it, accelerating the knife's movement toward the man's stomach. The man bent over, howling as the knife penetrated deep into his abdomen. Burns twisted the man's wrist, broke his hold on the knife, and kicked him in the face. The assailant fell on his back, arms flung to the side, the knife protruding from his belly. Blood spurted from the wound and pooled next to the body. *Might have caught an artery.*

Burns had dispatched the three people in less than a minute. He rotated toward the entrance of the parking lot, prepared to take on their leader, but the man was gone. Seconds later, the entrance filled with flashing blue and red lights as two police cars screeched to a stop and doors flung open.

FROM THE CAR on the right, Inspector Knecht leapt from the passenger door, a plainclothes officer from the driver's side. From the car to the left, Hall emerged from the passenger door, another plainclothes officer from the driver's side. Both officers had guns drawn. As Knecht and the police made their way toward Burns, he saw Hall open the back door of his car and Ackerman and Bernstein materialized in handcuffs. Burns stiffened. *What?*

Knecht stopped five feet from Burns and looked down at the three bodies on the ground. "I thought you give me your word you are not here on Mossad business and promised me no bodies."

"Take a good look before you," Burns said, breathing heavily. "Do you really believe I started a fight with three people, armed with knives, in a dark parking lot?"

"All right, I give you that. But what about not being here on Mossad business?"

"I'm not."

"What is your explanation for those two coming here?" Knecht said, turning his head to the front of the lot, nodding toward Ackerman and Bernstein.

"I told you before, and I'll tell you again. I'm here on a personal family matter. Those two agreed to help me. But, it's strictly off the books. It is not a Mossad operation."

The two men stared at each other, neither saying a word. Finally, Burns said, "Why are they handcuffed? Are they under arrest?"

"I am not sure what they are at this point. They also are on our watch list and were flagged coming into country. I had men follow them. When you checked into the Beau Rivage here in Interlaken, we were informed. Then we found Herr Hall from F.B.I. registered at same hotel. When I get call that tell me those two buy tickets also for Interlaken, my men follow them and I myself drive here. We took them in custody at car rental office, but they refuse to say anything. I call Herr Hall to meet me at police station to see if he can be of help."

Burns glanced at Ackerman and Bernstein. He could see them look at him and at their surroundings, assessing possible escape routes.

Knecht continued. "While we are trying to get them to speak, that man's cell phone rings," he said, pointing to Ackerman, "and he asks us to please answer it. I pick up phone to answer but no one there. That is when he tells us that this is signal you are in danger, where they are supposed to meet you, and we must come quickly here to help."

Knecht looked at the bodies on the ground. "Obviously, you did not need our help."

"They are all still alive," one of the plainclothes officers said in German to Knecht. Burns saw him out of the corner of his eye when he knelt to check their necks for a pulse. "But we need to get them to a hospital quickly, especially this one," he said, pointing to the bleeding man with the knife wound.

"Call it in," Knecht replied in German. He turned to Burns. "It is time you tell me what is going on. No lies. Herr Hall explained some of it. I know something happens to your uncle, so I want to believe you, that this is only family matter. I can help, but you must trust me, and tell me everything."

Knecht was right. Burns had to trust the man. But only about the kidnapping. His uncle's discovery was not on the table for discussion.

"Okay. Let's go to the hospital with these three and see if we can get some answers from them. Then, I'll tell you everything I can.

CHAPTER 21
February 24
Monday Night
Chalet Near Interlaken, Switzerland

S ANTOS' HEAD HURT. No, it more than hurt. A blinding pain shot from the back of his head to the back of his eyes. He opened his eyes, blinking to adjust to the low light and took in the room. It had stone walls and ceiling, with a single dim bulb. He tried to rise from the chair but couldn't move his body. He glanced down. Duct tape bound his body and feet to the chair, his arms pulled behind the back. Duct tape bound his wrists. *Where am I?*

Think. Tonight's events came back slowly. He had met the man called Burns in the pub, followed him to the parking lot, and gave his people instructions to follow him into the lot and grab the envelope with the disks. The man was a computer security salesman after all. He wouldn't be much trouble. "Don't kill him. I need him alive," he'd told them.

In a flurry of movement so fast it was almost a blur, Burns first put down one of his men and then the girl. That was the last thing he remembered before waking up tied to the chair.

He heard a latch click behind him. Hinges squeaked as the door opened.

"*Quien esta ahi?*" he asked, in Spanish. No response. He sensed, more than heard, someone in the room, somewhere behind him. He couldn't turn his head. *It's Switzerland. Maybe they only speak German.* Santos didn't speak German.

"Who is there?" he asked again, trying English.

"Not right question," the Collector said. "Right question... who you are and who send you to meet Burns."

Two hours later Santos told him, through broken teeth and swollen bloody lips, the plan was to get the disks and password from Burns, then kill Burns and his uncle. The Collector wasn't too surprised. But when Santos told him after he dispatched those two, his instructions were to also kill him, the Collector flew into a fit of rage.

He seethed with anger and took it out on Santos. He stabbed him repeatedly in the shoulders, arms and legs, purposely inflicting excruciating pain before ending the man's suffering by thrusting the knife into Santos' heart.

An hour later, upstairs in the living room of his rented house, he sat with eyes closed, breathing slowly, sipping a glass of vodka. The anger gone, his mind turned, working on what to do next.

He took inventory of his situation. He had the uncle in the basement, but the man served only one purpose now. Clearly, since he couldn't provide the long complex formula, his only use was bait, to draw in the nephew and the disks. The nephew was nearby in Interlaken with the disks and the password, but from what he'd observed in the parking lot earlier, he would not be as easy a pushover as the Collector expected.

Then there was Johnson and the Mexican drug lord Johnson worked with. According to Santos, they were going to double cross him and kill him so they wouldn't have to pay the $500,000 he was owed. If this were true, he couldn't let it go. It would be bad for business. A clear message had to be sent to Johnson and the Mexican drug lord that there were dire consequences for their attempt to double cross him.

The Collector stuffed the body in a large canvas bag, packed it with heavy weights, hauled it to the trunk of his car, and drove to nearby Lake Thun. He dumped it on the pier of a marina closed for the winter. Santos's body would be discovered soon enough. He'd be long gone from the area but word would get back to the drug lord. The Collector's message would be clear. *Don't try to fuck with me.*

He had to find out if what Santos said was really true. If so, he had to figure a way to get his money and get even with Johnson, and even more difficult, a well-protected Mexican drug lord. But that was for another day. He was patient. It would happen all in good time.

Next, maybe there was another way to capitalize on still having the Israeli scientist? Did the scientist have value to anyone else? Could he still get the disks and the password from the nephew? What could he do with the formula and password if he got his hands on them?

Pushing himself up from the leather seat, he polished off the rest of the vodka and moved to his desk. *Let's see if Santos lied to me.* He opened his computer and typed an email to Johnson.

After pressing the send button, a thought occurred to him. He typed a new email, this one to Bogden Bogdanov, a Russian criminal he'd befriended at the transit camp in Italy. They had stayed in touch over the years.

From his home base in London, Bogdanov ran a world-wide trade in black market goods, with connections in many countries. Lesser known, but also extremely lucrative, he acted as the intermediary between people held for ransom and those holding them. Perhaps, the Collector thought, he could still use the scientist and the nephew, as the American expression went, to make lemonade out of lemons.

CHAPTER 22
February 24
Monday Night
Police Headquarters
Interlaken, Switzerland

DOCTORS EXAMINED THE man and woman Burns incapacitated at the scene in the parking lot and told Knecht the injuries were not life threatening, although both patients would be in great pain for the next few days. They were each put in separate police cars, and with an escort leading the way, driven to the hospital behind the ambulance transporting the man Burns stabbed. On route, Knecht received a transmission from the ambulance informing him the patient had died. Knecht diverted the convoy to the local Interlaken Police Station.

Knecht ordered the man and woman be put in cells; the separate sections for men and women would keep them unable to communicate with each other.

Burns stood in the corridor as Knecht ushered Bernstein and Ackerman into a detention room and removed their handcuffs. He stationed four officers, armed with Heckler & Koch MP5 machine pistols, inside the room to guard them with two more positioned outside the door.

Knecht brought Burns to a private office he commandeered and instructed Burns to sit and wait for his return. Three officers also armed with Heckler & Koch MP5 machine pistol stood by the door inside the office. Knowing Burns and his training, Knecht instructed the guards to keep at least ten paces distance from Burns. Knecht knew Burns spoke fluent German and understood the instructions he gave the guards. He turned to Burns and told him to keep the same ten pace distance. Knecht walked to the door, hesitated before stepping outside, turned to the officers, and said, "If he comes closer than ten paces to your position, shot him."

Knecht made an effort to interrogate both prisoners. He tried German, French, and English. It became clear they didn't understand what he was saying to them. By their minimal responses, he thought they spoke either Spanish, Portuguese, or Italian. He didn't have an interpreter for any of these in Interlaken, and it would take hours to get officers who spoke each language to the station. He rejoined Burns in the office.

"What did you learn from them?" Burns asked when Knecht entered and sat at his desk.

Taking out his cell phone, Knecht dialed a number. "Nothing, I'm afraid. I don't know what language they speak, and they don't understand my questions."

Knecht held up his palm toward Burns to stop the conversation as he spoke into the phone. "I need you to get interpreters down to Interlaken who speak Spanish, Portuguese, and Italian. How fast can you get them here?"

"Just Spanish," Burns said.

Knecht snapped his head up. "How do you know that?"

"I heard them talking in the parking lot."

"You speak Spanish?"

"I do."

Knecht told the person on the phone to forget the request, hung up, and said to Burns, "Come with me."

As they exited the office Knecht spoke to the guards. "Follow us."

"Come on, Bruno. I'm not going to do anything."

"Sorry, but I think you lied to me, and I don't trust you anymore."

Knecht led Burns first to the man. Burns asked the prisoner, in Spanish, what his name was. He replied Miguel. Burns tried a few more questions, but he refused to respond to any of them.

They went to the woman's holding area. When Burns stepped in the cell, the woman cowered to the far corner of her concrete bed, her back pressed against the wall. After their encounter in the parking lot, it was obvious she feared him. Burns spoke calmly to her in Spanish, told her if she cooperated she had nothing to be afraid of, and asked her a series of questions. She told him what she knew, which wasn't much, and left more questions than answers.

She said she and the two men were members of the Charlin Clan of the Galencia crime families. The man who met with Burns was Santos Reyes, not part of their family.

"Reyes visits Spain three to four times a year," she said, "arranging drug shipments and overseeing the money laundering operation for a Mexican cartel leader named Moreno, who is the prime source of drugs to the Clan. I was told Moreno personally called their leader and requested he provide people for Reyes for something to be done in Switzerland."

She recounted their orders to follow Burns in Berne and down to Interlaken and Reyes orders to attack him in the parking lot, get the discs he carried in an envelope, but not kill him in the process. Reyes was insistent to keep him alive. She did not know why Reyes wanted the discs or why he wanted the man kept alive. She said she didn't know much of anything else. Burns believed her. As she talked, Burns gave Knecht a running translation.

Burns and Knecht were now back in the office he'd taken over. Knecht dismissed the guards since it was obvious from the woman's confession Burns didn't started the fight, and was, in fact, the victim.

"I owe you an apology. I thought you lied to me. Now I understand it was them and not you that began the trouble."

Burns shrugged. "No problem."

"Ah, well yes, there is a problem. I need you to tell me what's going on."

Since Burns had already decided earlier to do just that, he told Knecht everything, from the time he first learned something had happened to his uncle's lab, through receiving the discs, to getting the emails from the person who called himself the Collector. The only thing he did not disclose was what his uncle said the discs contained and what the discovery was. To those questions, when Knecht asked, he professed ignorance.

"So why is a Mexican drug leader after your uncle's discovery? And how does he know about it? And what would he do with it once he got his hands on it?" Knecht asked.

"I don't know, but there is someone who might help us find out."

"Who?" Knecht asked.

"Agent Hall. When I spoke to him, he mentioned the name Moreno as a person in Mexico connected to a man named Johnson in the United States. Those two are the ones involved in the money laundering ring Hall's trying to crack. I think we need to get him here and get all the information he has on them. Because, presuming you are going to release me, my next stop is Mexico where I'm going to ask Moreno those questions myself."

CHAPTER 23
February 25
Tuesday
Arizona

ELLIOT JOHNSON LOOKED again in disbelief at the email that had arrived from the Collector five minutes ago.
Why you send Santos to kill me?

What the hell is he talking about, Johnson pondered? The only thing he knew about anybody dying was the instruction from Moreno, which he forwarded to the Collector. That was to eliminate Shernicoff, and his nephew Burns, after he got the disks and password. As far as he knew, Santos didn't know about the Collector.

Johnson immediately sent an email back to the Collector telling him he had no idea what he was talking about. Breaking protocol, Johnson also sent the Collector the telephone number of one of his burner cell phones and asked him to call and explain the email. Ten minutes later, the cell phone in his middle desk drawer began to vibrate.

"Hello?"

"This is Collector. This is Johnson?"

"Yes."

"Why you send man named Santos to kill me?"

"I didn't, and I have no idea what you're talking about."

"Man named Santos come to where I am to meet Burns, follow him and try to grab disks and get password. That supposed to be my job. His people not get them from Burns, but I get Santos. It take time, but I persuade him to tell me what he doing. He tell me that plan is after I get disk and password and kill Burns and uncle, he instructed to kill me."

"I swear, I don't know anything about Santos being sent to kill you," Johnson said.

"Santos work for you, no?"

"No. No, he doesn't."

"Who he work for?"

Johnson held the phone in one hand while nervously rubbing his forehead with the fingers of the other, trying to decide who he was more afraid of, Moreno or the Collector.

Johnson made his decision. He took a deep breath. "He works for a man named Moreno. He's one of the leaders of a Mexican drug cartel. He's a very dangerous man. If he finds out I gave you this information, I'm a dead man."

"How you know this?"

"Because Moreno controls my company. Santos visited me before. He's Moreno's main man and muscle here in the United States."

"What you mean he controls your company?"

"He uses my company to launder his drug money."

"It is his idea to get formula from Shernicoff?"

"No, that was mine. If I can get the formula, I can make billions of dollars and break the hold Moreno has on me."

"So I not understand. If I get disk with formula and password why he want kill me?"

"I don't know. Maybe he doesn't want to pay you your money? Maybe you're just a loose end to him and he wants to get rid of you? I told you, he's ruthless."

"So how you know someday you not become loose end?" the Collector asked.

A bead of perspiration formed on Johnson's forehead. A small wave of nausea rippled through him. He'd asked himself the same question more than once. What would Moreno do when he or his company were no longer a use to the cartel?

"Don't think I haven't asked myself the same question," Johnson replied.

"I must think about all this," the Collector said. "I can call you back of this same number later?"

"Yes."

"I get back to you."

"Wait. What about Santos? Is he still trying to kill you?"

"Not anymore."

PART TWO

CHAPTER 24
February 27
Thursday
Washington, D.C.

M cGUIRE LISTENED STOICALLY. When Hall finished his pitch, McGuire shook his head. "It's too dangerous. You'll never get to him,"

"Maybe. But we want to try," Hall replied.

Burns and Hall were with Director of the Drug Enforcement Agency, Ralph McGuire, in his office in Washington, D.C. Hall had arranged the meeting. McGuire had agreed to the short notice request because he and Hall had history.

They had met two years before when Hall was the lead investigator of the F.B.I.'s taskforce charged with scrutinizing claims the D.E.A. laundered money for the Mexican drug cartels. Hall found the claims were technically true. Agents had deposited drug proceeds in accounts designated by traffickers or in shell accounts set up by agents. However, he determined the actions were clearly part of a sting operation to identify how criminal organizations move their money, where they keep their assets, and most important, who their leaders were. The D.E.A. kept meticulous records of every dollar they laundered, and he found no evidence of any unaccounted for money.

Some critics felt the D.E.A.'s involvement, regardless of the purpose, amounted to aiding and abetting a criminal enterprise. Hall made the judgment to report he found no credible evidence to support allegations of any criminal wrongdoing, and as such, earned the friendship and gratitude of Director McGuire. At the meeting that day, Hall was going to try to take advantage of that gratitude.

McGuire said to Hall, "Robert, you've got markers here, and you can cash them in any time you want. But this idea is insane."

Hall and Burns remained silent.

"What do you know about Moreno?" McGuire asked.

"Not much," Hall said. "I only know he is a big shot with the Sinaloa Cartel, and he's laundering money through a company in Arizona. I'm trying to break up the operation and put him and the guy who runs the company in Arizona in jail."

"And what about you?" McGuire said, looking at Burns.

"Nothing, other than he is somehow involved in my uncle being kidnapped."

"Well, then, let me tell you about him, and maybe you'll change your mind about going after him. Most of what I'll tell you has been verified, although I have to admit, some of his early childhood may be a narco fairy tale. "

McGuire put his feet up on his desk.

"The story goes he had a cruel father, a drunk, who beat his mother and him after spending afternoons drinking too much tequila at the cantina and how Moreno had to quit school at age eleven to work in the poppy fields, harvesting the plants that would be turned into heroin. They say by the time he was sixteen, he realized while he was breaking his back in the poppy fields, the drug dealers were becoming rich without having to break theirs and decided he wanted to be one of them.

"The next information we have on him is when he was seventeen, selling drugs for the Guadalajara Cartel in the border city of Tijuana. They say he was very shrewd and figured out the best places to sell marijuana to the gringos from across the border. His booming sales caught the attention of the bosses, who began promoting him. When disputes happened with dealers working for him, they say he preferred not to use violence, which was the norm, to solve them. Not that he had a problem killing when it became necessary, but he tried to settle problems peacefully. That's when he acquired the nickname, El Negociador, the negotiator."

McGuire got up from his chair. "You guys want water?"

Hall and Burns declined.

After grabbing a bottle from a small refrigerator built into a wall credenza and taking a drink, McGuire continued. "This part we know is true. When he was twenty-nine, they arrested Felix Gallardo, head of the Guadalajara Cartel, and sent him to prison. At a summit of other drug lords in Mexico, the Guadalajara Cartel was dismantled, and each boss got a certain region where they could traffic drugs to the U.S. Part of the territory was left open, and it was there the Sinaloa Cartel was formed. Moreno wanted to go back to his home area, so he joined the Sinaloa Cartel.

"Probably because of his talent of solving disputes without violence, he became a negotiator in the Cartel. We know one of the first tasks his bosses gave him was to forge alliances with Peruvian and Colombian drug suppliers. They say, because he did such a successful job at it, he became the dispute arbitrator within the cartel. We don't know if this is true, but supposedly he negotiated a peace agreement with the Gulf Cartel in northern Mexico. We know someone did, so it's possible it *was* him. He's also become legendary as a primary corruptor of government, military, and police officials for the cartel, although no one has been able to prove it."

The Director put his arms on his desk and leaned forward. "Moreno's had a lot of chances to rise to the top but seems satisfied with the number-two position. Maybe he's smart enough to see how the top guys end up getting arrested or killed and wisely chooses to maintain a low-profile and avoid a similar fate. Unlike most of his counterparts, he's never spent time in prison. In fact, as far as we can tell, he's never even been arrested. He's very discreet, the least visible of the Sinaloa capos. Because he doesn't want to be a lightning rod, his movements are invisible. This is why I don't think you have a chance of getting to him."

The Director turned his palms up and shrugged. "Now that you understand just who he is and what you're getting into, is there any way I can talk you out of this?"

They both shook their heads.

McGuire turned to Hall. "You understand you'll be operating without any official cover. If this blows up with the Mexicans, the D.E.A. is going to have to deny any involvement. You'll be on your own."

"I understand. I'm willing to take that chance," Hall said.

"And you," he said looking at Burns, "you understand if anything happens down there and our government does get involved, it's only to save Hall's ass. It will be up to your government to save yours."

"I understand," Burns replied.

"I hear you saying it," McGuire responded. "I just hope you really do."

McGuire turned to Hall. "Well, I tried, but it looks like I can't change your mind. Since I owe you big time, I'll give you the full support of the agency. But again, let me be perfectly clear. It will only be on this side of the border. Once you cross it, you're on your own."

"Understood," Hall replied.

McGuire threw up his hands. "Okay. I'll call the Phoenix office, let the Special Agent in Charge know to expect you tomorrow, and instruct him to give you guys whatever you want, no questions asked."

"Thanks," Hall said as he and Burns rose and shook McGuire's hand.

"Good luck," McGuire said, walking them to the door. "You're going to need it."

HALL HAD HIS hand on the doorknob of his hotel room, on his way to meet Burns in the coffee shop for a late lunch, when his cell phone rang. It was Agent Jack Collins.

"I take it you got something?" Hall said.

"Yes, sir. I intercepted an email from the Collector to Johnson. He asked why Johnson sent Santos Reyes to kill him. Johnson replied he had no idea what he was talking about and included a telephone number, asking the Collector to call and explain the email. This was a first. They've never communicated by phone before; it's always been by email. Also, the number he gave wasn't one of his office phones we've got a tap on. I figure it must be a burner."

"Shit."

"Maybe only partially shit," Collins replied. "Since his office is bugged, we picked up Johnson's end of the conversation. I've replayed the recording a few times, and just from Johnson's end of it, I think I've figured out what's going on."

"Tell me."

"Hold on for a sec." Papers shuffled in the background. Collins came back on the line. "Okay, first of all, these are direct quotes and they're on tape. Johnson told the Collector that Moreno controls his company. The Collector must have asked a question because next thing Johnson said, referring to Moreno, was, 'He uses my company to launder his drug money.'"

"And it's on tape? That's fucking great. We've got the son-of-a-bitch solid on money laundering."

"Yes, sir. But there's more. A couple of seconds later, I'm guessing the Collector asked him about the kidnapping of that Israeli scientist, because Johnson said it was his idea to get the formula. He said he could make billions of dollars if he had it and could break Moreno's hold on him."

"What else?"

"For that conversation, that's it. But, the Collector called back about a half hour later, and here is where it gets interesting. Hold on."

More shuffling of paper. Hall let out a sigh. *I've gotta have a talk with him. He's gotta learn to be more organized.*

"I'm back. Sorry, I have notes all over the place. Okay, I'm summarizing here, but from what I pieced together hearing Johnson's side of the conversation, I think this Israeli scientist is either going to be sent to Mexico, is on his way there, or is already there."

"Why?" Hall asked.

"I'm gonna read you the transcript of Johnson's side of the conversation. You decide if I'm right."

"Okay."

Collins cleared his throat. Hall heard him take what sounded like a drink before beginning.

"Here goes... Johnson. "

'Yes, originally your only job was to get the formula and some samples made with the formula but—

"'Okay. I know you couldn't do that, so I agree taking Shernicoff was the next best thing but—

"'What do you mean you don't want to babysit Shernicoff anymore?

"'Are you crazy? Moreno's not going to send a plane to Switzerland to pick him up and fly him to Mexico.'"

"Collins," Hall said, interrupting, "what was Johnson's tone of voice? Did he sound upset or mad?"

"No. At this point, I didn't pick up that he was angry or mad. But, he gets angry, or maybe upset is a better word, very soon. Let me read you why," Collins said.

"Okay. Go ahead."

"Here's Johnson again.

"'Hey, you don't threaten Moreno.

"'I don't care. He's got too much invested in this. Threatening to dump Shernicoff's dead body in a lake if Moreno doesn't send a plane is stupid.

"'You *are* crazy. Do you realize it's Moreno's money we're talking about, not mine? You can't expect him to pay you the rest of the money for a job you haven't finished.

"'I don't know anything about a hit out on you. But, I'll tell you right now, you're fucking with the wrong guy. Threaten him, and you can bet there will be.'"

Collins said, "Now he was raising his voice. I think he was really warning the Collector not to screw around with Moreno. I also think he was afraid the Collector might actually kill Shernicoff, and if that happened, he'd never get the formula, and out from under Moreno."

"Understood. Continue."

"Here's Johnson again.

"'Look, I can't make those decisions. I'll have to get in touch with Moreno and get back to you. Give me twenty-four hours.

"'Okay. Twelve hours. But don't do anything stupid with Shernicoff until you hear back from me.'"

"That's all I have on this," Collins said. "But now you know why I think Shernicoff is headed to Mexico. I don't think Moreno is going to let his financial investment in the Israeli end up dead in a lake somewhere in Switzerland."

"I agree. Great job, Collins. If you get anything more, get back to me pronto," Hall said before hanging up.

RIDING THE ELEVATOR down to the lobby, Hall thought about if he should say anything to Burns about the phone call. He decided he had to.

Hall spotted Burns in a booth in the coffee shop. "Did you order yet?" he asked, seating himself across from Burns.

"No. Waiting for you."

"Okay. But before we do, I've got something to tell you." He told Burns about the conversation he'd just had with Agent Collins. The cords in Burns' neck tightened, and his eyes grew narrow when he told him the part where the Collector said he would kill his uncle and dump him in a lake if Moreno didn't pick him up. Hall chose to remain quiet, giving Burns time to calm himself and digest the information.

Burns leaned forward and placed his forearms on the table. He closed his eyes and slowly drummed his fingers on the table, lost in thought. After a minute, he took a deep breath, slid from the booth, and said, "You'll have to excuse me. I'll see you at the airport tomorrow morning for the flight to Phoenix. I need to take care of something."

Hall decided not to ask what.

The following day, during the four-hour flight from Washington and the half hour drive to the Phoenix D.E.A. office, Burns hardly spoke. When Hall tried to make conversation, Burns firmly, but politely, asked Hall to please give him his space. Hall complied.

CHAPTER 25
February 28
Friday
Phoenix, Arizona

A UNIFORMED OFFICER ESCORTED Hall and Burns to Special Agent in Charge of the D.E.A.'s Phoenix office, Javier Ortega "Have a seat," Ortega said, pointing to two bridge chairs set up a few feet in front of him. He sat firmly on the front edge of a dented, olive green metal desk, dressed in a denim shirt, faded blue jeans, and a pair of scuffed cowboy boots planted solidly on the floor. He made no move to rise and shake their hands.

Burns and Hall seated themselves. Ortega asked the obligatory questions: how was the flight, how do like the Phoenix weather, and so forth. Hall sensed a chill in the air, as if Ortega was just going through the nicety motions. As he spoke, the agent's face had a hard look. His demeanor was stiff, and his tone of voice sounded almost hostile. Hall didn't understand the attitude, so he decided to cut off the small talk and get to the purpose of the visit.

"You spoke to Director McGuire, so you know why we're here?" Hall asked.

"I did and I do. And I agree with the director. Trying to get to El Negociador is insane. He thinks you're crazy to try it, and so do I."

Hall smiled. "We're not crazy. Well, maybe he is," Hall said, pointing to Burns. His attempt to lighten things up fell like a stone. Ortega's mouth didn't register a hint of a grin.

Ortega folded his arms across his chest. "And how exactly do you expect to get to him? He's one of the leaders of the Sinaloa Cartel and operates in a totally corrupt country. He pays off a lot of senior people in the federal and local governments as well as high-ranking officers in the military. Hell, he probably supports half the local cops in Sinaloa. We have a $10 million bounty on him, dead or alive, and so far no one has been brave enough, or stupid enough, to try and collect it. He even has rival cartels trying to find and kill him. And their doing it with no bounty involved."

His twisted his mouth in a sour expression. Unfolding his arms and jabbing a finger in the air in front of them for emphasis, he said, "And now you two waltz in here and expect to get to him, to do what no one else has been able to?"

Listening to the conversation, Burns leaned back in his chair and crossed his legs at the ankle. He sensed hostility from Ortega. He didn't know why, and he didn't give a damn. He had a mission and wasn't going to be deterred by some asshole with a stick up his butt.

"Excuse me, Agent Ortega," Burns said in a calm voice. "When Agent Hall and I met with your director in Washington yesterday, he told us he would call you and ask you to provide whatever help we need. No questions asked. Did he?"

"That's Special Agent in Charge, to you," he replied, glaring at Burns. "And yes he did. But—"

Burns cut him off. Snapping up the palm of his hand and leaning forward, he snarled, "Then with all due respect, I don't want to hear any fucking buts from you. You're either gonna help us or explain to your director why you didn't. Is that clear?" Ortega's eyes tightened, and his face redden. Burns didn't care.

Without giving Ortega a chance to reply, he said, "Your director said you have police, ex-police, and drug-traffickers working for you as informants. Is that true?"

Ortega flashed a cold smile. "Yeah, we do."

"Then get one of them to get us the information."

Ortega crossed his arms on his chest again and turned from Burns to Hall. "Even if I get one of our contacts to get the information, you're F.B. I. You work for the government, so you have to apply for permission from the Mexicans to operate in their country, and you have to tell them why. You can bet your ass, five minutes after you apply, the fucking cartel will know about it. Then what are you going to do?" He smiled smugly.

"You just get us the information," Burns interjected. "All we want to know is where El Negociador will be on a given day. We'll take it from there."

Ortega took a deep breath and let it out slowly. "First, I'm gonna talk to Director McGuire. I've got someone who might get the information you need. But, the minute he gives it up, he's a dead man. So before I ask him to commit suicide, the director and the U.S. Marshall's have to sign off on immediately putting him and his family in the Witness Protection Program here in the States. Only when that gets cleared will I get your fucking information. And if the director doesn't like it, he can fire me."

Ortega gave Burns a hard stare. Speaking through his teeth, with forced restraint, he said, "I don't know who the fuck you are or why the director is ordering me to do this. It's gonna cost me a valuable deep cover informant that took a long time to cultivate. So, in case you haven't guessed by now, I'm pissed."

So that's why the hostility. Burns shrugged. "Not my problem."

"Really? Not your fucking problem, huh?" Ortega lifted himself from the desk and stood in front of Burns, staring down at him. "Okay, you prick. McGuire said I had to help you, so I have to. But he said only on this side of the border. So fuck you and the horse you rode in on. As far as I'm concerned, it's all on you, and when you get your ass in trouble down there, and you will, the fucking cavalry ain't riding to the rescue. Are we clear?"

"Perfectly," Burns said.

"Then get the fuck out of my office."

THE NEXT MORNING, Ortega called Hall at the hotel and told him he'd heard from his contact in Mexico. El Negociador would be at his mountain estate in the hills near Badiraguato, his boyhood home, in two days.

Hall walked to Burns' room and gave him the information. "Have you figured out a plan? How are we going to do this?" he asked Burns.

"Sorry, Robert. There's no we. You can't come with me."

"You shitting me? Of course I'm coming with you. I've got a lot at stake in this too."

"You can't come. You heard what Ortega said. You're a U.S. government employee. You can't operate in Mexico without their permission. And to get it, you'd need to tell them why. You can't do that. I need the element of surprise working for me. Ortega was right. Five minutes after your request, the cartel and El Negociador will know."

"You can't expect to take on El Negociador by yourself."

"I'm not by myself," Burns said. "Yesterday after I left you at the coffee shop, I called Israel. A team of Mossad agents arrives in Mexico today."

"Are you kidding? Your government is going to let its agents operate in a country without getting its permission?"

Burns slowly shook his head. "Robert, tell me you're not that naive. Do you have any idea how many countries we operate in without asking for permission? Do you think Mexico is the only country that passes on information to the bad guys? Or doesn't want Israeli agents going after bad guys in their country?"

"But you don't have any resources. We can give you all the help you need."

Burns heaved a heavy sigh. "You think only your government can provide help? You think I don't have resources in Mexico?" he said sarcastically. "Robert, I have resources all over the world. They're called Jews."

Burns moved to the straight-back chair at the desk, turned it around, straddled it, and rested his arms across the back. "Let me give you a quick history lesson. In ancient history it was the Babylonians, Egyptians, and Romans. In modern history, the Germans, Russians, and Iranians. Know what they all have in common, the one connecting thread?"

"What?"

"The eradication of the Jews."

Burns took a deep breath; his eyes grew cold. "But we always have, and always will, survive. And you know why? Because the Nazis *were* right about one thing. We're a race. We're not just a religion. We're not just a culture. We're a race. For thousands of years, blood brothers scattered all over the world. Now, once again, we have a homeland. Israel. And there are tens of thousands of Jews around the world, ready and willing to help Israel survive in any way they can. We call them *sayanim*. In Mexico, there are well over a thousand. So don't kid yourself about me not having resources. I've got plenty."

CHAPTER 26
March 2
Sunday
Two Weeks Since the Kidnapping
Mazatlan, Mexico

B URNS' TEAM OF four agents left Israel at 12:10 a.m., arrived in Mexico City at 1:52 p.m., and flew on to Mazatlan. They picked up two SUVs at the airport's Avis lot and checked into the Pueblo Bonito Emerald Bay Hotel, the rooms and cars booked for them by a *sayan* travel agent in Mexico City. Ackerman and Bernstein were already at the hotel. Ben-Ami, at Burns' request, instructed them to fly in from Switzerland.

Five of the agents spent the afternoon and evening playing the part of tourists, swimming on the white sand beach, and eating an early dinner before retiring after a long day of travel. While the others were at the beach, in the late afternoon, the sixth agent, Mira Orsinski, drove to a private airfield eleven miles northwest of the resort. There, she met a *sayan* who owned a skydiving school in Mexico City. He'd contacted her an hour earlier, advising he'd arrived in Mazatlan.

Onboard his aircraft were six duffle bags and a molded plastic case containing a drone. Ben-Ami placed them in diplomatic crates, shipping them to the Israeli Embassy in Mexico City on the same flight as the four Mossad agents. The resident *katsa*, field agent, smuggled them from the embassy to the skydiving school. Thirty minutes later, the pilot took off for Mazatlan.

Orsinski loaded the bags and the drone into the SUV. "Here," she said, handing the pilot a disposable cell phone she'd purchased at a bodega on the way to the airfield. "Have the plane ready to go tomorrow night. As soon as I know, I'll call and give you our departure time."

Early the next morning, while Burns was in transit from Arizona, the team loaded into their SUVs and drove north on Route 150, the major highway hugging the west coast along the Gulf of California. Two and a half hours later, they switched to Route 10, northwest of Culiacan, the capital city of the State of Sinoloa, into the farmland area known as Rancho La Noria. Near a small forested area, they pulled off the road to set up their special piece of surveillance equipment.

The Israeli Military, working with Israel's high tech industries, had developed a cutting-edge drone. The body was constructed of fused nylon with curved wings, shaped to look like a bird. It came in four parts, which could be reassembled without tools. Its stealth configuration rendered it virtually invisible to radar. Powered by solar panels imbedded in its five-foot wingspan, it could remain aloft for more than thirteen hours. A powerful miniaturized nose camera could read the front page of a newspaper from a height of 4,000 feet, send the images back in real time, and save them to a flash drive in the operator's hand-held control panel.

Ze've Levine launched the drone, and within an hour, it flew in a lazy circle, 3,500 feet over El Negociador's mountain estate. To keep it from being recognized for what it was, Levine kept the drone at least two miles distance from the mansion. At that height and distance, it looked like a golden eagle, natural to the surrounding geography. To foster that illusion, he occasionally put the drone into a steep dive, like a bird of prey swooping in for the kill.

He guided the drone through the sky for three hours, taking pictures of the estate, the grounds, and the surrounding roads and paths leading to it. The camera, also equipped with thermal imaging and infrared capabilities, picked up the number of people inside the house as well as guards patrolling the area, those visible and those hidden in the woods and tree tops.

On the return flight, the drone scouted the mountainous landscape between Rancho La Noria and the estate, seeking the best ways to infiltrate. When Levine had everything he needed, he landed and disassembled the drone, packed it, and strapped it to the roof of one of the SUVs. They hid the SUV with the drone deep in the woods, covered it with branches for camouflage, and piled into the remaining vehicle for the return to Mazatlan.

On the drive back to the hotel, Levine thought about what he'd seen on the drone's display screen. The compound was completely encircled by a high chain link fence. The house was set back from the fence, surrounded by one hundred meters of open lawn, close to the length of a football field. There was no cover. From what he could see of guards, they were armed, and the team would be outnumbered probably by a factor of two to one.

Levine knew they'd have the element of surprise, and that was a very big advantage. But, if they lost that advantage, there could be a blood bath... and they'd be on the losing end.

Jorge Moreno Estrada, El Negociador, had built his mansion on a small plateau. An opulent 25,000 square foot hunting lodge, it was the largest of his sixteen homes, standing two-stories tall, with ten bedrooms, a media room, fully outfitted gym and sauna, and restaurant-sized kitchen. A twenty-five foot high window spanned more than fifty feet of the great room wall, offering a panoramic view of a manicured lawn the size of a football field, stretching to the forest behind the fence. Above the tree tops, the muscular peaks of the Sierra Madre Occidental Mountains stood like sentinels against the distant sky.

He'd named the lodge Casa Miranda after his third wife, although she'd never seen it. He had her ensconced in a seaside villa in Puerto Vallarta with their three children.

Casa Miranda was his favorite place to find respite, to escape, for a while, the day-to-day running of his organization. He'd often lament to his closest advisors his disappointment that he could spend only two to three days at the lodge each visit because his security chief insisted he had to frequently change his location. "You have enemies," his security chief reminded him, "and predictability is a luxury you can't afford."

He was sitting in the great room, sipping a glass of tequila over ice, starring out the large picture window. A golden eagle making wide lazy loops against a sky as clear as sapphire caught his attention. *How simple the life of that eagle. Roaming the skies, searching for prey. A predator, much like me, driven by survival instinct.*

The appearance of his head of security pulled him from his rumination.

"Perdoneme, jefe,"

"Ah, Dante. What have you got from the scientist?"

"Nada, jefe," replied Dante Navarro, Moreno's head of security and a trusted advisor. "He speaks to us only in words we do not understand. We think it is the language of the Jews in Israel. We tell him we know he speaks English, but he does not do it, even when Hector shocks him with the car batteries. I have our people in Mexico City looking for someone we can trust to translate the language of the Jews for us."

"It's been three days," Moreno said, "and we are still where we were before. The gringo Johnson says the Israeli scientist's invention is worth tens, maybe hundreds of billions of U.S. dollars, yet the scientist gives us nothing, and the man called the Collector destroyed his computers with the formula. Now, according to Johnson, I can get the formula only from the scientist who only speaks a language we do not understand or from flash drives the nephew has."

"Si, jefe," Navarro replied.

"Do we know where the nephew is now?"

"No, jefe. Santos and three others from the Charlin Clan were tracking him down in Switzerland, but Santos has not been in contact since you spoke to him a few days ago."

"Have our Spanish friends heard from their people?"

"No, jefe. I contacted them this morning. They think something is wrong. Their people should have checked in by now. Maybe they're right because we also should have heard from Santos by now."

"What do we know about the nephew?"

"Only what the man called the Collector told Johnson. He's a salesman for a computer security company from Israel and travels the world. I'm sorry, jefe, but so far there is nothing more on him. If he's still in Switzerland, I have our friends and associates in Europe tracking him down."

"Bueno. We will give our people two days to find the nephew. If they don't, I'm finished with this thing. We will kill the uncle and be done with it. I can't give this more of my time. I have other worries."

"But what of the money you've spent?" Navarro asked.

"I'll lose it. But our business will lose much more if I let this thing sidetrack me much longer. And who knows if this is all real or just Johnson's wishful dream."

Moreno rose from his chair, glanced out the window again at the golden eagle still visible in the sky searching for prey. "Two days," Moreno said. "When we leave here in two days, we either have the nephew and the flash drives or the scientist dies."

CHAPTER 27
March 3
Monday Night
Badiraguato, Mexico

B URNS USED A Canadian passport, taking the 9:55 flight the next morning from Phoenix to Mazatlan, landing at 1:02 p.m. local time. The same *sayan* travel agent in Mexico City arranged for a car at Avis as well as a suite at the Pueblo Bonito Emerald Bay Hotel.

By 3:30 that afternoon, the team gathered in Burns' room to review the images from the drone. They discussed the mission, and how to execute it, with everyone offering suggestions. By 5:00 p.m. the plan was defined, and each agent knew their assignment. To succeed, they needed the cover of dark. In this part of Mexico, at this time of the year, sunset fell at 6:21p.m., sunrise at 6:56 a.m. That gave them twelve hours to complete the mission.

Slipping out of the hotel at 6:00 p.m., Orsinski dropped Burns and the other operatives off at the private airport. She would leave the hotel at 5:00 the next morning and drive back to the forested area where they hid the other SUV.

Once on board the aircraft, the six agents removed camouflage fatigues from their duffle bags and changed out of their casual resort wear. They donned parachutes, each agent checking a colleague to insure they were attached correctly. Burns walked to the cockpit, handed the pilot a map, the co-ordinates of the jump zone clearly marked, and tapped him on the shoulder, signaling it was time to take off.

During the forty-five minute flight, they reviewed the plan. They would parachute from 15,000 feet, landing in the fields on the outskirts of Rancho La Noria. From there, they would drive the hidden SUV to the woods outside the small village of La Apoma, and trek through the mountains for fifteen miles to El Negociador's mansion. The informer warned Ortega there could be perimeter lookouts as far away as three miles from the mansion when El Negociador was there, so the first twelve miles would be easy. The rest would require stealth.

The red warning light flickered over the door indicating ten minutes to the jump point. Each agent clipped a twenty-foot tether strap to their duffle bag, attaching the other end to the "D" ring on a harness strapped to their waist. They slipped on night vision goggles, NVGs, before donning a specialized jump helmet with the face shield molded to fit securely over the goggles.

The pilot flashed the red warning light once more, signaling two minutes to the jump. With Burns in the lead, each agent rose and walked forward to the jump door, dragging their duffle bag. When Burns flung the door open, a loud, cold blast of wind assaulted the team. Burns pushed his bag to the edge of the doorway.

The green jump light glowed. Burns shoved his duffle bag out the door with his boot and leaped from the aircraft behind it. At 2500 feet, he pulled the ripcord, looked up to make sure the chute opened correctly, and pulled the brake toggles to slow his fall. He glanced above at the rest of the team floating behind him.

His NVGs lit up the landscape below in an eerie green as the ground rushed up to meet him. The duffle bag added weight and speed to his descent, so at fifty feet above the ground, Burns pulled hard on the chutes brake toggles, slowing his descent. The duffle bag hit the ground seconds before Burns' boots made contact. He quickly gathered up the deflating parachute and rolled it in to a bundle. Unhooking the duffle bag from the "D" ring, he released the straps fastening the parachute to his body, and dropped the bundled chute to the ground. Looking through the NVGs, he saw the rest of his team do the same.

Working as smooth as a well-oiled machine, the team began to gear up for the mission. They opened their duffels, removed Kevlar body armor, and Velcroed the sides tight to their bodies. Cinching utility belts to their waists, each hooked on a drop-down leg holster to the belt, and Velcroed the bottom to their thighs.

Burns lifted an aluminum case from his duffle. It held a suppressed H&P MP5 machine pistol set in protective foam cutouts. He slung the strap over his neck, muzzle down, and used a strip of Velcro to hold it across his chest. He pulled a suppressed Beretta from its protective cutout, inserted a ten round clip, and slipped it in the thigh holster.

From a second case, he attached a magazine pouch to the utility belt, and filled it with ten clips of H&P ammunition. He grabbed eight clips for the Beretta and jammed them into a leg pouch pocket. As he had told his team, you can never have too much ammo. He Velcroed two concussion and two fragmentation grenades to the chest panel of his body armor.

Twenty feet from his position, Ely Bergen and Rami Neumann, the explosives experts, packed bricks of Semtex and blasting caps into backpacks. Dov Ackerman pulled a rocket propelled grenade rifle from a duffle while Gabi Bernstein removed two aluminum cases, each packed with two RPGs.

Burns inserted the encrypted radio for communication, the telcom, in a pouch on his right shoulder. He popped in his ear-bud and pressed the transmit button for a radio check. The other five agents acknowledge comm was working.

Ackerman walked over to Burns. "What's that thing Levine's putting on?" Levine was strapping what looked like a miniature tank to his thigh.

"His new toy. It's called a Robotic Intelligence System. They designed the RIS to help the IDF do house-to-house combat in Gaza and the West Bank. It gets tossed through a front door or window so it can do a room to room search. You see how small it is? It can go most any place and not be seen. It protects from ambushes or planted booby-traps."

"How does it work?" Ackerman asked.

"It uses a laser, cameras, and a microphone to send back real-time high res images and sound to a handheld console the size of a smart phone. Our tech guys modified the rubber treads with special suction cups so it can climb walls and windows."

"Damn," Ackerman said. "That's one sweet piece of hardware."

"It is."

Burns addressed the team. "Okay, let's move it."

MAKING THEIR WAY to the hidden SUV, they loaded their back packs and cases in the cargo bay and piled in. Ze've Levine, one of the best wheelmen in the Mossad, drove to the outskirts of the small village of La Apoma. Using his NVGs, he had no trouble navigating the eighteen miles in the dark. It was 8:45 p.m. They encountered no traffic.

Reaching the village outskirts, they hid the SUV deep in the woods. With each member carrying a load of 30 to 40 pounds, Burns figured the fifteen-mile hike to the objective would take three and a half hours.

The team followed Burns in a single line as he led them though the forest for the first twelve miles of the trek. With three miles to go and the chance of encountering sentries growing, Burns spread them out with thirty feet of side-to-side spacing. Their NVGs illuminated the woods in green shadows as each followed the clearest path through the trees. He warned them to watch for small tree branches as they walked. The snap of an unseen branch breaking under foot would carry a long distance in the still night air.

They were a few feet from a clearing when Burns heard the *click, click* danger signal in his ear-bud. They all took cover behind trees and lowered to one knee, weapons at the ready.

"Guard coming toward me," Levine said over the com, standing thirty feet to Burns' left.

Burns scanned the trees in front of him. A guard, dressed in camouflage, emerged from the woods. A small caliber rifle, Burns thought a .22, dangled barrel down from his shoulder. He stopped, removed a pack of cigarettes from his breast pocket, and stuck one in his mouth. The flare of the match lit up his face, making him an easy target.

Not something someone expecting danger would do, Burns thought. *Small forest animals scampering in the underbrush were probably the most lethal thing he expects to encounter. Well, he gets too close, he'll meet something more lethal than that.*

"No guns," Burns whispered. He drew his combat knife from its sheath on his upper left arm. He glanced over to Levine through his NVGs and saw him do the same.

"No action unless he sees someone," Burns ordered, speaking quietly into his shoulder mike. "I don't want them sending out search parties for missing guards, so no dead bodies tonight if possible. But no one gets put in danger. "

The sentry approached a tree halfway between Burns' position and Levine's. The team remained perfectly still, eyes locked on the danger, breathing silently through their mouths. The guard leaned against the tree puffing on the cigarette. Its pungent smell hung in the still air.

Five minutes passed before the guard dropped the cigarette and mashed the hot tip in the ground with the heel of his boot. He unslung the rifle from his shoulder. Burns tensed, ready to lunge, but the man turned to face the tree, leaned the rifle against it, and proceeded to relieve himself. When he finished, he flipped the rifle back on his shoulder and meandered parallel to the trees where the team hid motionless. Within minutes, he was out of sight. The danger gone, Burns relaxed.

"That was close," Levine said softly over the com.

Bernstein moved over to Burns. "Why no guns?" she asked.

"We have to remain silent."

"But the MP5s have silencers built in."

"No such thing as a silencer," Burns replied. "You've fired them when you joined the IDF and in Mossad firearms training. Remember how loud they are?"

"Yes, but these have the additional silencers on the barrel."

"What's built in and attached to the barrel is actually a suppressor, not a silencer, and for good reason. You can only suppress, or minimize, the noise. You can't silence it. Only in movies can someone fire shots from a so called silenced rifle without any noise being made. In real life it doesn't work that way."

"But don't you use one when you're on a mission?"

"Yes, but it's a hand gun, a Beretta. It fires a sub-sonic round and the suppressor makes it pretty quiet. Not that a guy ten feet away won't hear it but someone thirty feet away, probably not. The bullet from the MP5 is traveling at 1100 feet per second. It breaks the sound barrier and you get a sonic boom, you know, that crack sound, as it moves through the air. A suppressor can't eliminate that noise. It can only lessen it, and with the MP5, not that much."

"Then what's the sense of having the extra suppressor attached?"

"Because we'll be working in the dark. When you fire, there's a big muzzle flash. The extra suppressor virtually eliminates the flash. The bad guys won't see where you are and target you. If you need to take someone down, and if you're close enough, the first option should be your knife. If they're too far away for that, the second choice is your Beretta. But, if you absolutely need to use your MP5, do it. No one dies tonight but the bad guys. Okay?"

Bernstein nodded and Burns watched her move back to her position. *Rookie questions. Did I make a mistake picking her? Will she be up to the mission?*

USING THE PHOTOS from the drone, Burns led the team to the edge of a small clearing in the woods about a mile from the mansion. He checked his watch. It was 12:38 a.m. They had made good time. Sunrise would be at 6:56, and he wanted to hit the place well before that.

He had learned through experience the best time to attack was shortly before dawn. It gave him a huge psychological advantage. Nothing is more disorienting to a target than being abruptly roused from sleep by the threat of danger, when their body is still halfway between sleep and wakefulness.

Burns motioned the team to gather around. "Take cover. Try to get some rest," he said. "We'll do a drone surveillance in about an hour and a half." Pointing to Bergen, Neumann, and Ackerman, he said, "You guys, set up in the trees, and take sentry duty."

Each man found a spot in the woods near the edge of the clearing and dropped their loads. Each slinging their MP5s over a shoulder, they picked a tree with thick foliage and lodged into crooks in high branches providing perfect surveillance of the area.

"Bernstein, you park over there," he said, pointing to a spot in the woods between the trees where Bergen and Neumann roosted. "Catch a cat nap if you want. Levine, take a spot over there," pointing to a spot near Ackerman's tree.

Ten minutes after the team settled into place, Burns circled the oval shaped clearing doing a perimeter check. He passed where Bernstein had bedded down, about five feet into the woods. She'd removed her plastic camo sheet from her rucksack, spread half the sheet on the ground, and covered herself with the other half. *Well camouflaged. I'd never notice her.*

After finishing his circuit, Burns sat with his back against a tree with an almost unobstructed view of the area. He laid his MP5 on the ground next to his leg and covered himself with a camo sheet. *My uncle better be okay or a lot of people will wish they'd never been born.*

Click, click.

Burns' eyes flew open when the danger signal sounded in his ear-bud. He shook his head. *Must have dozed off.*

"Where?" he whispered into his mic.

"Coming into the clearing. One guard. Your two o'clock," Neumann replied.

Burns remained as still as a stone. Only his eyes moved, shifting, looking in the direction Neumann indicated. He was a few feet outside the clearing and a small bush blocked his line of sight. He couldn't see anyone. He dropped his hand, grasped the Beretta from his thigh holster, and slid it onto his outstretched leg. He slipped his finger onto the trigger.

"No one move," he whispered into the comm. "No action unless he becomes a threat."

There he is. The man emerged slowly through the trees to the right of Burns' position, and stopped. He wore a white shirt, blue jeans, straw cowboy hat, and western boots. An AK-47, known as "*cuerno de chivo*" or "goat horn" because of its distinctive banana-shaped magazine, was slung over his shoulder. Strapped to his waist, a scabbard held a machete. *He's gotta be a wide perimeter guard,* Burns decided, because they were still a mile from the target. *This isn't a bored sentry like earlier,* Burns realized. *This is a pro.*

The guard stood still for about a minute, looking over the area. His head swiveled left and right, taking in the open space in front of him.

Snap. The man jerked his head sideways, cocking his ear. Burns heard it too. A branch snapped. The sound came from the direction where Bernstein had bedded down, about eighty feet from where he sat.

The narco whipped the AK-47 from his shoulder and pointed the barrel in the direction of the sound. Burns' grip on his Beretta tightened. The narco edged slowly across the clearing toward were the sound had come from, the AK-47 sweeping back and forth before him. He stopped and dropped to a knee, a little more than halfway across the clearing. It was clear he was peering into the trees in front of him, trying to see what had made the noise.

Apparently not finding anything, he swiveled his head, scanning the entire opening. At one point, he looked in Burns' general direction.

But Burns knew that, covered by his camo sheet, the narco wouldn't spot him.

Snap. Another branch broke near Bernstein's location. *What the hell is wrong with her?* Burns thought. *She shouldn't even breathe, never mind move.*

The narco leapt to his feet and dashed toward the sound and Bernstein. Burns couldn't see her from his position, but now she was in danger. The narco moved fast. He'd be on her in seconds. Burns bolted up from his position, braced his arms against the tree to hold his Beretta steady, and prepared to take the narco down. He knew using a pistol from this distance was a hard shot, but going for his MP5 would take too long.

Before he could pull the trigger, the *crack* from an MP5 pierced the quiet night. The left side of the narco's head exploded; his body spun in a half circle and dropped to the ground. To Burns, the shot sounded as loud as the crackle of overhead thunder.

"Damn it. Who the hell took the shot?" Burns yelled into his com.

"I did," Ackerman replied. "I thought he was—"

Burns interrupted, his tone tense. "It's done. Everyone stay alert. We're only a mile from the target. We're screwed if they heard the shot and come looking."

Burns raced across the clearing to the body. Grabbing both legs, he dragged the dead man into the woods. If someone came to investigate the sound, he had to get the body out of sight. About five feet into the woods, walking backward while pulling the body, he stumbled over a log. The log jerked upright. It was Bernstein, pointing a Beretta at his head.

"What the hell?" she said.

"What the hell yourself?" he replied. "Why didn't *you* take the shot with your pistol?"

"What shot?"

"At him," Burns said, turning his head to the body he held by the legs.

Her eyes popped wide. "What happened?"

Burns stared at her, and then it dawned on him. "Were you sleeping when I tripped over you?"

"Yes."

"You didn't hear the double click?"

Bernstein's hand flew to her ear. The ear-bud wasn't there. She looked down. It lay in her camo sheet. "Must have fallen out when I was sleeping," she said, holding her head down, unable to meet his eyes, her voice weak. "'I'm sorry."

"Forget it. The good news is, if the shot Ackerman took didn't wake *you*, maybe the guys around the mansion didn't hear it either. Come on. Help me drag him in deeper and cover him up with those dead leaves."

After disposing of the body, Burns found the team huddled together at the edge of the clearing. "Launch the drone," he told Ze've. "Get it up quick and fly tight 360's over our position and then widen the circle. Search for any guards between us and the mansion." It was 1:55 a.m.

Levine assembled the drone, calibrated the monitor and controls, and launched their spy in the sky. Clearing the tree tops, it disappeared in the dark sky. As the altitude increased, he widened the curve of the circle and changed the pattern of flight to irregular shaped loops.

When the drone reached a cruising altitude of 4,000 feet, a height at which the cameras could cover an area of sixteen square miles, it began sending back pictures of the mansion and its grounds.

Burns expected people to come looking for the dead guard, but after an hour had passed, no one had. In fact, no guards were picked up patrolling anywhere near their location.

The team digested the data pouring back from the drone. It picked up six two-man patrols circling the mansion. They calculated how long it took each patrol to make a full circuit around the building. The thermal imaging camera located two one-man sniper nests in trees outside the chain link fence surrounding the perimeter and one guard in a booth at the front gate.

At night, the cool air and ground made thermal imaging sharper than it had been the day before during the warmer daytime. The drone picked up the distinctive heat signatures of five men in the lodge on the ground floor, three on the second floor, and one in what appeared to be a basement under the kitchen.

If that's my uncle down there, he's alive. Dead men don't give off heat.

Burns diagnosed the night's images and picked the place where he wanted to break through the fence. Once inside, they would split into three two-man teams. They could breach the house at multiple entry points. Feedback from the RIS would provide the best place to do it.

Burns' watch showed 3:00 a.m. He fingered his comm button. "Let's go. I want to be in position by 5:30. That'll give us at least an hour before dawn to hit them."

CHAPTER 28
March 4
Tuesday, Early Morning
Badiraguato, Mexico

THE TEAM GEARED up, donned their NVGs, and moved out, spread out in thirty foot side to side tactical spacing. "I'm taking the lead, twenty paces in front," Burns said, as they left the clearing.

When he came to the chain link fence, Burns whispered into the comm, "Everyone hold in place." He looked at his watch. It was 3:30. *Made good time.*

He slid parallel to the barrier until he found the place where trees pressed to within a foot of the fence. The spot sat beyond the view of the sniper nests. He focused on the house across the expanse of open lawn. Directly in front of him lay the large picture window seen in the drone images. The room behind the glass was dark.

The plan was to cut the fence at this spot and crawl through. If the chain link metal proved to be too hard to cut, the backup was to either scale the fence or climb the trees and drop down on the other side. Neither were great options. They could become deadly exits if a battle broke out on the other side, and they needed to get out fast.

"Link up on me," he said into the comm.

With the team assembled, he told Ackerman to cut an opening

in the fence. Ackerman removed a bolt cutter from his rucksack and extended it toward the links closest to the ground to start making upward cuts. Suddenly, Burns' hand darted out at Ackerman's arm, like a striking cobra, and yanked him backward.

Ackerman spun his head. "What?"

"It's hot," Burns said, pointing to the almost invisible wire woven through the links at the bottom.

"Shit," Ackerman said.

Bergen squatted next to the fence, lifted his NVGs to his forehead, and examined the wire. He rose and let his eyes scan the fence from the bottom to as far up as he could see. "Give me a minute," he said to Burns.

Walking around the closest tree, he found a low hanging branch. Jumping, he grabbed it and hooked a leg over the limb. Swinging his body onto the branch, he reached above to grasp another branch for support and tight roped his way around the tree until he was almost on top of the fence. He squatted on the branch, examined the fence, reversed his route, and dropped to the ground.

"I've got good news and good news. There are no wires at the top. That one," he said, pointing to the wire at the bottom "is the only one. The other good news, I can neutralize it."

"How?" Burns asked.

"If you look closely at the wire, at about three foot intervals, the insulation is stripped off, and the copper core is wrapped around a link. That's how they keep it electrified. I'm going to by-pass the connections."

Bergen removed a spool of wire, wire cutters with a built in wire stripper, a set of alligator clips, and a pair of lineman's insulated gloves from his duffle bag. Kneeling next to the fence, he rolled out ten feet of wire from the spool, cut it, used the stripper to remove a half inch of insulation from each end, and connected the alligator clips.

Donning the insulated gloves, he attached one of the alligator clips to an insulated part of the electric wire. Squeezing the tips of the clip, he forced its jagged teeth through the insulation, making contact with the inner copper core. He shuffled sideways on his knees, dragged the ten foot length of wire with him, and repeated the process.

"Here goes," he said, extending the wire cutter. With a deep breath, he squeezed the handle and felt the pressure of the blades engage the wire between the two alligator clips. *Ping.* The wire split in two. He shuffled on his knees eight feet to his right and cut again.

Bergen looked up and grinned. "Done. The juice is by-passed where Ackerman is going to cut. If there's an alarm to alert them of a break in the wire, the by-pass kept the circuit closed. They won't know."

Ackerman cut the fence to a height of five feet. Next, he made two-three-foot horizontal cuts, one at the bottom, and one at the five-foot mark. Folding back the fencing, the team scrambled though, dragging their equipment bags behind them. After the team reached the other side, he refolded the fence and planted a radio beacon in the ground. Tuned to channel two on their comm equipment, it would direct them to the opening in the dark when it was time to exfiltrate.

"What happens if one of the sentries notices the cut?" Bernstein asked.

Burns shrugged. "Can't do anything about it, so let's hope they don't. If they do, we'll have to deal with it. "

Pressed close to the fence, Burns looked at the open expanse of the manicured lawn stretched in front of them. There was no cover. Once they broke for the mansion, they'd be completely exposed, visible to any security looking in their direction.

"Ze've, the RIS," Burns whispered. It was one thing to have the images from the drone, now he needed more up-close information.

Levine unstrapped the unit from his thigh and placed it on the ground. He pulled the control console from his breast pocket and turned on the power. Maneuvering the joysticks, the tiny RIS crawled across the lawn.

When it arrived against the mansion, the camera picked up a two-foot shadow on the ground around the outside of the building. Levine glanced up from the console, peering at the structure. "The roof overhang is casting a shadow. So, unless the RIS moves, as long as I keep it in the shadow, no one walking within a foot of it will notice it."

"Okay," Burns said. He tapped Levine on the shoulder. "See that narrow window to the left, about three feet off the ground? Can you get a look inside?"

Levine maneuvered the RIS along the grass to a spot under the window. He pressed a button, and suction cups extended out of the rubber treads. The RIS climbed the concrete wall at the base of the building, rolling over a small indentation and onto the stucco siding. When it reached the center of the window, the suction cups held it in place. Levine rotated the cameras to look inside.

Burns peered over Levine's shoulder at the video display and stiffened. It looked like his uncle, but he couldn't be sure. "Zoom in," he said.

Dressed in what looked like hospital scrubs, the man on the bed was turned away from the window, so Burns couldn't see his face. He was partially bald like his uncle and looked about the same height. *He must have lost fifteen pounds since I last saw him*, Burns thought. A chain was clamped to his ankle, the other end attached to a bolt in the cement floor.

Burns felt heat flush through his body, then a sharp pain in his left hand. He looked down. He'd dug his finger nails into his palms. He forced himself to take deep breaths.

He glanced at his watch. "Everyone, sync your watches on my count."

He waited until they all had their fingers set. "On my count it will be 3:52 in..." he said, pausing to allow the team to make their calibrations, "five, four, three, two, one... mark. We all get that?"

Each nodded in acknowledgement.

"Levine is with me. The rest of you know your assignments. Move out. We'll radio you as needed with updates from the RIS. I still want to breach by 5:30. That gives you an hour and a half to get your jobs done. Be careful. Stay close to the fence, but don't touch it. It's still hot beyond here."

"Before we go, what are the rules if we run into bogeys before we breach?" Bergen asked.

"Try to not engage. We need surprise working for us. If you're forced to engage, remember the battle isn't won with the first shots. It's won with the first accurate shots. So stay focused, and be selective. They die, not us. These people are no different from Hamas or Hezbollah, and we're not taking prisoners. Any questions?" There were none.

Neumann took some of Bergen's explosives and packed them in his duffle. "Let's go," he said to Bernstein. They took the rest of their equipment, lowered their NVGs, and headed left.

Bergen took his explosives duffle and joined up with Ackerman who had the RPGs. They lowered their NVGs and moved off to the right, into the dark night.

Burns tapped Levine on the shoulder. "Okay. Let's see what the RIS gives us."

Levine lowered the RIS from the window to the grass below and guided it along the wall of the mansion listening for sounds through the microphone and panning the cameras back and forth.

It took the unit a half-hour to make a complete circuit of the building, the cameras and microphone picking up the movements and conversations of the guards on patrol. It confirmed there were six two-man patrols. The property was so large, the guards only crossed paths every ten minutes. It also confirmed there were no dogs patrolling.

Their plan of attack was simple to execute. But Burns knew, once the action begins, most plans tend to go out the window.

CHAPTER 29
March 4
Tuesday Morning
Badiraguato, Mexico

THE DRONE OVER-FLIGHT and RIS showed a large metal lattice gate at the front entrance. A guard booth stood inside the gate, next to the long driveway leading up to the house. The RIS's infrared camera picked up one guard inside. Two SUVs parked on the driveway ten feet from the guardhouse, hoods angled toward the gate in a V shape, served as a roadblock.

Neumann and Bernstein moved along the perimeter fence, approaching the guard booth from its blind side. Neumann quietly dropped his equipment bag and slid twenty feet to the door, taking a position on its hinged side, combat knife drawn. When he was set, Bernstein threw a small stone at the top of the gate. *Clang.* The noise wasn't very loud, but Neumann knew the guard heard it. He picked up the sound of the guard's shuffling feet inside the booth.

The door cracked open and the barrel of an AK-47 poked through. A few heartbeats later, the guard followed, stepping outside, his back to Neumann. Neumann took three quick steps, clamped his hand over the guard's mouth, and slashed his throat with the razor sharp blade. Twisting the convulsing body to the side to avoid spurting blood, he dragged the guard back into the booth. Bernstein arrived in seconds, yanking Neumann's rucksack inside with her.

After stashing the body in a corner, Neumann removed three blocks of Semtex and four blasting caps from his rucksack. He cut one block into two equal pieces and inserted a remote controlled blasting cap into the four pieces. Slipping from the booth, he attached one full block of Semtex to the hinge side of the gate and one to the lock side. He moved to the SUVs and peered inside. The keys were in the ignition. He lay on his back and attached a half block of Semtex to the undercarriage of each vehicle.

While Neumann was doing his job, Bergen was doing his. He made his way around the property fence, stopping thirty yards from a tree holding a sniper in a hunting blind, twenty feet off the ground.

Working quickly, Bergen connected three steel plates, each two inches thick, forming a triangle. To one side of the triangle, he attached a block of Semtex and inserted a remote controlled blasting cap. He edged his way along the fence to a location underneath the tree. The hunting blind's flooring prevented the sniper from looking straight down and seeing him. The fence was still electrified, so Bergen couldn't touch it nor reach the tree on the other side of the fence holding the sniper. He didn't need to.

He positioned the explosive side toward the fence and the tree, the steel triangle creating a shaped charge. With the Semtex angled upward, the blast force would be aimed in that direction. The powerful concussion wave from the explosion would either kill the sniper or so disorient him, he'd be useless in a fight. Moving along the fence, Bergen repeated the same task under the second sniper's perch.

BURNS LOOKED AT his watch. Eighteen minutes since the others left. It was time to make a move for the house. Once they broke from their position against the fence, they would be totally exposed as they dashed across the open expanse of lawn. They unslung their MP5s, waiting for the right moment.

Four minutes after a two-man patrol passed and were gone from sight, Burns said, "Let go." They bolted for the house.

In training, Burns could run the hundred-yard dash in twelve seconds. He estimated the lawn at twice that. But in training, he wasn't weighed down with protective gear, weapons, and other equipment, so it might take thirty to forty seconds to make it to the house. That was a long, dangerous time to be in the open. He told Levine to run in a straight line. The usual zig-zag path would add more time and create more movement, increasing the chances of being spotted.

Hurtling across the lawn, they made it to the house in thirty-six seconds. Hearts pounding, they gasped for breath, their lungs straining to replenish depleted oxygen. They leaned against the house, positioned back to back, scanning the landscape for any signs they'd been seen. Everything remained placid.

As their heart beats approached normal and their breathing became less labored, Burns whispered, "Send the RIS that way," pointing toward the front of the house and the door to the kitchen. He'd picked that entrance to breach because it was better to enter at the end of a building rather than the middle, limiting possible threats from the sides. He estimated it to be fifty feet from where they stood.

Burns watched the RIS through his NVGs. It moved slowly in the shadow cast by the roof overhang. Ten feet from the kitchen door, it stopped. Burns jerked his head toward Levine.

"What?" he whispered.

Levine put a finger to his lips and then tapped his earphones.

"Hear guards. Close," Levine mouthed.

Burns flattened his back against the wall, slung his MP5 across his chest, and pulled his Beretta from the leg holster.

Burns heard a voice. "Espera un minuto. Necesito usar el baño."

Great, thought Burns. *Now he needs to use the bathroom?*

His NVGs picked up two guards heading to the kitchen door. One of them stepped inside; the other rested his rifle against the wall beside the door, leaned back, and lit a cigarette. The RIS sat motionless five feet from his boots.

If he looks down and sees it, we're screwed. With his back flat against the building, Burns inched forward toward the guard, reducing the fifty foot spread between them. Thirty feet from the guard, he froze in place when the man leaned over, dropped his cigarette to the ground, and crushed it out with his boot.

"Hola, Carlos," the guard called out to his companion. He stuck the upper half of his body inside the door and yelled, "Vamonos,"

"Un minuto," came the reply from inside.

While the guard leaned inside the door calling for his friend to hurry up, Burns threw caution to the wind and sprinted across the thirty feet between them. The guard apparently sensed or heard someone behind him because he jerked upright and started to twist away from the door, reaching for his rifle. He was too late.

Burns clamped his hand over the guard's mouth, jammed the suppressed Beretta's muzzle into his right eye, and fired. Death was instantaneous. Burns pulled the twitching body away from the doorway and lay it against the building. *Did Carlos hear the shot,* Burns wondered?

"Miguel, quiere una botella de agua?" a voice called from inside.

He didn't hear the shot.

Burns moved back to the side of the doorway keeping out of sight from inside, placed his hand over his mouth to muffle and distort his voice and replied, "No, gracias."

He heard footsteps approaching from the kitchen inside. He reholstered the Beretta and pulled his knife from the shoulder scabbard. Crouching, he waited for the man named Carlos to appear. When Carlos's body filled the doorway, Burns lunged, thrusting upward, driving his knife into the man's midsection below the rib cage. The blade severed the aortic artery and plunged into the lower chambers of the heart. The momentum of attack propelled them inside to the kitchen. Falling on top of the guard, he yanked the knife free and sliced the man's throat, severing the carotid arteries and windpipe.

Jumping to his feet, Burns scanned the kitchen, listening for anyone coming to investigate. The only sound he heard was the soft gurgling of blood bubbling from the open throat of the body at his feet. In seconds, all was quiet.

CHAPTER 30
March 4
Tuesday Morning
Badiraguato, Mexico

Burns wiped the blood from the knife on the guard's shirt and slipped it back in the scabbard. Hustling outside, he lugged the first guard's body back into the kitchen, kicking the door shut behind him. Dragging the body to a far corner, he returned to the body of the man named Carlos. Grasping the man's legs, he pulled him to the same corner, leaving a wide swath of blood trailing on the floor behind. Burns wasn't worried about anyone seeing the blood. His concern was not to slip on the sticky wetness if he had to rush out.

The RIS's sensors showed, if it was his uncle in the basement, he was unguarded. Burns' plan was to get to him as fast as possible without coming in contact with anyone. Get him out of the house, back to the fence opening, and be on their way through the forest to the SUVs before anyone knew his uncle was gone.

About to head for the basement, he heard a noise coming from the hallway on the right, the one leading to the main part of the house and the basement door. He crouched against the kitchen counter, drawing the suppressed Beretta from his thigh holster. He'd left his NVGs outside before attacking the first guard. Now, he was as blind in the dark as everyone else.

A light went on in the hallway, momentarily blinding him. He'd used his NVGs or normal night vision for so much tonight, the light hurt his eyes, causing him to squint repeatedly.

A man came into view. Short, maybe five-feet-six inches, drooping mustache, big belly, a pistol strapped to his waist. Burns raised his Beretta, taking aim at his head. The man stood next to the basement door, scratched his groin, opened the door, and disappeared from sight, closing the door behind him. *Shit.*

He rose from his crouched position, and took a step toward the basement door when the outer door creaked open behind him. Burns whirled and leveled his pistol, ready to kill whoever came through, when he caught sight of a hand placing the tiny RIS over the threshold. *Levine.* He forgot to give him a situation update. *Probably thought I was in trouble.*

Burns tapped his comm unit. "Levine, I'm in the kitchen. It's clear. Get in here fast."

Levine slipped in the door, closed it behind him, picked up the RIS, and moved to Burns.

"Plan changed. Someone just went down to the basement," Burns whispered. "We can't go there now. If there's shooting and anyone in the house hears it, we'll be trapped down there. There's only one way in and out. We're gonna have to clear the house first."

"Okay," Levine said in a hushed tone.

"The drone picked up five on the ground floor and three on the second," Burns said. "I figure the guy who went to the basement is one of the five. We hit the four on the ground floor first. Let's see where they are. If the shit hits the fan, the ones upstairs need to come down the single staircase to get to us. Should be easy to handle them. "

Levine gave Burns an ear-bud so he could listen to the units microphone then lowered the RIS and guided it out of the kitchen into the hallway. Walking shoulder to shoulder so both could see the monitor, they followed ten paces behind as Levine maneuvered it down the corridor. He stopped the unit next to an open door. The microphone picked up two distinct sounds, one of loud snoring, and one of very heavy breathing. He turned the unit into the room. Twin beds. The cameras picked up arms and legs extended beyond the mattresses, each bed occupied. *There's two,* he thought, looking at the hand held monitor.

Levine backed the machine out of the room, continuing down the hallway. He moved it to two more open doors, pausing at each. No noise from the rooms. The RIS came to a closed wooden door, and he stopped it for five seconds to see if the mics picked up any sounds behind the door. Hearing nothing, he continued moving the unit down the hallway until it reached the last doorway at the end. Levine paused the unit at the open door, picking up light snoring.

Maneuvering the machine inside, the cameras scanned the room. Twin beds again. The bottom half of a leg stuck out from beneath the blankets from the bed of the man snoring but picked up no one on the other bed.

Burns motioned Levine to back the unit out of the room and head back toward the kitchen. Levine brought the RIS back with him.

"Okay. We don't know where the fourth guy is, but we can't waste time. I'm gonna take out the three we know about. You wait here," Burns said.

"You mean kill them? In their sleep?"

"That's what I mean," Burns replied. "These guys are in the house, so Moreno trusts them. He would only trust men who killed for him. They're scum who not only kill, but torture their victims. We're not taking prisoners."

Burns put on Levine's NVGs, moved down the hallway, and slipped into the first room with the two men. He approached the bed with the man who was breathing heavy, placed the tip of the suppressor an inch from the base of the skull where the spinal column connects to the brain, and pulled the trigger twice, severing the spinal cord. Death was instantaneous. Even with the suppressor, the noise sounded like two loud coughs.

The man in the other bed was snoring loudly, so deep in sleep the noise didn't cause him to stir. Burns moved over and executed the snorer.

Edging his way to the last room, he peered inside. He could make out the one body on a bed. As expected, the other bed was empty. *Where is he?* Gliding into the room, Burns killed the sleeping man. *The other guy better be upstairs, or we're screwed.*

He began working his way back to Levine when the only door that had been closed suddenly swung open. Burns swiveled toward it, taking aim with his pistol. A rush of adrenaline heightened his senses. The sound of running water and a pungent odor assaulted his nose. *The bathroom.*

The man in the doorway stood open-mouthed, eyes wide. Before the startled man could react, Burns lunged. He grabbed a handful of the man's shirt, pushed him back inside the bathroom, jammed the suppressor into his eye, and fired. As the body slumped, Burns held the shirt tightly and slowly lowered the dead man to the floor.

Moving quickly back to the kitchen, he found Levine waiting anxiously. Burns nodded.

"All three?" Levine whispered.

"I found the fourth," Burns said quietly. "Let's get upstairs."

They made their way to the end of the corridor, Levine in front, holding the RIS. He lowered the unit and maneuvered it to the foot of the stairs leading to the second level. Slowly and quietly, the RIS climbed the stairs. It took four minutes to make it to the top landing.

Standing next to Levine, Burns watched the monitor as the camera scanned the hallway. A man sat slumped in a chair, fifteen feet away, next to a set of double doors. His chin was down, head tilted to the side, sleeping. An AK-47 lay across his lap.

Levine moved the unit to the entrance of an open bedroom doorway, twenty feet past the guard. "Look," he said, tapping the display. The unit's infrared camera picked up the sleeping form of the second of the three people on the top floor.

Burns pondered the situation for a few seconds... then made a decision.

"Here's what we're going to do," he told Levine. "When we get to the top of the landing, I'm going for the guard. You cover the far bedroom. If there's any noise and someone steps through the doorway, you take him down. Otherwise, keep me covered, and I'll get him next. After that, I'm going after whoever is inside the bedroom. I'm betting it's Moreno. Any questions?"

Levine shook his head, and started to the stairway. Burns grabbed his arm.

"Hold on," he said.

Burns tapped his comm. "Check in" he whispered. All four agents reported in.

"All assignments complete?" Each replied yes.

"I'm downstairs. I eliminated one of the two-man patrols. Things might go to hell fast in here," he said into the comm. "When I yell *go, go*, execute immediately. Confirm."

The agents all acknowledged.

"Okay," he whispered to Levine, "let's move."

THEY CREPT UP the stairs, Burns holding his suppressed Beretta in his outstretched arm. Reaching the landing, he moved his back against the wall on the side of the corridor where the guard sat. Levine lowered himself flat on the hardwood floor in the middle of the corridor, raised his MP5, sighting the weapon on the doorway of the far bedroom.

Burns holstered the Beretta, eased his knife from the shoulder scabbard, and inched his way along the wall. Five feet from the guard, he stepped on a loose floorboard, which groaned with a loud *squeak*. The guard bolted upright in his chair, twisting his head in the direction of the noise.

Burns lunged. The guard swung his weapon toward him. Burns lashed out with his left arm to block the AK-47 from pointing directly at him and plunged the blade into the guard's chest.

Before Burns could wrestle the AK-47 from the dying guard, the man's muscles contracted, and his finger reflexively squeezed the trigger of his weapon. A burst of bullets sprayed harmlessly across the opposite wall. But inside the quiet house, the noise from the unsuppressed weapon assaulted his ears like the explosive cacophony of jet engines.

Fuck. Everyone had to hear that.

He punched his comm. "Go, go!" he shouted into the comm.

Brief seconds later, Burns heard explosions outside. He shifted his attention to the last bedroom. The occupant, woken from his slumber by the sounds of the gunshots in the hallway and the explosions outside, rushed into the hallway gripping an AK-47. Levine fired and the man crumpled to the floor.

Burns yanked his MP5 from across his shoulder, pointed it toward the double doors of the bedroom protected by the dead guard, and kicked them open. He was shocked at the sight in front of him.

Crouched in a corner, quaking and quivering like an abused dog, was the man he presumed to be Moreno. The leader of one of the deadliest cartels in Mexico, reputed to be responsible for personally killing scores of people and ordering the deaths of countless others, held his trembling hands above his head, shouting, "Por favor, no me mates." Please don't kill me.

Sorry pal, no prisoners. With his weapon tight against his shoulder, he quickly swept the room for other occupants before aiming the laser sight's red dot center on the man's forehead.

But, in the split seconds it took to sweep the room, Burns' training kicked in, his brain working like a super computer. *If you can improve your exit strategy, do it. They'd lost the element of surprise,* he reasoned. *Moreno may be more useful alive.*

Lowering his weapon, the red dot resting on Moreno's chest, Burns screamed in Spanish, "Get up! Now!"

"Who are you?" the man asked, his voice quaking. As he struggled to his feet, Burns could see the fear written on his face.

He didn't answer as he closed the gap between them. Two feet from the cowering man, Burns grasped his MP5 in both hands and jammed the stock into his stomach, causing the man to double over in pain, gasping for breath.

"Not another word from you, or you'll get worse. Understand?"

"Yes," he gasped, clenching his teeth in pain and nodding.

Burns reached into his cargo pants and retrieved a zip tie, which he used to fasten the man's hands behind his back.

"Don't even think of fucking lying to me. You're Moreno. Right?"

He watched the man's eyes. It looked like there was a millisecond when the man thought of how to respond before he mumbled, "Yes."

Burns jabbed him in the stomach with the barrel of the MP5. "What? I didn't hear you."

"Yes," the man said louder. There was no arrogance in this once powerful man's tone. He was defeated, for the moment, broken. But Burns knew, given the chance, Moreno would try to regain his sense of power, his manhood.

Outside, the noise of explosions and gunfire continued.

"Come on," Burns said, pushing Moreno in front of him, the barrel of his weapon pressed against his spine.

Making sure a jittery Levine didn't shoot him, Burns tapped his comm. "Levine, coming out with a prisoner."

Marching Moreno out of the bedroom, Burns pushed him toward the stairs. "Let's move it," he said to Levine. "We need to get to the basement fast."

CHAPTER 31
March 4
Tuesday Morning
Badiraguato, Mexico

O NCE THE TEAM outside heard the shots from inside the house, and the, "Go, go," message from Burns, they sprang into action.

Bergen set off the Semtex charges beneath the sniper nests, rendering the occupants dead, unconscious, or disoriented. From his position on one side of the mansion, near the fence and forty feet from the first sniper nest, he lay on the ground, his MP5 at the ready. Ackerman's job was to be in the same position near the second sniper nest.

As anticipated, one of the two-man patrols appeared within minutes of the explosions. With near calm, Bergen killed them both. The bark of his suppressed MP5 got lost in the chaos of the explosions caused by Neumann and Bernstein at the front of the mansion. He presumed Ackerman enjoyed the same success. If so, that was three teams down, counting the one Burns eliminated, leaving three more to watch for.

Neumann and Bernstein were huddled in the guard shack when the, "Go, go," signal came. Stepping out of the guardhouse, Neumann heard Bergen's explosions taking out the snipers. He pressed his remote, blowing the explosives on the front gate, knocking it flat to the ground.

Next to him, Bernstein raised the RPG weapon to her shoulder, taking aim at the mansion's massive wooden front door. With a loud *whoosh,* followed seconds later with a deafening *boom,* the once ornately carved front door was reduced to a pile of splinters.

Using the guard booth for cover and bracing their MP5s against the edges of the structure to hold them steady, both agents had their weapons at the ready, Bernstein on the right, Neumann on the left. As expected, guard patrols raced to the front of the mansion where it sounded like the main assault on the house was occurring.

Taking aim on the first guard team to show on the right, Bernstein took a deep breath, calmly steadied her aim and put a round into the head of the lead guard, a microsecond later doing the same to the second one.

Neumann didn't do as well. He killed the first guard to appear around the corner of the mansion on the left, but he was too anxious. He took the shot before the second guard broke completely into the open. He'd pulled up short and threw his body backward, just as Neumann's shot bounced off the building, just missing him. Seconds later, the barrel of the guard's AK-47 appeared around the corner, blindly spraying bullets indiscriminately across the lawn.

The comm units came alive.

"I just got two," Bergen said over the comm.

"I got two," Ackerman echoed.

"Me too," Bernstein said.

"I've got one down, but the second has cover and is firing," Neumann said. "He's at the front left side of the house if you're facing the front. Can any of you get to him?"

"I'm near that side," Ackerman replied. "I'll try to make it over there, but by my count, we still have one more two-man team out there. Anyone got eyes on them?"

"Negative," came the response from the others.

INSIDE THE MANSION, Burns pushed Moreno in front of him as they walked down the stairs to the first floor. Levine followed, holding the RIS.

When they reached the door to the basement, Burns moved Moreno past the door and told Levine to cover him. Positioning himself to the side, Burns reached down, grabbed the handle of the door, and yanked it open. It took a half a minute before a hail of bullets flew up from inside, striking the wall and ceiling of the stair landing opposite Burns.

Covering Moreno with his MP5, Burns told Levine to send the RIS down.

Placing the unit next to the door, Levine guided it over the threshold, across the small landing and down the stairs. The room was pitch black, rendering the RIS's regular camera useless, but not so the infrared one. When the unit reached the bottom of the stairs, Levine began the infrared scan of the room.

Near the left wall, the one closest to the outside, it picked up the image of a body lying flat on a bed. Kneeling on the floor next to the bed, using the body on the bed as a shield, the infrared sensors picked up the glow of the top half of a man, as well as the heat image from his recently fired pistol glowing bright red in the camera.

Yelling down to the man in the basement, Burns shouted in Spanish, "Come out with your hands in the air!" The man replied with a single gunshot to the wall next to the stairs.

Jabbing Moreno in the stomach with the rifle barrel, Burns said, in Spanish, "Tell him to drop his weapon and come upstairs."

Moreno stared at Burns for a second, grinned and shook his head. "No."

"What did you say?"

"I said no. You may have me, but now I have something you need. Cut me free and maybe I'll help you."

Burns' eyes narrowed like a feral cat. "Really? You think you can bargain with me?"

He pulled his Beretta from its holster and shot Moreno in the foot.

Moreno let out a blood-curdling scream as the bullet pierced his instep. He leaned down to grasp his injured foot, but Burns placed the hot tip of the suppressor under his chin, pushing him upright. The man bellowed in agony, twisting his head away from the metal searing his neck. A blister formed under his chin He leaned against the wall, standing on one leg, holding the injured foot inches above the floor. His eyes watered, and he sucked in air with rapid gasps, trying to alleviate the intense throbbing from his foot and neck.

"Next time you think you're in control," Burns hissed through clenched teeth, "I'll put one through your knee cap and cripple you for life. Do you understand?"

"Si," Moreno whimpered.

"Good. Now let's try it again. Tell him to drop his weapon and come upstairs."

Moreno complied and yelled for the man downstairs to do as the gringo instructed.

"Cover him," he told Levine as he moved to the edge of the basement door. Hearing no movement downstairs, he shouted in Spanish, "Get up here. Now!"

Why was he taking so long to comply with an order from his boss? A shiver passed through Burns' body, his sixth sense kicked in again. He had a bad feeling.

"He just stood up," Levine said, his eyes flickering from Moreno to the RIS monitor.

Bang, Bang.

"Oh, shit," Levine muttered.

Burns didn't wait to ask Levine what happened. With his weapon leading the way, he flipped on the basement light switch and charged downstairs, two steps at a time. When he hit the bottom, he threw himself to the ground, rolled in a practiced maneuver, weapon up, ready to fire.

The Mexican lay on the floor, a pool of blood forming around the gaping head wound. He shifted his gaze to the bed. Blood dripped over the edge of the mattress onto the floor.

"No!" he screamed, scrambling to his feet, rushing to the body of his uncle. As he ran, with a rage more intense than he'd ever felt, he lowered the weapon and emptied a full clip of bullets into the already dead Mexican.

Eyes filled with tears, Burns grabbed the body of his uncle in his arms and rained kisses on the face covered in blood from the head wound. His pain was beyond description. Bile rose in his throat from the metallic taste of his uncle's blood coating his lips. He rocked back and forth, holding the body tight.

"Oh, my God! Oh, my God. How could I let this happen to you," he said repeatedly.

Seconds passed as remembrances of his uncle flooded his head. Just as quickly, his mind switched from grief and anger to the here and now. *I have to get my men out of here, and I'm bringing Seth home, back to Israel.*

His thoughts momentarily shifted, from his uncle to Moreno. "You're responsible for this," Burns muttered to himself. "You'll pay. You'll suffer pain like no human has ever gone through. Before I'm done, you'll beg me to kill you."

He gently lowered his uncle to the cot and wiped the tears from his eyes. Burns searched the room for something to clean his uncle's blood shrouded face before he brought him upstairs. He spotted towels on a table across the room. Saturating one of them in water from a pitcher, he returned to the bedside. Eyes brimming once more, he reverently began washing the blood obscured face.

Within seconds, as more of the face was revealed, Burns gasped. "It's not my uncle."

Part Three

CHAPTER 32
March 4
Tuesday Morning
Route 15, Sonora, Mexico

H E ANSWERED ON the second ring. "F.B.I. Agent Hall."

"Good Afternoon, Robert."

"Burns? Where are you? Still in Mexico?"

"I am. But on my way back."

"With your uncle?"

"No."

"Why? What happened?"

"Long story. I'll fill you in when I get there. The reason I'm calling is because I need help getting into the U.S."

"Fly back. There are no alerts out on you here."

"No can do. I need to come by land and can't go through Mexican border check points. I need you to get Ortega to slip me in without any hassle from the Mexicans or U.S. Border Patrol."

"You're shitting me, right? Ask Ortega? Did you forget a few days ago he told you to go fuck yourself, and if you got in trouble down there, the cavalry—meaning him—isn't riding to the rescue?"

"He'll ride to the rescue this time. I've got Moreno with me."

"Moreno! You've got Moreno?"

"Slightly wounded but otherwise intact."

"Oh, man. I'll bet he'll send the cavalry for this. Where are you now, and how can I get back to you?"

"I'm headed north on Route 15, just past Hermosillo in Sonora. According to my GPS, it's about three hours from the Arizona border. If I continue on 15, it takes me to Nogales on the Mexican side, but I'm probably pushing my luck staying on this road much longer. By now, Moreno's people know shit went down at his place this morning. I'm betting, along with the cops and military the cartel has on their payroll, they're looking for him. "

"What do you want me to ask Ortega to do?"

"Get me to a place where I can cross the border. I'm not worried about the Mexican border guards. They probably don't give a crap about their people crossing into the States. But I don't want some trigger happy I.C.E. agent taking shots at me or trying to lock me up if I get caught crossing with Moreno. Have him pick a place where I can cross and meet *his* people."

"Okay," Hall said. "I'll get back to you ASAP." Burns gave him his satellite phone number and disconnected.

HIS THOUGHTS DRIFTED back to what had happened over the last eight hours.

After discovering the man in the basement wasn't his uncle, Burns rushed upstairs.

"Let's move it," he yelled to Levine.

"Your uncle. Is he...?"

"Let's go," Burns shouted, ignoring Levine's question, jamming the barrel of his MP5 into Moreno's back and pushing the limping man to the door leading outside.

Burns pressed his comm button. "Sit rep outside?" he asked the agents.

Neumann advised that the one remaining two-man patrol was still unaccounted for and one guard was still firing at him and Bernstein from the left corner of the house.

Levine pushed open the kitchen door and poked his head cautiously around the doorframe. "Looks clear," he said over his shoulder and started to exit.

"Hold it," Burns said, grasping his arm. "Send the RIS out first."

Levine lowered the unit and moved it outside. The infrared camera scanned the area and soon picked up the heat signatures of the two-man patrol, huddled near the cut in the fence the team used to enter the compound. Levine tapped the monitor, showing Burns their location.

"I'm going through the door first," Burns said. "You keep Moreno covered. I want him alive if possible, but if he tries anything, kill him."

Burns put a fresh clip in his weapon, took a deep breath, lowered his body into a crouch, and lunged through the open door. Twisting his body, he landed on his shoulder, rolled to a prone position on soft grass and began firing at the guards.

The guards returned fire and clumps of dirt and grass kicked up around him. He felt a sharp pain above his right eyebrow and instinctively closed his eye. He wiped away a chunk of dirt. When he opened his eyelid, the eye was irritated, his vision blurry. Relying on muscle memory and instinct, he fired blindly in what he hoped was the right direction.

"Aieeeh!" The sound of pain filtered into his ear. *I hit one.* His clip ran out. As he reloaded, he realized no more gunfire came from the direction of the guards.

"Burns, the infrared picked up the guards squeezing through the cut in the fence," Levine shouted. "They're on the run,"

Before he could respond, Burns heard gunfire coming from the other side of the mansion.

"I got the one shooting at Neumann," Ackerman shouted through the comm. "He's down."

Burns, vision now clear, rose to a knee and let loose a full clip in the direction of the fence's opening. By now, the guards were out of range. He wanted them to keep running and not re-engaging.

"Listen up," Burns said over the comm. "The guards went through our fence opening. They probably kept running. But, they may have figured that's how we have to get out of here and are waiting to ambush us. When we go through the fence I want everyone extra alert."

"Burns, this is Neumann. We've got another way out."

"How?"

"They left two SUVs set up as roadblocks, keys in the ignition. I rigged them with Semtex to blow them before we left so they couldn't follow. I can disarm the explosives, and we've got wheels out of here."

"Do it," Burns said.

By the time the team all gathered at the guard booth, Neumann had removed the explosives from the SUVs, and their engines were running.

"Levine, you take the lead," Burns said. "Bernstein, you go with him. I want your RPG up front in case we run into anything ahead. Ackerman, you're with them."

"Bergen, you drive this one," Burns said, walking to the second SUV. "Neumann, you take the passenger seat. I'm in back with Moreno. Let's move out."

The vehicles drove slowly over the ornate gate lying across the mansion's entrance. Once clear, the convoy moved cautiously down a long gravel driveway in close formation, headed to the main road. Windows down, weapons at the ready, the team scoured the surrounding landscape for any sights or sounds of danger.

Moaning softly, the drug lord sat curled against the rear door, gently rubbing his injured foot. Ackerman had put a field dressing over the bullet wound. A dark circle from seeping blood stained white gauze. "Moreno may have a permanent limp," Ackerman had told Burns, "but the wound was not life threatening."

The convoy had moved about a quarter of a mile when Burns heard the loud rumble of an engine coming from around a bend in the driveway.

"Levine. What's that?" Burns barked over the comm.

"Don't know. We'll check it out."

The lead SUV coasted to a stop.

"I'm on it," Ackerman's said.

Burns leaned forward and watched through the windshield. Ackerman, wearing his NVGs, exited the SUV. He'd moved ten paces from the vehicle when the noise suddenly stopped. Dropping to a knee, he swept the barrel of his MP5 side to side across the driveway ahead. Seconds ticked by before he rose, cautiously crept forward again, and disappeared from sight around the bend.

"It's a tractor," Ackerman whispered at last over the comm. "It's blocking the end of the driveway at the entrance to the main road. I picked up two men using it for cover."

Burns tapped his comm button. "Bernstein, take it out."

Bernstein slipped from the lead vehicle, rested the RPG launcher on her shoulder, and hustled up the driveway. Burns lost sight of her when she turned the bend.

Burns' tension was palpable as he waited for a report. Time crept like a river of molasses. Suddenly, an ear-splitting explosion shattered the night air, followed by the sound of small weapons fire.

"Report, report," Burns screamed into his mic.

No reply.

"Neumann, you've got Moreno," he yelled, opening his door and leaping from the SUV. The gunfire stopped before he reached the bend in the driveway.

"Ackerman. Bernstein, report," he commanded.

"Bernstein took out the tractor," Ackerman replied. "I've got one dead behind what's left of it. The other one is gone. There's a blood trail leading into the woods. Should I go after him?"

"Negative," Burns replied. "Get back to the SUVs. Let's get out of here."

Burns figured the two men were probably the guards who went

through the fence. The wounded one would head to the nearby village where he'd summon help. They needed to get out of the area fast.

The convoy worked its way around the mangled tractor, swung onto the main road, and headed to their hidden SUVs at the outskirts of La Apoma, fifteen miles away. When they reached the hiding spot, Burns pulled Ackerman to the side.

"When you get back to the hotel, have Mira go to my suite. I put an envelope with some discs in the safe in the closet. The code to open it is 1812. Have her wait until tomorrow, then fly to Phoenix, Arizona, with the discs. I'll give you my sat phone number. Tell her to call me every day at 10:00 a.m. and 4:00 p.m. until we connect. If she doesn't get in touch with me in four days, tell her to give the envelope to Ben-Ami."

He watched the team pack their gear into the SUVs. "Get in touch with the pilot. Have him get that," he said, pointing to the drone case, "and the other equipment back to Mexico City so the embassy can get it back to Israel. I want all of you to stay in your tourist roles at the hotel for two days, then head back to Israel."

The team left for Mazatlan in one of Moreno's SUVs and one of the rentals. Burns took the other rental. *Less likelihood of someone stopping me with rental plates.* Before setting out, he gave Moreno an injection of chloral hydrate to put him to sleep, laid him in the cargo bay, and covered him with a camo sheet.

THE RING OF the satellite phone snapped Burns back from his musing.

"Burns?" Hall asked.

"Yes," he said, glancing at the clock on the dashboard. Thirty-five minutes since they spoke.

"We're set. I think Ortega had an orgasm when I told him you had Moreno," Hall chuckled. "There's a soccer stadium south of Nogales in Aqua Zarca, Exit 97 on Route 15. The stadium is eighteen miles from Nogales, Arizona. Call me twenty minutes before you think you'll get there."

"Why?"

"Because Ortega is sending a D.E.A. chopper into Mexican airspace to pick you up. It's an unauthorized flight, which means if the Mexicans spot it, shit will hit the fan, and we'll have a major international incident. It's roughly fifteen minutes flying time each way. The chopper has to be in and out fast, so you need to be there on time, ready to board. When you call, the chopper will take off."

"I'll be there," Burns replied.

Two hours later, and twenty minutes from the stadium, Burns called Hall and told him to get the helicopter on its way. When he pulled into the stadium, the chopper sat idling in the middle of the field. The crew helped him put Moreno inside, and they lifted off within two minutes of his arrival. Seventeen minutes later, flying at rooftop level, the chopper hovered over the Nogales, Arizona, airport.

Fifty feet over the tarmac, Burns saw the red and blue flashing lights from four black Suburbans and one grey sedan. To the rear of the landing circle painted on the blacktop sat an ambulance, red lights blinking.

The chopper settled, and Burns exited, ducking clear of its whirling blades. Hall, who had been leaning against an SUV next to Ortega, pushed off to greet him. They shook hands. "Welcome back."

Ortega, standing slightly behind Hall, moved forward and put out his hand to shake Burns' hand, but Burns refused to take it.

Glaring at the man with cold eyes, Burns said through gritted teeth, "Fuck you, Special Agent in Charge," using the title Ortega insisted Burns call him when they met. "You think I don't know you never would have sent the chopper for me if I didn't have Moreno?"

Burns shifted his gaze back to Hall. "The grey one yours?"

"Yes."

"Then let's get out of here before I do something to this arrogant prick we might all regret."

They walked to Hall's car. Burns paused before getting in and turned back toward the chopper. The ambulance crew, surrounded by four D.E.A. agents, loaded Moreno on a gurney and wheeled him to the ambulance.

The helicopter's engine had shut down. Except for the Suburban's idling engines, the tarmac was quiet.

Standing next to Hall's vehicle, Burns said, his voice booming, "By the way, Ortega. I did exactly what you insisted couldn't be done a few days ago. I brought Moreno back. Something you made a big deal of pointing out no one else has been able to do, including you."

He fixed Ortega with a hard glare. "The D.E.A. owes me the $10 million bounty. Make the check payable to the State of Israel. And when it's ready, I'm going to ask Director McGuire to have you personally hand deliver it to the Israeli Ambassador in Washington. Have a wonderful day, you pompous asshole."

Burns meant his words to embarrass Ortega because every D.E.A. agent heard everything he'd said. Burns grinned. It appeared he'd succeeded because Ortega's face turned as pale as wax, and he looked as if he had bitten into a lemon. Satisfied, Burns slipped into Hall's car, and they sped out of the airport.

CHAPTER 33
March 4
Tuesday Afternoon
Phoenix, Arizona

"What happened down there?" Hall asked, as they headed back to the F.B.I. field office in Phoenix.

Burns told him most of the story, leaving out only the parts relating to the specialized surveillance equipment they used.

"So if the dead man wasn't your uncle, what was Moreno doing with him?" Hall asked.

"I can't be positive, but I have a theory," Burns replied. "Based on the intercepts your people made, the Collector found out Moreno planned to screw him out of his fee and kill him. So I think he double crossed the double crosser and sent a man who generally fit my uncle's description. This way, he still has my uncle and gets his fee."

"I hate to ask this, but do you think the Collector killed your uncle?"

"It's possible, but I don't think so. It would be out of character for him. Look how he scammed Moreno. From what little we know about him, he seems to be smart, cautious, and a businessman."

He paused as eight Harley Davidson's sped by, their engines

roaring and making conversation momentarily impossible. When the blare subsided, Burns continued. "I think he still believes he can make money from my uncle. He knows about his discovery, and it could be worth billions. He also knows I have the discs and the password for them. If I were him, I'd use my uncle to draw me out to get them… like he tried before. I think he's smart enough to understand the only way that all works is if he keeps my uncle alive because I'd require proof of life."

"I buy that," Hall said. "What do you want to do going forward?"

"I need to get word to the Collector that Moreno's out of the picture, that I know the man he sent to Mexico wasn't my uncle, and I want my uncle safe and unharmed. The only way I know how to do that is through Johnson. He's the only one we know of with the ability to contact him."

"I agree. Johnson's the key to making contact. How can I help?"

Burns had a few ideas. They discussed them for half an hour before settling on the details. After their conversation, Burns decide a call to Ben-Ami at Mossad Headquarters was overdue.

"Where the hell have you been?" Ben-Ami screamed. "I tracked down your team, and all they could tell me is you had Moreno with you, and you drove off with him. Your Aunt Miriam is a nervous wreck. Simon Bloom keeps calling me to give her updates."

"I've been pretty busy on my end, and frankly, updates were the last thing on my mind."

"Did you forget that I'm your friend as well as your boss and my neck is also out on the line? I sanctioned an unauthorized mission, using classified weapons," Ben-Ami said, his tone more moderate. "And if you didn't think it was important for me to know, shouldn't you let your aunt know what's happening?"

Burns took a deep breath and rubbed his forehead. Ben-Ami was right. He did stick his neck out for him, and his aunt had to be going through hell. He should have reported in before.

"You're right," Burns said, "I'm sorry. I'll fill you in."

He began by telling Ben-Ami his uncle was not in Moreno's

custody in Mexico and never was. "Please tell Bloom so he can tell my aunt."

Burns continued with everything that had transpired since his arrival in Mexico, leaving out only classified weapons information because Hall was next to him and could hear the conversation.

"Either you or Bloom tell my aunt I'll call her when I can, but it might not be for a few days. Make sure she understands I feel positive Uncle Seth is alive, and I'm going to find him. I'm convinced the Collector still has him, and we're going after Johnson to get to the Collector," Burns said, finishing the conversation.

After he disconnected he asked Hall, "You heard what I just said about Johnson. Have you thought about how to approach him?"

"Oh, yes," he said, a grin stretching his lips. "If he can contact the Collector, I know just how to make him cooperate."

DURING THE DRIVE from Nogales, Hall laid out his idea on the approach to use with Johnson. Burns offered a few suggestions but said, in the end, it was Hall's show to run.

With more than two hours to go before they arrived in Phoenix, Burns leaned his head against the car window, saying he was going to rest his eyes for a bit. Within minutes, the steady hum of the tires rolling over the smooth blacktop ribbon of the interstate put him to sleep.

Hall decided not to head to the F.B.I. office in Phoenix. Instead, he took the downtown by-pass spur, past Sky Harbor Airport, and merged onto Interstate 17, which headed west before bending north.

Burns woke about ten minutes later, but having no interest in the passing terrain, kept his eyes closed and his head resting against the car window. He was thinking about his uncle. *Did the Collector still have him? Was he okay? Where was he?*

The clicking turn signal, and shift in direction as the car changed lanes, snapped him out of his contemplation. He looked through the windshield at the approaching overhead sign. Exit 207, Glendale.

"Glendale? Why Glendale?"

"Johnson's office. I have an agent on the floor below his, with orders to call me if Johnson left the building. No call while we've been on the road, so he's still there. Since you need him to make contact with the Collector, we might as well get the ball rolling now."

Leaving the interstate, Hall spotted an empty space on the street. "That's where his office is," Hall said, pointing to a multistory office building a half a block away. "No sense pulling into their open parking lot in a car that screams Feds."

They walked to the building and climbed two flights of stairs to the suite the Bureau rented as the listening post. Hall knocked on the door. A few seconds, later the knob turned, and the door opened a crack. Someone on the other side obviously recognized Hall, because the door opened all the way to let them enter.

When they stepped inside, Hall said, "Agent Jack Collins, say hello to Eric Burns."

Burns appraised the agent as they shook hands. He looked like a college kid. A baby face emphasized by smooth shaved cheeks. He had a tight military haircut, so maybe he was just out of the service, not college.

Wasting no time, Hall had Collins gather copies of the transcripts of the emails and conversations between Johnson, the Collector, Moreno, and Gomez. Hall read them, marking select passages with a green highlighter. Handing the papers back to Collins, he instructed the agent to make a recording from the files containing the sections indicated. Thirty minutes later, Hall slipped the small digital recorder/player containing the information in his coat pocket.

"Let's go," he said to Burns and Collins, heading to the door.

They took the stairs to the third floor and moved down the corridor to the corner office with Energy Renewables stenciled on the mahogany front door. Standing outside, Hall choreographed in his head everything he'd do when he entered in the next few seconds. It would be a classic Bureau entry, intended to intimidate and frighten. Taking a deep breath, he yanked the door open and burst inside, followed closely by Collins and Burns.

"F.B.I.!" he bellowed, his credentials held above his head. "Everyone stay seated."

He made a beeline to the only interior office, a set of closed double doors at the rear of the four-foot high cubicle dividers. He pushed through the doors, followed by Collins and Burns,

"F.B.I.! Sit down!" he screamed at Johnson who began to rise from his chair at the sudden intrusion. Like a shot, Hall was alongside the bewildered man. Pulling him to his feet, he forced Johnson face down across the desk and handcuffed his wrists behind his back.

Hall lifted Johnson from the desk and shoved him back in his chair. He noticed the front of Johnson's pants. *The pussy pissed himself.*

The stunned man asked, "What's going—"

"Shut up," shouted Hall, keeping up the intimidation. "We know all about you, Moreno, and the Collector. You're going away for a long time. You'll do hard time, a minimum of twenty years. And I'll bet within three months you're going to be some lifer's personal bitch."

"I don't know—"

"Shut up, you lying piece of shit. Don't say another word!" Hall yelled.

"I want a lawyer," Johnson was able to get out before Hall could stop him.

Once Johnson made the request for his lawyer, Hall was obligated not to speak with him without the presence of the attorney. He'd expected Johnson to make the demand at some point, and he and Burns had worked on a plan to skirt the issue.

Handing Burns the digital recorder/player, Hall and Collins left the office.

"I demand to call my lawyer right now," Johnson said, defiance in his tone, his mouth twisting in a smirk.

Burns moved to within two feet of Johnson, glared down at the man, and lashed out, backhanding him across the cheek, knocking him sideways in the chair.

"Listen to me very carefully. I'm not law enforcement, and I don't have to play by their rules. There's no law in the room now. It's just you and me, so no one is violating your rights to have a lawyer present during questioning. Just shut the fuck up and listen to the tape I'm going to play for you. And while you're listening, keep in mind the guys who just left the room may be your only chance for you to not spend the next twenty years of your life bent over your bunk servicing the men in your cell block."

"Who are you?" Johnson asked, his voice trembling, the smirk and defiance gone.

"My name is Eric Burns."

Burns saw Johnson's eyes widened and his complexion ashen.

"I see you know who I am. So just listen to the fucking recording. We'll talk after."

Burns pressed the play button, and for the next thirteen minutes, Johnson squirmed in his chair, listening to recordings of his taped conversations and Collins narrating transcripts of emails between him, the Collector, Moreno, and Gomez. As the minutes passed, Johnson sagged lower in his chair. When the recording finished, Burns hit the stop button and gave Johnson a few seconds to absorb the amount of evidence against him.

"Now you know. The F.B.I. has you dead to rights on money laundering, S.E.C. stock fraud with Gomez Securities, conspiracy, and about ten more charges they can throw at you. You're going to prison, there's no getting around that. For how long and where you end up, that depends on your co-operating with Agent Hall outside. But he can't work with you if you insist on having your lawyer present."

Burns grabbed Johnson under the chin and tilted his head up so he could look the man directly in the eyes. "This is a onetime offer, expiring in sixty second. Would you like to cancel your request for your attorney?"

Johnson nodded his head.

"You have to verbalize the request."

Burns held a prepared statement in front of Johnson. Hall told Burns the declaration might not hold up in court, but they had enough solid evidence to get a conviction anyway.

"Go ahead," he said, and pressed the record button on the digital device.

"My name is Elliot Johnson. I make this declaration of my own free will. I understand my right to have counsel present when talking to F.B.I. Agent Hall, and I voluntarily give up my right to do so."

Burns opened the office door and motioned Hall inside. He handed him the recorder.

Hall moved next to the desk and peered down at Johnson. "You're gonna send the man you call the Collector a message."

"I don't know if he'll pay attention to me anymore," Johnson said.

"You'll send it anyway," Hall replied.

He pulled Johnson to his feet, uncuffed him, and pushed him back down into the chair. From his jacket pocket, he removed a sheet of paper with the message Burns had composed a half hour ago.

"Send this to the Collector, exactly as it's written."

CHAPTER 34
March 5
Wednesday Morning
Local Time
Switzerland

THE COLLECTOR WASN'T expecting any more emails, but checking twice daily had become a ritual. Placing the steaming second cup of morning coffee on his desk, he turned on his monitor and desktop computer.

Two days ago, he had received an email from Bogdanov with the name of the last bidder for the Israeli and his formula, bringing the total to four countries and one corporation. He sipped his coffee waiting for the machine to boot up and thought of how well things worked out. Moreno had deposited the money he owed in the numbered account. And by now, Moreno must realize he'd been swindled, getting an imposter. He smiled to himself. Payback was a bitch.

He still had the Israeli and five groups willing to bid for the formula. He gave Bogdanov a broad outline of what the formula would do and instructed Bogdanov to inform interested parties bidding would begin at twenty-five million U.S. dollars. None of them balked at the figure.

The Collector had one major obstacle. At some point, he'd have to provide concrete proof the formula would do as claimed. And for that, he needed the discs and the password. The problem... how was he going to get them?

The glow of the monitor announcing completion of the boot up pulled him from his thoughts. He typed in the security protocols for his email account. His forehead furrowed. He had a message from Johnson. The time stamp indicated Johnson sent it last night at 8:17, Arizona time.

Why is Johnson sending me an email? he wondered. Our business ended when I sent the imposter to Moreno and collected the money owed. *Could it be a trap? Did it have a virus that would trace back to his location? Did Moreno set this up to get revenge?*

The Collector moved the pointer to the delete button. *No sense taking any chances,* he reasoned. *On the other hand, what am I afraid of? My email security is excellent. They can't trace me,*

Seconds of indecision passed, his finger resting on the mouse, ready to click delete. But, his curiosity won out. He moved the pointer to the email, and opened it. He read it, shook his head in amazement, and leaned back in his seat. Taking a deep breath, he moved forward and reread the message to insure he read it right the first time.

I am in my office with Eric Burns. You know who he is. He has the discs and the password. He wants to meet with you to exchange them for his uncle. He said to tell you he knows the man you sent to Mexico wasn't his uncle and that Moreno is in police custody. He wants proof of life, that his uncle is still alive. He will meet with you anywhere, at any time, but you better not try any tricks like you did with Moreno. If you get back to me tomorrow by 5:00 p.m., Arizona time, he'll know you got the email and want to deal. If he doesn't hear from you, he'll presume his uncle is dead and will destroy the discs so no one will have them. Johnson.

The Collector shook his head and smiled. *How lucky can I get,* he thought? His biggest problem with the bidding plan was getting his hands on the discs and password. To do that, he needed to find the nephew, and the solution just fell in his lap. The nephew wanted to find him.

CHAPTER 35
March 5
Wednesday Morning
Local Time
Phoenix, Arizona

AFTER JOHNSON SENT the email to the Collector, Hall asked Johnson if he would willingly consent to come to the field office in Phoenix. Willing consent meant Hall did not have to place him under arrest, which might legally complicate matters. Johnson knew he had to cooperate, so he agreed. They held him overnight, handcuffed to a cot, with Collins guarding him.

The next morning, they took Johnson back to his office, arriving at 8:30. This insured all email exchanges between the Collector and Johnson would be on the office computer in case the Collector had a way of knowing differently.

Presuming the Collector was still somewhere in Europe, there was an eight or nine hour time difference with Arizona, depending on what country he was in. It was now afternoon over there. If the Collector received the message, there should be a reply waiting for them.

Hall ordered Johnson to check while he and Burns peered over his shoulder.

"There, that's from him," Johnson said, pointing to the fourth message from the top.

"Open it," Burns said. The message was short and to the point.

Received message. Uncle still alive. Will send proof of life. When satisfied, will send instructions for exchange of disks and password for uncle.

Burns let out a deep sigh of relief. They had made contact, and the Collector claimed his uncle was still alive. He looked at Hall and mouthed a thank you. Hall nodded back.

Twenty minutes later, three messages appeared in the inbox. Two junk advertisements, the third from the Collector. The heading read "proof" and indicated it had an attachment.

Burns pulled Johnson out of his chair, sat in front of the screen, and opened the message and the attachment. He drummed his fingers on the desk, waiting for the attachment to open.

A picture of his uncle unfolded. He was sitting in a straight back chair, holding a copy of *20 Minuten*, the largest Swiss daily newspaper. Burns enlarged the photo and scanned the page. He found the date. It was today's. Burns' body relaxed into the chair. With a smile he couldn't contain, he tilted his head to the ceiling and uttered a soft, "Thank you."

Hall turned to Collins, who was standing by the door. "Take him to the outer offices," he said, nodding at Johnson. When they were alone, Burns asked Hall what he intended to do with Johnson.

"I'll follow your lead on this. What do you want to do? Eventually I have to charge him, but I can put it off for a while, until things play out with the Collector."

"Thanks. There's not much I can do until we get an email from him with how he wants the exchange to work," Burns said. "The proof of life photo came back quick. He had the newspaper handy, so it looks like they're still in Switzerland. I'll probably need Knecht's help, but I'll hold off on contacting him until I hear from the Collector, in case he picks a different country for the exchange."

Burns glanced at the computer, willing a new email from the

Collector to be there. The screen remained blank. He pushed himself from the chair." I need some alone time. I'll be back in a few minutes."

Moving to the hallway outside the front door of Energy Renewables, he slouched back against the wall. The elation he immediately felt knowing his uncle was alive had morphed into concern about what would surely come next. *If I were the Collector, I'd want proof I have the discs. He'll probably ask me for something from them he can verify. And I can't give it to him, because I don't know the fucking password to open them!*

Burns lightly banged the back of his head against the wall. *Damn it, Uncle Seth. I know you. Somewhere, somehow, you gave me a clue. But where?*

BURNS RETURNED TO Johnson's office. He'd been waiting about an hour for the Collector to send the meeting details when his satellite phone rang. It was Mira. She was at the Phoenix Airport with the discs. Burns looked at his watch. It was 10:00 a.m. He covered the mouthpiece and spoke to Hall, "One of my people is at the airport with an envelope for me. Can one of your agents from the Phoenix office meet her and bring it here?"

"No problem. Have her hold while I arrange it. "

Hall called the office and explained what he needed. The Agent in Charge placed Hall on hold and called the reception desk at American Airline Admirals Club in terminal A. The Club agreed to admit Mira while she waited. After confirming an agent was on his way, Hall gave the information to Burns, who passed it on to Mira.

The agent who picked up the envelope from Mira arrived at Johnson's office an hour and ten minutes later. Burns placed it on Johnson's desk, next to the monitor.

At 12:07 to be precise, the email arrived from the Collector.

Check in once more to Grand Hotel Beau Rivage, in Interlaken. Be there in two days.

Too soon to put anything together, Burns thought. *I need to buy more time.*

"Robert, can you keep Johnson under wraps for at least four days?"

"Can do."

Burns typed a reply.

Discs held in safe place. Need time to retrieve. Can be there in three days. Confirm.

Ten minutes later came the reply.

Confirmed.

"I just bought three days. Now I've got to figure out what I'm going to do," he said to Hall.

"Good. Let's go get something to eat. I'm starved, and you haven't eaten in a day and a half."

"No, you go. I'm not hungry, and I need to think this thing out."

"Well, you'll do it better with something in your stomach."

"No, you go."

"You need to eat. Jesus, now I sound like a Jewish mother. You've got to have lunch. You need to— "

Burns caught his breath. He jumped to his feet. "That's it!" he shouted.

"What? What's wrong?"

"Nothing. Nothing's wrong," he said, unable to contain his excitement. "I think I know the password."

Burns grabbed the envelope with the discs off the desk, removed disc number one, and inserted it in the computer. When the 'enter password' prompt appeared, he typed, took a deep breath, and tapped the enter tab on the keyboard. The monitor screen went white, followed by a page filled with strings of chemical formulas, with detailed explanations typed before and after each one.

"Yes!" Burns shouted, jumping from the chair with a fist pump, then turning and bumping knuckles with Hall.

"How did you finally figure it out?" Hall asked.

"You. You triggered it."

"Me? How?"

"When you said you sounded like a Jewish mother."

"What does that—?"

"Look at this."

Burns inserted disc number six and found the file his uncle included, the only one not needing the password. He scanned the message left for him, until he found the passage he was looking for and pointed.

"There," he said.

As I write this, even though you've grown, I can't help thinking of you as the bright boy your aunt and I spent the summers with at the kibbutz each year with your mother and grandmother. I remember how you made your grandmother laugh when she yelled out the window for you to come eat, calling to you in Yiddish, and you'd pretend you didn't understand.

I think about how you showed signs of persistence and remarkable intelligence even as an eight-year-old, and how those traits served you so well as you became an adult. I recall when I taught you about computers, how you became fascinated by the simple power of 3 words.

Maybe I'm being too paranoid about all this. But just in case, keep these drives in a safe place.

"See this," he said to Hall who was looking over his shoulder at the screen. Burns pointed to the last line, "*fascinated by the simple power of 3 words.*"

"So?'

"If you're like most people, you probably try to use the same password so you can remember it, even though that's not very safe, or smart, to do. And, if you make up passwords with random upper and lower case letters, numbers, and symbols like most sites require, they're complex and hard to remember."

"True," Hall said, "but most sensitive sites won't let you enter and use a password that isn't complex and difficult."

"I agree, but they're wrong. You can have safe and easy to remember passwords, and that's where the power of 3 words comes in."

"Meaning what?"

"Meaning that to make usable passwords, all you need to use is just three words, something simple to remember. For example, let's make up a simple three word password like 'this is fun'. Trust me on this; it would take a hacker 2,500 years to crack it."

"Wow. I never knew that. Okay. So you thought the password would be three easy to remember words. But how did you know what the three words were?" Hall asked.

"That my friend was thanks to you."

"Thanks to me?"

"Yeah, you. Take a look at this," Burns said, pointing to the screen and the words *"grandmother laugh when she yelled out the window for you to come eat, calling to you in Yiddish, and you'd be pretend you didn't understand."* When you made the comment about sounding like a Jewish mother, it clicked. What about sounding like a Jewish grandmother?"

"What do you mean?"

"Like it says here," Burns said, pointing to the screen, "my grandmother would call me for lunch or dinner, in Yiddish. She'd yell '*boychik, kumen esn.*' Loosely translated, it means 'little one, come eat.' Three words. They can be in any language, as long as they're easy to remember. Why else would my uncle make reference to both things in this message to me?"

"I'll be damned. It sounds so easy now," Hall said.

"Well, the trouble is, I can't do anything with it until the Collector sets up a face-to-face meeting in Interlaken."

CHAPTER 36
March 7
Friday
Switzerland

BURNS ARRIVED AT Zurich International at 10:30 in the morning. He spotted Knecht sitting on a plastic bench outside the security exit doors when he entered the main terminal.

"How was the flight?" Knecht asked, shaking his hand.

"Long. I'm exhausted."

"I understand. But we need to talk. You leave message to tell me you return to Switzerland to save your uncle, need my help, and will explain all when you arrive. This is a bit dramatic, do you not think?"

"Well, hearing you say it that way, I guess so. But it's a long story, not something I wanted to discuss over the phone. Look, Arizona to Zurich, with a two and a half hour layover in New York, is a tiring trip. I got maybe two hours of sleep. And this is something I can't cover in ten minutes. How about I grab some shut eye first, then we'll talk?"

"I wait this long, I suppose a little more is okay. I got you room in Central Plaza Hotel since you are not expected in Interlaken until tomorrow. You rest and we meet for early dinner to talk?"

"Sounds great. Thanks."

At 6:30, Burns entered the King's Cave Grille, located in the cellar of the hotel. He spotted Knecht at a table toward the back.

"Did you sleep?" Knecht asked.

"I did. I think I went out the minute my head hit the pillow. That, a shower, and fresh clothes is just what I needed."

"Good. Then now to business. So now you tell me what is going on." His mouth set in a hard line. "And unlike last time, you tell me everything."

"I will. You deserve that."

For the next hour, interrupted only by waiters refilling their water glasses and bringing fresh bowls of pretzels, Burns told Knecht everything that had happened since his uncle's kidnapping. He told him about the formula, the Collector, the trips to Switzerland, and Mexico, Johnson and Hall's involvement, and the latest emails bringing him back to Switzerland.

Except for a couple of questions for clarification or occasional sips of water and popping pretzels in his mouth, Knecht gave Burns his uninterrupted and undivided attention.

When Burns finished the tale, Knecht leaned back in his chair. "This is some story," he said.

Burns shrugged. "Yes, it is."

"So, this Collector, he wants you to go to in Interlaken and stay at the same hotel as before? This would suggest he and your uncle are somewhere in that area."

Burns turned his palms up. "That seems logical. But with this man, you can't presume anything. Based on the last time, I think he's pretty shrewd. He could be holding my uncle far from Interlaken and using the location only as a safe negotiating place. Or, he may have told me to stay at the same hotel, only to tell me once I'm there to come back to Zurich, or Berne, or Lucerne, or someplace else. Until he makes contact tomorrow, there's no sense in speculating. At this point, he's holding all the cards."

"What do you want me to do? How can I be of help?" Knecht asked.

"To start, can you have some plainclothes men in Interlaken?"

"Of course. And I will have our best technical people on standby to see if they can trace his email to a location here in Switzerland."

"Not sure that's going to happen. I've had our best computer experts trying to do it for two days without success."

"What makes you think my computer—"

"I mean no offense, Bruno, but trust me. If my people can't, your people can't. It's not by accident people call the strip between Tel Aviv and Haifa the second Silicon Valley."

Knecht nodded. "So I have heard. What else can I do to help?"

Burns took a deep breath. He knew his next request would not be palatable to Knecht.

"Can I have some of my people come to Switzerland to help?"

"Some of your people? Who?"

"Come on, Bruno. You know who. Mossad."

Knecht sat up and shook his head. "Sorry, my friend, but I must say no. It is usually bad when you show up. But when you also have your people here, it always means trouble. Trouble as in bodies."

"Bruno, please? This is my uncle's life we're talking about. I'm not taking anything away from you or your people, but mine are, how do I say this, more seasoned than yours. You know, or can guess, that I've worked on many operations with my people, and we work as a team. Bruno, this time the stakes are personal. I need them. Please?"

Knecht went poker-faced and fiddled with his watch.

Seconds ticked by.

"How many?" he asked at last.

"Eight."

"Two."

"Bruno, please. I need eight."

"Three, and that's final."

"Okay, and thank you."

Knecht nodded, but with a tight expression, as if he was not yet fully committed. "Don't thank me yet. You still have to get them here before the Collector makes contact tomorrow."

"You're right. I hope I can."

Burns felt a twinge of guilt. Knecht was helping him out of friendship. What would happen to that friendship if he ever found out that four Mossad agents, one more than agreed to, were already in Switzerland? After the final contact from the Collector instructing him to come to Switzerland, Burns contacted headquarters with an update, and at Ben-Ami's insistence, the agents were sent.

"I make a suggestion," Knecht said. "It is unlikely the Collector waited at the airport here in Zurich to follow you. He may be watching for you, or have people watching for you, but most likely not before you reach Berne or Interlaken. You are two blocks from Central Train station. Take train as before to Berne and Interlaken. I will put plain-clothes police on train as passengers with you to Berne and switch to different ones for Interlaken. I will drive to Interlaken and station myself at local police barracks."

"Sounds great," Burns said. "Thank you, Bruno."

With that, they picked up their menus and ordered dinner. They parted two hours later.

He left Zurich for Interlaken mid-morning. The clock on the wall showed 1:07 p.m. when he arrived at the front desk of the Grand Hotel Beau Rivage.

"Welcome back, Herr Burns," the desk clerk said, handing him a reservation form to fill out, while taking his passport to copy.

When the clerk returned, Burns handed him the completed form as well as his credit card. "That will not be necessary, Herr Burns," the clerk said. "The room is prepaid for a three day stay."

"Prepaid? By who?"

"One moment, please," the clerk said, looking down and typing on his computer. "Our records show the reservation was made by a Dr. Seth Shernicoff and paid for with his American Express Card."

"Shernicoff?" Are you sure? Did you check the American Express Card?"

The clerk wrinkled his brow. "Yes, that is the name, and the American Express Card charge was approved. Why do you ask? Is there a problem?"

"No, no," he responded. Thinking fast, he said, "He's my uncle, and he told me the other day he lost his card."

The frown disappeared from the clerk's face. "Well, the computer shows the reservation was made over the phone. He must have received a replacement card."

"Yes, that's probably what happened. He asked me to meet him here, so I guess that's why he felt obligated to pay for my room."

The Collector made the reservation. He wants me to understand he's in control of my uncle.

The clerk smiled and handed Burns the key card to his room "You have a generous uncle." Glancing down at the computer screen, the clerk said, "If you will please wait, I see we also have an envelope for you. Perhaps from your uncle. Let me get it."

The clerk returned from the back office and handed him a small white envelope with the name Eric Burns hand printed in block letters. "This is for you. Enjoy your stay with us."

Burns walked to the elevators, taking in the people in the lobby. He wondered if one of them was the Collector. Or maybe some of Knecht's people. If Knecht's people were there, they were very good at blending in. He hadn't spotted any of them during the train ride from Zurich through Berne to Interlaken.

He entered his room and immediately pulled the detecting wand disguised as a battery-powered shaver from his suitcase and swept the room for listening or video surveillance devices. The room was clean.

He sat at the desk and tore open the envelope.

Murphy's Irish Pub on Hauptstrasse. 7:30. Last booth on right facing the bar. Don't be late. Come alone or uncle dies.

The exact instructions he gave me last time, Burns thought. Same place, same time, same warning.

Burns called Knecht and gave him the time and place of the meeting.

Next, he called Shlomo Bar-Nathan, the leader of the four-man team Ben-Ami sent to Switzerland. He'd worked with Shlomo, an excellent field agent, during the Adwar operation in San Salvador a few weeks ago.

"Bar-Nathan, it's Burns. Is the team all settled in?"

"We are."

"Let me talk to Rozen," Burns said when he finished giving Shlomo the details of that night's meeting.

Ori Rozen was the best analyst in the Mossad. A math and computer prodigy in grade school, he graduated college at eighteen and had earned a Doctorate in Mathematics by twenty-two. Mossad psychiatrists diagnosed his lack of social graces, combined with his computer and math genius, as possible borderline Asperger's syndrome. All Burns cared about was that he was great at his job.

Rozen rarely worked in the field. There were only a handful of people he would interact with, and only those he decided he liked. For whatever reasons, Rozen liked him. Burns learned over the years that Rozen would become excitable when taken out of the comfort zone of his computer lab at headquarters. Burns needed to speak to him calmly, sometimes like a small child, to get him to focus on tasks.

"Shalom, Shalom, Burns," Rozen said.

"Shalom to you, too, Rozen. Did you have a good trip here? Do you like your room?" Burns replied.

"Yes, yes. This is fun. I like it."

"Good. I'm glad. Ori, did you bring the equipment I asked for?"

"Yes, yes. I have it. I linked the cell phone with my computer. The microphone they inserted will let me hear you even when it's not being used as a phone. It has your same telephone number so you can still get calls."

"Good. And the other stuff?"

"Yes. Yes. The ring camera and small ear-wig"

"Good. I want you to give everything to Shlomo so he can bring it to me."

"Why can't I bring them to you?' Rozen asked, clearly sounding disappointed. "I'm your friend. I want to bring them."

"No, Ori. It's very important that you always be near your computer," Burns said. "I need you to be watching over me, to keep me safe." It was a small, but necessary, lie. He had to make Rozen feel he was key to the mission's success.

"Oh, okay. I'll watch out for you."

"Good. Can you put Bar-Nathan back on the phone?"

"Yes, Burns?" Bar-Nathan said.

"Get the equipment from Rozen. Have a messenger service deliver it to me at the hotel. We don't know if the Collector or someone he hired is watching the hotel or is in the lobby. I can't have anyone from the team show their face. You know what you have to do for the meeting tonight?"

"We're all set. I'll get the items over to you."

Burns looked at his watch. He had four hours before the meeting. He kicked off his shoes, set the alarm for two hours, lay back on the bed, and went to sleep.

THE KNOCK ON the door woke him. He glanced at the clock. He'd been asleep for an hour and fifteen minutes.

He grabbed his pistol from the top of the night table and moved to the door. Looking through the peephole, he saw a young man in a uniform.

"Who is it?" he asked.

"The bellman, sir. I have a package for you."

The package from Bar-Nathan.

Burns slipped the revolver into the waistband at the small of his back. He opened the door, took the package, and tipped the bellman.

When he dumped the contents of the package, a cell phone, small red box, and a clear plastic envelope fell on the bed.

The cell phone was an exact duplicate of his own. He retrieved the battery-powered scanner from his suitcase and swept it over the phone. The devise didn't register any electronic signal coming from it. *Shit. The damn thing is broken.*

The ring inside the red box looked like a college graduation ring with a large ruby stone in the middle. A thick gold band on either side was tapered down to normal size. They'd stamped the date of his graduation from Technion Institute on it. Folded flat on the bottom of the case, he found an instruction sheet. It lay on top of a black cloth, with a wire inserted into the cloth at one end and a USB plug at the other end.

Point the stone to take a picture. Press down on the date etched into the ring to activate the camera. To send pictures, wrap the ring in cloth, plug USB into a computer, and log-on to the following website. The website was unfamiliar. Burns put the ring on, pointed the stone at the bed, and squeezed the date as instructed. He didn't hear a click. He squeezed again. Still no click. *Damn it. This is broken, too?*

The last item, in the clear plastic envelope, was the ear-wig. Burns could not believe how small the device was. It looked to be no more than a quarter of an inch long, and an eighth of an inch in diameter. He removed it from the envelope and pushed it into his right ear. He moved to the bathroom sink and stood in front of the mirror. Turning his head to the left, he searched his right ear for the ear-wig; it was not visible.

He walked back to the bed and looked down at the phone and ring. Shaking his head, he let out a sigh. "Just fucking great. I'm supposed to rely on this shit, and the phone and ring don't work, and

I have no idea if the fucking ear-wig works either," he said, talking to himself.

"The phone works fine," the voice in his ear said.

Startled, Burns' hand flew up and over his right ear. "Who's this?" he said.

"Me. It's Rozen. Who did you think?" the voice in his ear replied.

"Ori? How can you hear me? The phone doesn't transmit."

"Yes, it duuuz," he said, drawing out the word.

"But I ran my scanner over it. There is no signal transmitting."

"Hah, hah. That's so funny. You're so funny."

"Rozen, this isn't a joke. How are you hearing me?"

"I just told you, from the phone. The lab developed a transmitter, which once inserted into the phone, broadcasts your voice over a secure frequency. It's made out of specialized ceramic and platinum that works without using electromagnetic waves. That's why your scanner didn't pick it up. And if your scanner can't pick it up, no one else can either. Neat, huh?"

"I'll say. But how can they do that?"

"Well, first they had to—"

"Forget it. I don't want to know. What about the ring?"

"Did you do what the instructions said?"

"I did but never heard the camera click."

"I doesn't make any noise, silly. If it did, the bad guys would hear it."

"You're sure it works?"

Silence.

"Rozen, are you sure it works?"

Silence.

"Rozen? Rozen? You still there?"

"I'm still here," he said, his voice soft, almost hesitant.

"What's wrong?"

"Why do you think I wouldn't test everything before I gave it to you? Do you think I want you to get hurt? Do you think I don't know any better?"

Oh, boy. I don't have time to deal with this shit now. His feelings are hurt. He's acting like a child.

"No, Rozen. I know you better than to think that. It was just a rhetorical question. I didn't mean anything bad. Do you forgive me?"

"I guess so," he said, with a moody tone.

"Good. I've got to get ready to go. I'm relying on you to keep me safe. You're very important to the mission."

"Okay. I'll make sure to keep you safe," he said, sounding more upbeat. "Don't worry."

CHAPTER 37
March 8
Saturday
Interlaken, Switzerland

BURNS STOOD OUTSIDE the restaurant and checked his watch before walking inside. It was 6:47 He glanced in the direction of the booth where he was to meet the Collector. *If he shows up. He didn't last time.* Approaching, he saw an elderly couple sitting in the booth, so he took a seat at the end of the crowded bar, adjacent to them. Empty coffee cups, small dishes, and crumpled paper napkins lay on the couple's table.

Burns couldn't tell if the couple had just sat, and needed to have the table cleaned, or if they had finished their meal. A few seconds later, he had his answer. A waitress put down the black folder with their check protruding partially from the bottom. Waiting, Burns aimed his ring at the people sitting at the bar, as well as all the tables he could clearly see, squeezed the ring, and took pictures of all the patrons. He recognized two of his team members sitting at a table eating dinner.

It took five minutes before the elderly couple paid their bill and left. Before anyone else had a chance to move, Burns quickly stepped from the bar and slid into the vacant booth.

A busman arrived a few minutes later with a large plastic tub, cleared the dishes, cups, and napkins, wiped down the table with a damp dish towel, and left a menu on the table. When the man was finished, Burns placed the manila envelope he'd carried from the hotel in plain sight on the table. He wanted the Collector to see he'd brought the disks.

Shortly after, the waitress appeared and asked if he wished to order now. "Nein," he replied. He was expecting a friend, he explained, and would wait until he arrived to order, but he would like a beer while he waited.

Burns glanced at his watch. 7:28. A half hour since he sat and almost the appointed meeting time. No sign of the Collector. He sipped on his second stein of beer. The minutes seemed to drag by. He looked at his watch again. 7:55. He drummed his fingers on the table. *He's late.*

When he next looked at his watch, it was 8:25. The Collector was a no show. He put enough Euros on the table to pay for his drinks and a large tip, to make up for any money the waitress lost by him taking up the booth. Picking up the envelope, he left the pub and walked back to his hotel.

He heard the phone begin to ring as he opened the door to his room. .

"Burns. What happened tonight?" Knecht ask. "What happened to the Collector?"

"I have no idea. I followed his instructions. He didn't show. Wait a minute. How did you know he didn't show?"

"I had three agents inside the pub. They reported to me a few minutes ago that no one made contact with you."

"You had three agents there? Maybe he spotted them and got spooked."

"I do not think so. One was the bartender, one was the waitress that served you, and the other was the busman who cleared your table."

"Those were your people? You're right. I don't think the Collector spotted them as police. I sure as hell didn't. "

"What is the next move?" Knecht asked.

"I just have to wait until he makes contact again. He's paid for my room for three days, so he knows I'm here for that long. I'm sure I'll hear from him when he's ready. I'll keep in touch."

Burns disconnected and lay back on the bed to think. *Was he testing me to see if I was alone?*

Five minutes later, the phone rang. He bolted upright. With his feet planted on the floor, he sat on the edge of the bed with his hand hovering over the receiver, letting it ring three more times. *Can't have the Collector think I'm worried or anxious that he didn't show up.*

After the fourth ring, he answered. "Burns."

"It's Bar-Nathan. What happened tonight?"

Damn. His shoulders sagged.

"I don't know," he said, running his hand across his forehead. "I just went through this with Inspector Knecht. Maybe he was testing me. Maybe he got held up. Who knows? See anything on your end?"

"Nothing suspicious. We got there as planned, three hours before the meeting. I sent two of our people inside to have dinner."

"I know. I recognized them."

"I was across the street in an alley, taking pictures of everyone that either passed by or went in the pub while I was there. The agents inside used mini cameras to photograph everyone in the pub in case I missed anyone or my pictures weren't clear. Rozen downloaded all the pics we took onto his laptop, linked them to his computer at the Office, and is running the facial recognition analysis program he developed to see if anyone pops up."

"I'm not holding out much hope on that. We have no idea who this guy is, never mind what he looks like. Look, I'm tired. I'm sure the Collector will get in touch with me again. He set up the meeting and paid the hotel room for three days. He wants the formula and the password, but it looks like it's going to be on his timetable. Since I have no control over that, I'm going to try and get some sleep. I'll be in touch as soon as I hear from him."

Burns undressed and slid under the covers. He looked at the clock on the night table. 9:05 p.m. He rolled over and fell asleep in minutes.

RING, RING. BURNS rolled on his side and looked at the red numbers on the bedside clock. 5:29 a.m. *The Collector.* A jolt of adrenaline shot through his body. He became instantly alert. Swinging his legs to the floor, he sat on the edge of the bed, took a deep breath, and answered.

"Burns."

"It's Bar-Nathan."

Damn it. Not again.

"What the hell do you want now?" he replied, tersely.

Before Shlomo could respond, Burns said, "Sorry. Didn't mean to snap at you. I was hoping the call was from the Collector and was disappointment it was you, not him. What's so important you had to call me this early?"

"We think we know who the Collector is."

"What!" Burns shot to his feet. "Who? How?"

"Rozen's facial recognition software got a hit. Someone I shot a picture of going into the pub, and you and the agents took pictures of inside the pub. He was sitting near the opposite end of the bar from where you were."

"Who is he?"

"His name's Yuri Elson. We have him in our files because he came to Israel from Russia years ago and applied for citizenship under the Law of Return. Three months after it was granted, he moved to the United States. But, a few years ago, he bought an apartment in Caesarea. He stays there a few times a year, sometimes a week or two, sometimes a couple of months."

"Why do you think he's the Collector?"

"Because he came back to Israel eight weeks before your uncle's lab got blown up, and he's disappeared."

"But that doesn't mean any—"

"Let me finish. As I said, he's in Israel eight weeks before someone blew up the lab and kidnapped your uncle. Your uncle had to be smuggled out of Israel, because there is no record of him leaving the country. It stands to reason there would also be no record of the person who smuggled him out of the country leaving either. Elson is now in Switzerland, and there's no record of him leaving Israel. How did he get there? Add to that, both times the Collector wanted meetings, they were in Switzerland. "

"You're making a good case, but—"

"Stop," Bar-Nathan said, raising his voice. "I'm still not finished. When Elson left Israel, he moved to Brooklyn, New York, which has a big Russian immigrant population. A few hours ago, Rozen hacked into every three-letter U.S. Government agency, and the New York City Police Department's data bases. Elson's got an extensive file with the NYPD. They haven't been able to prove anything, but they're sure he's part of the Russians gangs there. He's been brought in for questioning in four murder-for-hire cases and a host of other crimes. Noteworthy among them, he was a suspect in thirteen cases of kidnapping for ransom."

Burns moved back to the edge of the bed and sat, absorbing what he'd been told. All the pieces seemed to fit.

"Thanks. Great job. Have someone bring me over a picture of Elson. Oh, by the way, is Rozen there?"

"Yes, but he's sleeping."

"Okay. Don't wake him. But when he wakes up, do me a favor. Tell him I said, 'Thank you,' for everything he's done, that he did a great job and when I'm back home, I'm taking him out to dinner. Tell him I said, 'Thanks for having my back.'"

"Okay," Bar-Nathan said. "I'll take care of it."

"I'm going to contact Knecht and let him know what we have. Hang tight. I'll get back to you soon."

After Burns disconnected the call, he began to assess the situation. If all that Bar-Nathan reported was true, he was close to getting his uncle. He needed only one more piece of information.

BURNS DIDN'T CALL Knecht immediately after speaking to Shlomo. His bedside clock showed 6:02 a.m., too early in the morning to call him at his house. Actually, Burns was more concerned about Frau Knecht getting upset than Knecht. He waited until 9:00 before making the call.

All Burns told Knecht of his conversation with Shlomo was that they had reason to believe the Collector's real name was Elson. "If Elson is in Switzerland, he has to be staying some place. Is there any way you can track him down?" Burns asked.

"Of course. I will get to work on this immediately. After all," he said, with a chuckle, "what is good being Chief Inspector of Swiss Federal Police if I cannot put my minions to work when I wish to?"

Three hours later, Knecht was back on the phone with Burns. "I have his location. Herr Elson, eight weeks ago, has rented a chalet in Grindelwald, twenty kilometers from Interlaken. What action do you wish me to take?"

"No direct action for now, but I need you to do two more things. First, have a local police car with two officers drive by the chalet. Tell them not to stop. Just drive by slow enough for the passenger to take as many pictures of the building as possible... without being obvious. Tell them not to drive by a second time. I don't want to arouse any suspicions in Elson if he sees a police car more than once."

"That will be no problem. What is the second thing?"

"Is it possible to get a blueprint or drawing of the chalet, from the building department or whatever agency would have them?"

"Yah, this can easily be done."

"Great. How soon do you think you can get the blueprint and the pictures to me?"

There was a pause before Knecht answered. "It is now 9:20. I think I would be able to bring them to you at hotel by early this afternoon, maybe one o'clock."

Burns thanked Knecht for all his help before hanging up.

He went downstairs to the dining room and ordered breakfast. Now it was just a matter of waiting for the blueprints, the pictures, and the Collector to contact him. In the meantime, he had to figure out what he was going to do and how he was going to rescue his uncle. Knowing who the Collector was and where he was most likely holding his uncle was a major breakthrough. Over breakfast, Burns devised a plan.

When he entered his room, he saw an envelope on the floor just beyond the door, his name printed in large block letters across the front. *From the Collector.*

He read the note inside.

Murphy's Irish Pub on Hauptstrasse. 7:30. Last booth on right facing the bar. Don't be late. Come alone or uncle dies.

The exact instructions he gave me yesterday, Burns thought. Same place, same time. He's being cautious, probably running counter-surveillance, to make sure he's not being followed.

KNECHT ARRIVED AT Burns' room at 12:50. He wasted little time, spreading out photos of the chalet on the desk and unrolling a large blueprint of the chalet on the bed. They reviewed the blueprint, which indicated the ground floor was comprised of a Finnish sauna and a steam bath with a whirlpool. It also indicated an oversized wine cellar made of stone, built to resemble a medieval dungeon. The wine cellar was adjacent to a two-car garage.

The first floor, accessible by elevator and stairs, had three double bedrooms and an office, all with access to a large terrace. The top floor was an open living area with the kitchen and a large dining area. The master bedroom was located on this floor.

Knecht provided eight by ten colored prints of the pictures his officers took of the chalet, which Burns now turned his attention to. He laid them on the blueprint, matching them up to their corresponding locations on the diagram. He studied the pictures, turning his attention to the area surrounding the outside of the chalet, plotting potential entry points. He was pondering the various attack options when Knecht coughed, snapping him out of his pensive contemplation.

Burns jerked his head to the side. Knecht was studying him.

"Sorry. I did not mean to startle you," Knecht said. He glanced at his watch. "You've been quiet for almost five minutes. What is it you are thinking?"

"About the best way to enter the house. The Collector sent me the same meeting instructions as yesterday. I figure the best time to breach the chalet will be when he leaves to meet me tonight. I'd bet if he has my uncle in the chalet, he's holding him in the wine cellar. I'm not worried about alarms. I can by-pass those. I'm more concerned he may have wired the place with explosives."

"Do you have plan?" Knecht asked.

"Right now, just a rough one. Can you arrange for your same three people to work the pub tonight? If he sees different people from last night, he might get suspicious."

Knecht nodded. "This can be done. The owner is most co-operative,"

"Good. So, here's what I'm thinking, and I want you to see if you pick up anything I missed that could go wrong. You said the chalet is twenty kilometers from Interlaken. I make that about a half hour drive. Sound right?"

"Yah, about that if no traffic."

"Okay. That means he should leave around 7:00, unless he decides to go earlier and set up surveillance at the Pub. If I'm waiting near the chalet by five o'clock, I'll be ready to make my move as soon as he leaves, even if he goes earlier. If there are no booby-traps, and my uncle is in the wine cellar, I should be in and out, fifteen minutes tops. Am I missing anything?"

"Nein. Nothing about the chalet. But what about the Collector? He will expect you to be at the pub at 7:30."

"Here's where you can help. Can you have a helicopter standing by somewhere near the chalet and fly me back to Interlaken? It should only take fifteen minutes. This way, if he has my uncle someplace other than the chalet, I can still make the 7:30 meeting. He won't know I was at the chalet, and my uncle won't be put in danger. At that point, I'll have to go to plan B."

"I can arrange for helicopter. But what is plan B?"

"Negotiations. I'll give him a small piece of the formula to verify it's legitimate. He'll have to come back with proof my uncle is still alive. Then we'll arrange a swap of the formula disks for my uncle, each of us with conditions to insure the other holds up their end of the deal. That will all take a day or two. If my uncle isn't at the chalet, maybe while all those things are going on, Elson will lead us to my uncle before the swap, and we can try for a rescue. As a last resort, I'll make the swap."

"What will you do after you make the swap?"

Burns' eyes grew cold, his jaw firm. "I'll track Elson down and kill him."

CHAPTER 38
March 9
Sunday
Three Weeks Since the Kidnapping
Grindelwald, Switzerland

AN UNMARKED POLICE car dropped Burns off at the Grindelwald train station. He lifted a ski bag from the roof rack fitted on the top of the car for the trip, then retrieved a boot bag from the rear seat. Walking to the driver's side window, he leaned down, shook the driver's hand, and in a loud voice, thanked him for the ride. To anyone watching or listening, he was just one more skier, dropped off by a friend, to enjoy the slopes of the Eiger Mountain.

As he walked to the center of the village, the steeple clock of the white church next to the village green chimed four times. Propping the ski bag in a rack outside a small café half a block from the church, Burns settled inside at a table next to the window where he could keep a close eye on the bag. Neither the ski bag or the boot bag sitting on the floor by his foot under the table contained ski equipment.

The long bag outside held a suppressed sniper rifle with a mounted optical scope, a bulletproof vest wrapped tightly around it. The boot bag held powerful Swiss Military night-vision binoculars, chemically activated hand and foot warmer packets, and protein bars.

All the items had been provided by Knecht, and the Swiss Federal

Police, including the Swiss Army knife tucked in the zippered pocket of his black ski jacket. Also in the bag were specialized items, these courtesy of the Mossad. Burns' personal suppressed Beretta sat nestled in the small of his back, held firmly in place in the waistband of his thermal insulated ski pants.

He ordered a cup of tea and pretended to read the local newspaper, keeping an eye on the ski bag. He glanced occasionally at his watch, biding time. When the digital numbers indicated 4:42, Burns decided it was time to get moving. Dropping Euros on the table to pay for the tea, he gathered the boot bag, left the café, and grabbed the ski bag outside. He strolled down Endwegstrasse to the Hotel Glacier. To anyone paying attention, he was just another skier returning to his lodging with his ski bag slung over his shoulder and boot bag in hand.

The Collector's chalet was located a short distance from the hotel's parking lot, situated behind the building. Reaching the rear of the lot, Burns entered the stand of canopied trees, bordering open farmland. He found it on the satellite images he'd accessed that morning. He worked his way through the trees until he reached a large blue spruce with a thick trunk, thirty meters from the rear of the target chalet.

From his vantage point, Burns could also see the driveway. He unwrapped the vest from around the rifle and leaned it against the tree trunk. He pulled off his ski parka, slipped on the protective vest, and quickly re-donned the parka. Grabbing a protein bar from the bag, he nibbled on it, waiting for the Collector to leave. The air became chilly as the sun sank low in the sky. Colder temperatures would not be not far behind.

Darkness had fallen at 5:37, and so had the temperature. Twenty minutes before, the cold had so penetrated the soles of his boots, he had used two of the chemical foot warmers to keep his feet warm. The packets had a forty-minute life. He hoped he wouldn't be here that long. Nibbling on another protein bar, he scanned the chalet grounds through the night-vision binoculars, fingers warmed by the chemical packet he'd inserted in his gloves five minutes earlier.

Burns' body stiffened. Headlight beams suddenly lit up the driveway, quickly followed by a car pulling out of the garage and slipping down the chalet's driveway. He tapped a side button on his watch. It illuminated the dial in the dark for three seconds. 6:24.

Bet he's heading out early to scout out the meet location.

Burns tossed away the remainder of the protein bar and called Knecht. "I'm behind the chalet. A car just pulled away. If it's Elson, he's probably leaving early to set up surveillance. Have your people in place at the pub now, and tell the copter pilot to start warming it up. I have the cell number of the officer in the unmarked car that brought me here. He's stationed in the hotel lot. Let him know I'll be calling very soon. I'll need him to pick me up fast, and get me, and I hope my uncle, to the helicopter so I can be on time for my meeting at the pub."

After Knecht told him he'd handle it, and they disconnected, Burns called Shlomo, told him Elson was on the move, and instructed him to get the team in position.

Burns grabbed the rifle, slung it over his shoulder, and pulled the Beretta from beneath the ski jacket. Picking up the boot bag, he crept carefully toward the rear of the chalet. He couldn't be sure it was Elson who drove away. Maybe it was someone else. Or maybe it was Elson, and if his uncle was in the chalet, maybe he left someone there to guard him.

He'd scanned the surrounding area. The pictures he had reviewed earlier, taken by the passing police car, showed the closest buildings, but there was no scale. Now he could see they were at least 250 meters away, almost three football fields. It was very unlikely someone would see him and raise an alarm.

Burns climbed the stairs leading to a balcony on the first floor, slipping across the concrete deck to a French door. After having studied the blueprints of the building, he was sure if his uncle was here, Elson would hold him in the wine cellar on the ground level on the other side of the chalet. First, he had to make sure there was no threat from any guards, or Elson, if that wasn't him that left. He'd need to go room to room, clearing the chalet, before moving down to ground level, and the wine cellar.

Setting the bag down, he removed a wand and ran it around the perimeter of the door, searching for a current, indicating an alarm. A small red light on the handle blinked rapidly when it passed over the upper right edge of the door. *Alarm.*

Using the wand as a guide, he attached a glasscutter with a suction cup, close to the magnetic alarm latch. The cup would prevent the cut glass from crashing to the floor. After he removed a six-inch circle of glass, Burns reached through the hole and slid a thin magnet between the wired magnet on the door frame and the one attached to the door. This maintained a closed circuit, rendering the alarm inoperable.

It took him twenty seconds with a lock pick to open the door. He pushed the boot bag inside with his foot, easing in behind it. Holding the night-vision binoculars to his eyes with one hand, gripping the Beretta with his other, he began the task of clearing the house.

Starting on the first floor, he moved swiftly through the three bedrooms. Those cleared, he proceeded to the second floor and the kitchen, dining area, and the master bedroom. Empty. He looked at his watch. It had taken five minutes to clear the upper part. It was also 6:50, and he had an appointment with Elson at the pub in Interlaken at 7:30. He sprinted downstairs, taking them two at a time, descending to the ground level.

He checked the sauna, steam bath, and whirlpool rooms. Empty. Now he stood at the door leading to the wine cellar, steeling himself for what lay behind it, or what might not be there. He pressed his ear to the door. No sounds. He turned the handle. *Locked.*

He turned to head back to the first floor and his lock pick, then stopped. *Fuck it.* He spun back, took two long steps, raised his foot and kicked the door near the handle with all his might. It flew open and there, chained to a wall, stretched out on a cot, was his uncle.

FROM THE BACK seat of the police car bringing them to the waiting helicopter, Burns called Knecht and gave him an update. "Thanks for having a physician with the chopper. My uncle was drugged, and he is unconscious. The doctor examined him before putting him on board and said he was stable but suffering from fatigue, malnutrition, and dehydration.

"It is good to hear your uncle is alive," Knecht said. "Everything is in place in Interlaken for your meeting."

After disconnecting with Knecht, and well before the car reached the helicopter, Burns called Bar-Nathan. To insure the police officer driving would not understand, he said in Hebrew, "Execute Exodus."

When the chopper settled on the ground in Interlaken fifteen minute later, Burns called Knecht again. "The jet that brought my team to Switzerland is at the airport in Berne. Do I have your okay to use it to get my uncle back to Israel right away?" he asked.

"Of course," Knecht said. "I will speak to helicopter pilot and authorize him to fly your uncle to Berne. I will next call airport to clear jet's departure." Burns hugged his uncle, told him he would see him in Israel in a couple of days, and watched the chopper take off for Berne.

A waiting unmarked police car dropped Burns off two blocks from the pub. He walked to the pastry shop across the street from the pub. The clock in the window showed 7:26, four minutes before the appointed meeting with the Collector. He checked his phone. A text message from Bar-Nathan. *Exodus executed.* Burns smiled. *Game on.*

Inside the pub, Burns saw Knecht's undercover agents. The bartender, waitress, and busman from the night before, were going about their business. The owner, or perhaps the waitress, kept the last booth un-occupied. Burns moved to it quickly and sat as expected, waiting for Elson to arrive, although he knew the man would not be coming.

Earlier, at breakfast, Burns had come up with a plan if his uncle, alive or dead, was in the chalet. He called Bar-Nathan and laid out the operation he code named Exodus. In this case, it would be for the departure of just one Israelite, not a whole nation.

Bar-Nathan and his team had been waiting for Burns' phone call earlier that evening. Hearing the code "execute Exodus," the agents had intercepted Elson driving on the road to Interlaken. He had offered little resistance to his own kidnapping. They gave him an injection to knock him out, drove him to the airport in Berne, and smuggled him on board their jet, fuelled and ready to take off. As soon as Burns' uncle arrived by helicopter and was on board, they departed for Israel leaving Burns behind to continue his charade.

At 7:35, Burns ordered a beer from the waitress. At 8:10, he ordered another. At 8:30 he signalled the waitress for the check. "It seemed the person I'm waiting for is not coming."

When Burns arrived back at his hotel, Knecht was waiting. Grasping Burns by the elbow, he guided him to a set of chairs at the far side of the lobby. "What happened? Why did not Elson come to the pub?"

Burns shrugged, shook his head, and rubbed the back of his neck. "I don't know," he said, sounding frustrated.

"Do you think he see my people and get suspicious?" Knecht asked.

"I don't know. Maybe. But there could be lots of other reasons. Maybe he's still playing a game with me. Who knows?"

"What do you want to do now?" Knecht asked.

"By now, I'm sure he's discovered my uncle isn't at the chalet. He's probably trying to figure out how we found out about his hideout and my uncle, and how much we know about him. There's no doubt he's on the move now. Either he's gone into hiding here in Switzerland, or more likely, he's already out of the country. I'm going to have to go home and begin searching for him all over again." *I hate lying to this man.*

"I understand. You know, if I can be of any help, all you must do is to call."

"I know, Bruno. You've been terrific. I couldn't have asked for any more that you've given."

This sucks.

They stood and shook hands. Burns promised to call Knecht with any breaks in the case. Making Burns feel even worse than he already did about deceiving this fine man, Knecht insisted on having a police car drive him from Interlaken to Berne the next morning for his flight home.

CHAPTER 39
March 10
Monday
Tel Aviv, Israel

BURNS LANDED IN Tel Aviv the afternoon following the rescue of his uncle and the abduction of the Collector from Switzerland. At the time, he couldn't have imagined the surprises and revelations that would soon follow.

The first thing he did when he got off the plane was to call the hospital and ask for an update on his uncle's condition. All they would tell him was a standard, "He's resting comfortably," and his room number. When he asked to be connected to the room, he was told doctor's orders were no phone calls until the next day. Ignoring all the voice mail and text messages from Ben-Ami, Hall in the United States, and Knecht in Switzerland, Burns rushed to see his uncle at the Hadassah Hospital on the outskirts of Jerusalem.

He arrived at the hospital an hour after landing and bullied his way through security, walking into his uncle's room on the third floor. The first thing he saw was his Aunt Miriam sitting in a chair next to the bed, holding his uncle's hand. His uncle's eyes were closed, the rhythmic rise and fall of the bed covers indicating he was asleep. Standing next to his aunt's chair was Simon Bloom.

His aunt became aware of him standing in the doorway. She

leaped to her feet and hugged him tightly. "Thank you, thank you," she said, looking up at him. "You said you would get him back safely and you did." She held his head in her hands, smothering his cheeks with kisses, before returning to her chair and grasping his uncle's hand again.

"Has he said anything?" Burns asked Bloom, glancing at his uncle.

"No. I was about to ask you the same question. Has he told you anything about who was behind his kidnapping? Why they did it? What they wanted?"

"He didn't, but I know some of it. A man named Elson, he's also called the Collector, was hired to steal, or collect, if you will, Uncle Seth's invention. Elson was hired by a man named Johnson in the United States. Arizona. This guy, Johnson, was trying to develop the same algae solution for low cost fuel as Uncle Seth. Somehow, Johnson found out Uncle Seth was about to succeed."

Burns let out a sigh of frustration. "There are a lot of unanswered questions. How did Johnson know Uncle Seth was close to success? What's the connection between Johnson and Elson? Is there anyone else involved? How did Johnson and Elson always seem to be one step ahead of me, like they knew what I was planning to do?"

Burns heard a sound and turned toward the bed. His uncle's body squirmed and he muttered something unintelligible. It sounded like he was dreaming, or maybe having a nightmare.

Turning back to Bloom, Burns said," Before I forget, thanks for being there for my aunt and relaying the information about my progress. You took a big load off of me."

Bloom smiled. "Happy to do it. So, what's next?"

"After I leave here, I'm headed back to Tel Aviv. I've got Elson, and I'll wring every bit of information out of him. The F.B.I. has Johnson in custody in Arizona. They have so much evidence against him for money-laundering and other crimes, it's only a matter of time before he starts talking, looking for leniency. He'll begin to fill in some of the blanks. I expect we'll get a break on this very soon."

"That sounds great. Look, now that you're back, I have to get back to the university. Spending time with your aunt, I've neglected a lot of my work."

Burns again thanked Bloom for all his help and walked him to the door. After Bloom left, he pulled up a chair next to his aunt and sat with her for an hour before saying goodbye. He was going to Tel Aviv, he told her, but would be back as soon as he could.

WHEN HE GOT to Mossad Headquarters, the receptionist said Ben-Ami had left orders for him to come to his office immediately upon arrival. Burns knocked on Ben-Ami's closed door and walked in without being invited.

"Where have you been?" Ben-Ami growled. "I've been trying to reach you."

"At the hospital with my uncle and aunt."

"Anyone else there?" Ben-Ami said, leaning back in his chair.

"Just Simon Bloom. I filled him in on what we had to date. He left to go back to the university. He said he's been neglecting his work while staying close to my aunt. Why?"

"While you were in Switzerland yesterday, and not checking your messages or emails, I received a very interesting phone call from your friend, F.B.I. Agent Hall."

"Interesting, meaning what?"

"Interesting meaning Johnson talked, and gave Hall everything. Including who told him how close your uncle was to the breakthrough, the person responsible for putting the whole plot in motion," Ben-Ami said. He sat silently, hands folded on his desk, waiting for Burns to speak.

"Gideon, don't sit there like a smug fucking asshole. Who was it?"

"Bloom."

"Bloom? What do you mean Bloom?"

"He's the man. He's the one who called Johnson and told him how close your uncle was. He's the one that told Johnson to get someone to get the formula. He's the one who told Johnson to kill your uncle after they got the formula. The whole time he made believe he needed the information on our progress to comfort your aunt. He's been telling Johnson everything we've been doing to track down your uncle. That's how the person he knew as the Collector was able to stay one step ahead of us."

Burns banged his fist on the arm of the chair and pushed himself out of the seat. "That prick. And I let him just walk out of my uncle's hospital room, thanking him for all he's done. I'm going to the university. I'm gonna kill him."

He wheeled around and rushed toward the door when Ben-Ami yelled, "Hold it. He's not at the university. We had Shin Bet put a tail on him as soon as I got the information from Hall, to see if anyone else was involved. I don't know what you said to him at the hospital, but it spooked him. After he left, he headed straight to Ben Gurion Airport. Shin Bet picked him up, trying to board a plane for South Africa."

"Where is he now?" Burns asked.

"Here. Downstairs in an interrogation room. I'll let you speak with him but only if you promise not to hurt him. I'm being serious here. You do not lay a finger on him. Are we clear?"

Burns felt blood pounding in his ears, his heart beating rapidly. He knew he had to calm down, or Ben-Ami wouldn't let him near Bloom. He would promise Ben-Ami he'd behave, but when he got in the room with Bloom, he'd kill him with his bare hands.

"Okay. I'll be good," Burns said.

"I don't believe you. Look at you. Your face is red, you're clenching your fists." Ben-Ami leaned to the side and removed a stun wand from a desk drawer. "I'm coming into the room with you. I'm going to stand behind you, and this will be in your back at all times. There will be three other agents in the room armed with tasers. I'm not kidding. If you make one move to harm Bloom, we'll stop you. This man is going to be tried, and there will not be one mark on his body. Are we clear?"

Burns held up his palms. "Okay, okay. I'll behave."

Ben-Ami picked up his phone and punched in some numbers. "We're coming down now," he said.

STEPPING OFF THE elevator on the third floor, they moved down the corridor, stopping at a heavy wooden door. Before entering, Ben-Ami tapped the stun wand gently against the small of Burns' back. "Behave."

In the center of the room sat a six foot metal table. Simon Bloom was slumped forward in a chair bolted to the floor, his wrists manacled to a chain looped through a U-shaped bar welded to the table top. Stationed on either side of Bloom were two men with stun guns held at their side. A third agent stood just inside the door, similarly equipped.

When the door snapped shut, Burns surveyed the room, his senses heightened. He took in the location of the agents and watched Bloom's eyes track him as he moved to the chair across the table and sat. Burns felt the light warning brush of the stun wand in the middle of his back as Ben-Ami took a position behind him.

"Wanna tell me why?" Burns asked.

Bloom shrugged and said nothing.

"Simon, listen to me very carefully," Burns said, speaking in a soft, measured tone. "I had to promise not to lay a hand on you. Gideon and the men in this room have stun guns. They're not for you. They're for me. They'll use them on me if I make a move toward you. You will notice I'm not handcuffed. That was a mistake on their part. Trust me. I could get across the table and kill you before they could react. And death would come with a lot of pain and not quickly. Just so you know, I'm about one heartbeat from doing it, so when I ask you a question, you'd be smart to answer. Do you understand me?"

Blooms eyes were wide with fear. He nodded.

"Once again. Wanna tell me why?"

"Money and jealousy."

"Explain."

Bloom tilted his head and shrugged. "The money part is easy. The discovery is worth billions, and auctioning it off would make me rich beyond my wildest dreams. I told you in Ben-Ami's office after your uncle was kidnapped, there are countries and businesses that would pay a king's ransom for the formula, either to use it for themselves, or to stop it from ever being used.

"Think about it. If you were a country like China, importing huge amounts of oil to fuel your manufacturing, having your own unlimited cheap supply of oil would give you a fantastic competitive advantage. And, if you were one of the Gulf States, Saudi Arabia or the UAE, you'd want to stop it from ever being used and destroying your oil-based economy. How much do you think owning the formula would be worth?"

"But you told me in Ben-Ami's office both of you would own the patent. You'd be rich from that."

"I lied. I was never going to have my name on the formula. It was you uncle's discovery."

Burns was doing everything in his power not to take his chances against the stun guns and leap across the table.

"Explain the jealousy," Burns said.

"Are you that naive?" Bloom said, shaking his head. "I'm the chairman of the department. Your uncle works for me. And he's smarter than I am. He'd be the one getting all the accolades, maybe even replace me as chairman."

"You couldn't just steal the formula, sell it, and think my uncle would let you get away with it. How did you think you could pull that off?"

Bloom remained silent.

"Well?"

Bloom dropped his head, his chin on his chest.

Burns slapped his palm on the table. *Crack*. "Answer me, you son-of-a -bitch."

Bloom's head jerked upright, tears in his eyes. "I told Johnson to kill your uncle after he got the formula. I'm sorry," Bloom said, his voice breaking in a small sob.

The man just admitted to ordering his uncle's death. Every lesson, every instinctive reaction drilled into him as a *kidon*, screamed at him to leap across the table and kill him. But he didn't. He just stared at the man for a few seconds, shook his head, rose from his chair, and left the room.

WEEKS LATER, DUE to the sensitive nature of the discovery and national security implications for Israel, the Central District Court ruled Bloom's case "highly classified, top secret." A special panel of jurors appointed by the Prime Minister tried him in a secret session behind closed doors, the transcripts immediately deposited in the court's vault. They found Bloom guilty of conspiracy to murder Shernicoff, kidnapping, and attempting to steal State secrets. They sentenced him to thirty years in prison. Bloom argued that in reality, based on his age, that was a life sentence. The judge agreed with him but did not change the ruling.

Before the trial, they pressured Bloom to write a letter of resignation to the president of the university, stating he was leaving his position to pursue other opportunities. A personal phone call from the Prime Minister to the president of the university followed, requesting that, as a matter of highest State security, the university not make any additional inquiries into the resignation.

A similar phone call followed a day later by Ben-Ami, who made the same request. Ben-Ami's call was phrased in a way to give the impression Bloom was engaged in clandestine activities for the Mossad.

The same jurors impaneled for Bloom tried Elson, also known

as the Collector. Elson argued that, while he was indeed an Israeli citizen, he was a longtime resident of the United States and requested to be tried in that country. The judge refused the request, saying he was an Israeli citizen and had not given up his citizenship when he moved to the United States. They found him guilty of the same crimes as Bloom. The judge sentenced him to life in prison.

They sent both men to Unit 15 at Ayalon, considered to be Israel's supermax prison. Each man was "disappeared," stripped of his name and identity, and given a pseudonym. They were incarcerated in suicide-proof cells, video-monitored round-the-clock, and held in complete and absolute isolation from the outside world.

CHAPTER 40
Two Months Later
May 15
San Salvador

BURNS WAS BACK in San Salvador to finish what he hadn't done last February. He'd lost Adwar then. It wouldn't happen again. Nothing was going to stop him from executing him this time.

The *sayan*, Sanchez, had made hotel reservations for Adwar's return to San Salvador on May 15th, and Gideon sent Burns back with a team of four people. Zvi Levi and Shlomo Bar-Nathan were in San Salvador and would also assist.

The team landed on May 10, five days before Adwar's scheduled return. They rented three cars from the same *sayan* in the car rental business and went to a safe house Levi had borrowed from a *sayan*, who would be out of the country for four months.

Gideon told Burns before he left, "Put everything that happened with your uncle out of your mind. We want to know who the arms supplier is that Adwar's meeting with at the Guatemalan Embassy. Get the information if possible, but your orders are clear. Your primary objective... *execute him.*"

For the five days before Adwar's arrival, the team re-traced the same route Adwar had taken to the embassy in February, as well as the streets surrounding the hotel and the embassy, re-familiarizing themselves with the area.

Adwar arrived on May 15 as scheduled, and they followed him for two days. His routine remained the same as in February. He would leave the hotel between 9:30 and 10:00 a.m., walk to the Guatemala Embassy, stay until 8:00 at night, and walk back to the hotel.

Burns decided the date for the execution. It would be that night, May 18th.

THAT AFTERNOON BURNS and Zvi Levi sat alone in the living room of the safe house, waiting for the rest of the team to return from a lunch break so they could go over the plans, once again, for the mission. The clock on the piano chimed 4:00 p.m. when the team gathered.

Burns prepared to take the team through the plan for the sixth time that day. He'd laid out the basic plan earlier in the day. "This has to be done in a way that no one can point a finger back at Israel. Being in El Salvador should make it easy. The country has a bad reputation with regard to crime, with one of the highest homicide rates in the world. We're going to make the execution look like a random act of street crime, like a robbery gone wrong. They'll blame the gangs for it."

Burns studied the team. He sensed they felt they were ready and didn't want to go through another rehearsal. "Look, I know you think you're ready, but let's do it one more time. Practice makes perfect," he told them. "We go over it and over it, until we just do it, we don't even think about it."

Turning to Yinon, one of the surveillance specialists, "Go," Burns said.

"I'll be in a parked car across from the embassy, and radio Zvi when Adwar leaves the embassy."

Shai, the second surveillance specialists said, "I'll be parked on the block where Adwar makes the turn to Avenue Magnolias toward the hotel. I'll radio Zvi when he does."

Levi said, "I'll signal you so you can time your move onto Avenue Magnolias. If Adwar looks in your direction, it will seem like you just turned onto the street, that you're not someone lurking on the sidewalk waiting for him.

THE TIME WAS now 10:30. There had been a chilly drizzle for most of the day, and Burns was dressed in a dark blue, plastic poncho. He leaned against the driver's door of Levis car, parked at the curb, three feet from the corner where he would start his walk. Levi looked up at Burns through the open window. "How are you doing?" he asked.

Burns knew the question was more of a way to pass the time than of any real concern.

How am I doing? Like I always do on a mission. My stomach feels like an acid factory and my bladder might let loose any minute.

Burns leaned down and looked at Levi through the open window, forced a smile, and whispered, "I'm fine. No sweat."

"Clink, clink."

A surge of adrenalin coursed through Burns' body, the hairs on his neck tingled. He spun toward the direction of the noise, instinctively reaching for his weapon. A cat sauntered between trash bags piled at the curb, and the bottle it knocked over rolled into the gutter.

He could hear the pounding of his own heartbeat roaring in his ears, his breathing rapid. The waiting always worked on his nerves. He tried to relax, taking deep breaths, knowing the longer the delay, the better the chance something could go wrong.

Calm down. You're too tense.

Earlier, Levi had received a call on the secure radio frequency from Yinon, waiting outside the embassy. Burns listened in. "Adwar's routine changed. He left with two people and walked to a restaurant. I'll let you know when they leave."

He looked at his watch again. 10:45. *This is taking too long,* he thought, as he paced between the car and the corner.

Five minutes later, Levi whispered out the driver's side window, "We're on. I just heard from Yinon. Adwar left the embassy. Be ready to move in about ten minutes. Yinon said he's carrying a briefcase. He's never carried one before. It may be important."

Burns was a professional, and as he was trained, he'd do things by the book.

BURNS SLIPPED HIS hand under the poncho to the small of his back, grasped the butt of his .22-caliber, high-powered Beretta, and pulled it free from its holster. Easing the weapon through the side of the poncho, he thumbed the magazine eject button and caught the clip in his free hand. Checking that it was fully loaded, he slammed the magazine back in. He then pulled the weapon's slide back and heard a round rack into the chamber.

Satisfied, he pulled out the specially designed silencer for the Beretta, screwed it to the barrel, then released the safety. He slid the silenced weapon back under the poncho where it would remain in his right hand until ready to use. He moved to the corner of the street and waited.

Stay calm. Deep breaths.

Waiting at the corner, the chill drizzle washed his face, and he felt a small shiver. *Was it the rain or what he was about to do that caused it?* His thoughts should be laser focused on what lay ahead. Instead, they drifted back to that day years before when Adwar masterminded the suicide bombing that killed his wife and child. He could still picture them that morning, before he left for his training mission.

This is for you. Tonight you get justice.

Funny how the mind works. He thought of his dead family, of

getting justice, and no longer heard the sound of his own heartbeat roaring in his ears. He felt his heart rate lower to normal, his breathing slow, and a sense of calm spreading through him.

"Burns, go," Levi said as he pulled away from the curb. He would meet him after, one block away.

Burns began the march which would end with Adwar's death. Moving with hunched shoulders against the chilly drizzle, he appeared like a man seeking shelter from the rain, heading toward the protection of the hotel lobby. Keeping his head tilted slightly down, his eyes never left the figure of Adwar walking toward the hotel from the opposite direction.

Walk at the pace you practiced. Keep the timing. Don't rush it.

He methodically closed the distance to the hotel entrance, knowing he would get there twenty paces ahead of Adwar. When he reached the hotel entrance, instead of turning into it, he moved quickly past, right at Adwar.

Now I've got you, you bastard. You're a dead man.

Burns raised his head for the first time and glared at Adwar, his eyes catching an umbrella in Adwar's right hand and a large leather attaché in his left.

Good. Even if he has a weapon, he won't be able to get to it fast.

Pulling the Beretta through the side opening of the plastic poncho, Burns raised the silenced weapon and pointed it at Adwar's face. The distance between them now could not be more than ten paces. He focused on Adwar's face, his wide open eyes, mouth agape, staring at the silenced pistol pointing at him. It was as if his mind was unable to process the events taking place before his eyes.

Burns picked up his tempo until he was not more than three paces from Adwar. Pointing the weapon directly at Adwar's left eye, he said "For Tamara and Saul," and pulled the trigger quickly three times. All three shots hit Adwar's face. One entered the forehead above the left eye, one entered the left eye, and one entered the left nasal cavity.

The bullet in the left eye was the kill shot. After passing through the eye socket, the .22 caliber round did not have enough power to exit the back of the skull. Instead, it ricocheted around inside, severely shredding the brain. Adwar was dead before his body fell halfway to the pavement.

Training kicking in, he dropped to a knee. Rolling the body on its side, he placed the silencer to the nape of Adwar's neck where the brain stem enters the skull, pulled the trigger, and severed the spinal cord.

He rolled the body on its back, pushed up the left sleeve of the suit jacket, and removed Adwar's watch. Reaching to the inside jacket pocket, he removed the terrorist's wallet and passport, then pulled a thick wad of U.S. dollars and Salvadorian colons from the pants pockets. He stuffed everything he took off the body into the briefcase that had fallen to the sidewalk.

Burns rose and walked at a brisk pace, no need to run, toward the far corner where Levi waited, and he slipped into the passenger seat. Levi pulled away from the curb slowly, rounding the corner before jamming his foot on the accelerator and speeding away from the scene. When the body was found, it would look like a street gang robbery and murder, adding another grim statistic to the country with the highest homicide rates in the world.

Eric leaned back in the seat, head slumped against the backrest, eyes closed. A feeling of elation swept through him. *Rest in peace, my loved ones.*

EPILOUGE
Ten Months Later
New York City

THE PRIME MINISTER had assembled a closed door session of select advisors. After twenty-five minutes of raucous debate, he made his decision. No official delegate would attend the meeting. The government needed plausible deniability if things did not go the way they hoped. He would send Burns and Shernicoff as surrogates to represent the government's position.

Ben-Ami delivered the news to Burns. "In two days, a secret meeting will take place in New York at the United Nations. The Prime Minister selected you and your uncle as Israel's representatives."

"Me? Why me? I'm not a diplomat."

"You think we don't know that? That's why he chose you. This meeting is not for a diplomat. They nuance things. We need someone who won't mince words, someone who will make them believe we mean what you say."

"And what exactly am I going to say?"

Ben-Ami held up a palm. "In a minute. First, I need you to tell me you'll go."

"Please, Gideon. This isn't me. There has to be someone else."

"Maybe. But no one else has had as much of a personal stake

in this as you and your uncle. Believe me, you're definitely the right messengers. "

"Why does my uncle need go?"

"To answer any technical issues raised."

"Technical issues? Exactly what do you want them to agree to?"

When Ben-Ami told him what the council decided, Burns' right eyebrow shot up. "You're kidding, right? You don't really think they'll go for it? Do you?"

"That's why we're sending you. Convince them."

JUST AFTER NOON, Burns and his uncle met newly promoted Special Agent Robert Hall for lunch at the Carnegie Delicatessen on Seventh Avenue, near Fifty-fifth Street, in Manhattan. Burns had not seen Hall since he had left Arizona and flew to Switzerland when he rescued his uncle.

Burns introduced his uncle to Hall who had asked Burns to set up a meeting with his uncle when he found out they were coming to New York.

"It's nice to finally meet you, Dr. Shernicoff. This may not come out the way I mean it, but if it wasn't for you being kidnapped and allegedly taken to Mexico, a lot of bad guys on this side of the Atlantic might not have been caught."

Shernicoff gave Hall a mock salute. With a grin and a twinkle in his eye, he said, "Glad to be of service. If you ever need more help, let me know. I'll see if I can arrange to be kidnapped again."

Burns and Hall smiled.

"Seriously," Shernicoff said. "I wanted to meet you, to thank you personally. From what my nephew says, if it wasn't for your pressure on Johnson, we never would have found out who was behind this."

"I'm glad I could help." Turning to Burns, Hall said, "What happened with Bloom and the Collector?"

"Bloom was tried and sentenced to thirty years," Burns said.

"And the Collector?"

"He got away. We have a team of agents working to track him down, but so far nothing. You know our reputation. We'll get him eventually."

Burns didn't want to lie to Hall. But, if Bruno Knecht ever found out the true facts of what happened in Switzerland and that the Collector was in an Israeli prison, it was quite possible the Israeli-Swiss relationship, as well their personal friendship, would be destroyed. He needed Bruno Knecht to believe the Collector was still at large.

The Mossad also wanted the criminal world to believe the Collector was still open for business. It took some time, but Elson finally gave them his secret email address and the names of the two people who knew it. The Mossad had monitored them ever since and passed the information on to appropriate law enforcement, thwarting future contracts requested by Elson's unsuspecting clients.

"So give me an update, Robert. What's been happening?" Burns asked, changing the subject.

"Johnson rolled on everyone. He pled guilty to money laundering, tax evasion, and other charges. He got fifteen years at the federal prison in Allenwood, Pennsylvania. Gomez, the stock broker from Chicago, got ten years for stock fraud and money laundering. He's doing time in Marion, Illinois."

"What about Moreno?" Burns asked.

Hall paused, taking a bite of a half sour pickle, when the waiter came to take their order. When he left, Hall continued. "Moreno had so many charges against him, he knew he couldn't beat them. El Negociator didn't even try to negotiate. He pled guilty. He's doing one hundred years at the federal supermax prison in Colorado. He spends twenty-three hours a day locked in his cell and one hour a day of solitary outdoor recreation."

"Couldn't happen to a nicer guy," Burns quipped.

"Yeah, well it all worked out for me, too. Thanks to everything that happened, the Bureau promoted me. I'm now Special Agent in

Charge of all financial crimes for the Southern District of New York. Big job, big promotion."

Burns reached across the table and patted Hall's arm. "Congratulations."

"Thanks. But I'm not quite done. I've got one more for you. About your friend Ortega."

Burns' expression soured, his brows drew together.

"Relax," Hall said, holding up his palm. "It's good. You'll like it. After you left for Switzerland, I called Director McGuire. I gave him the complete story, how Ortega handled our meeting, what he said, his attitude, everything. Then I pointed out the D.E.A. owed you the $10 million bounty. I told him you wanted the check payable to the State of Israel, and you wanted him to make Ortega personally deliver it to the Israeli ambassador in Washington, because he'd been such a pompous ass."

Burns tilted his head. "What did McGuire say?"

"First, it must have taken him a minute to stop laughing. I mean, I've known him for a lot of years, and I've never heard the man completely lose it like that. After he stopped laughing, he told me he'd order Ortega to deliver the check as requested."

"Good," Burns replied.

"It gets better. McGuire was so pissed off at the way Ortega handled everything, he promoted him."

Burns recoiled in his chair. "What? He promoted him. But you just said—"

Again, Hall held up his palm. "Stop. It's not what you think. McGuire promoted him to lead all D.E.A. activities in the Mid-East. He's now stationed in the garden spot of the Mid-East, Kabul, Afghanistan."

Burns laughed so loud, heads turned to look at them.

At that moment, the waiter arrived with their food. Corned beef sandwiches on rye bread, with side orders of potato salad and fried onion rings. Burns ate with gusto, savoring everything Hall told him.

After lunch, the men parted outside the deli. The Mossad and F.B.I. agents gave each other a brief hug and promised to keep in touch.

BURNS AND SHERNICOFF walked a block and a half to Sixth Avenue and Fifty-fifth Street, back to the scene of the crime. At least that's how Burns' uncle told him he chose to think of the New York City Hilton Hotel.

It was there, one year ago, at the same Conference on Renewable Energy Development, his uncle and Simon Bloom had met Elliot Johnson. Overhearing Shernicoff tell Bloom how close he was to making the breakthrough on renewable energy, Johnson initiated the events leading to the destruction of his uncle's lab and his kidnapping. In its wake, relationships were broken or damaged, and people were dead or in prison.

"Listen to him," Shernicoff said to Burns, tilting his head toward the speaker on the dais. The speaker was droning on about the need to find low cost alternatives to oil.

Shernicoff shook his head. "He makes it sound so easy. It took me seven years and a lot of luck to make everything come together. And, what no one ever gives thought to is the ramifications of that kind of discovery... the economic and social upheavals that will occur."

"You're right, but that's a fight for others to work out," Burns said. "Today we have our own upheaval to address."

They were meeting with the oil ministers of Saudi Arabia, Russia, China, Iran, Venezuela, and Exxon/Mobil representing the American Fuel and Petrochemical Manufacturers, the AFPM.

With the exception of AFPM, the other attendees had contacted the Collector, prepared to bid for his uncle's discovery and perhaps even his uncle. According to the Collector, none had reservation with bidding starting at twenty-five million U.S. dollars. This day, the negotiations would not be for money. The stakes were much higher.

Three weeks ago, using the discs sent to him for safekeeping, his uncle replicated his discovery and produced six, one-gallon samples. The Israeli ambassador to the United Nations hand delivered them to the U.N. ambassadors of the five countries and one to a representative of the AFPM.

The Ambassador provided a report detailing what their scientists would find when they examined the samples. Proof positive of a low cost renewable energy as an alternative to oil pumped from the ground. He also submitted a spreadsheet analysis clearly supporting the facts that the oil could be produced at well under four dollars per barrel.

The Israeli ambassador admonished each recipient that testing must take place within eight days or the samples would become worthless. When asked why, the Ambassador could not answer; he said he was repeating what he had been told.

What the Ambassador did not know is that Shernicoff had triggered the on/off switch, the one he called the suicide switch, with each sample. This would destroy the samples eight days after receipt, preventing other scientists from trying to backward engineer them and discovering the process he'd invented.

The Israeli ambassador proposed a meeting of all parties to take place at the United Nations in three weeks, after their respective people confirmed the accuracy of the claims made. All parties responded within ten days. They would attend. The meeting was set for this afternoon.

BURNS AND SHERNICOFF left the hotel and hailed a cab on Sixth Avenue. The taxi took them across town on Fifty-fourth Street to Second Avenue, weaving through heavy traffic and around double parked cars. Going south on Second, it took the cab fifteen minutes in stop and go traffic to move fourteen blocks to Forty-second Street. Burns was in a foul mood when they finally arrived at the entrance to the United Nations on First Avenue and Forty-sixth Street, thirty-five minutes after getting in the cab.

The Israeli ambassador met them at the security desk and ushered them to Conference Room Ten, reserved for the meeting. The room had a large elliptical table seating thirty-four people. However, for today's meeting, they would use the rectangular secretariat table in the center of the room, with seating for ten.

Burns sat at one end of the table, his uncle at the other end. This would force the other participants to sit across from each other, forcing them to have to swivel their heads to look at either Burns or his uncle. Mossad psychiatrists believed this seating arrangement provided Burns and his uncle a physiological advantage. Burns didn't know if it would... and he didn't care. He had one objective at the meeting. Either he would accomplish it... or he wouldn't.

At precisely three o'clock, the door opened, and the invitees entered. The Israeli Ambassador rose from his chair to greet them. The Ambassador turned and introduced Burns and Shernicoff. As preplanned, both of them remained seated. By not rising Burns set the tone for the meeting. He was the power in the room, the one in charge. After the invitees sat, as instructed by his government, the Israeli ambassador excused himself and left the room.

Burns addressed the attendees. As agreed, the chosen language for the meeting was English. "Thank you for coming. I'll make this as brief as possible. I take it each of your respective scientists examined the samples?"

Each man nodded.

"Since you're here, I'll presume it's safe to conclude the samples lived up to our claims."

The representatives from Exxon and Venezuela nodded. The others sat still and stone faced.

"Let me lay out a few statements of fact. First, any country in the world that wishes to produce oil for themselves can use our technology to do it. That means, with the exception of China, each of your countries, which combined produce the majority of the world's oil, will lose your monopoly. A country as small as Malta or as large as you, China, can use the technology."

Burns paused, letting what he had said sink in.

"Anyone here doubt that?"

The room was silent.

Burns continued. "Second, we gave you the figures. I'm sure they were reviewed carefully. Anyone not convinced by our figures that the oil can be produced for less than four U.S. dollars per barrel, raise your hand?"

There was some shifting in the chairs, but not one hand rose.

"This leads me to point number three and the most important to all of you. If Israel makes our discovery available to the world, again with the exception of China, it will devastate each of you economically."

Burns saw the attendees' bodies tense and lean in his direction, as if to catch every word. *Good. Now they're paying attention.*

Burns cocked his head and steepled his fingers. Looking directly at the respective representatives, he said "Russia and Iran, if you think sanctions caused your economies to tank, you haven't seen anything. This will be worse by at least a magnitude of ten."

Swiveling his gaze, Burns continued. "Saudi Arabia, you and the rest of the Gulf oil producing countries will go back to the third world countries you were before oil fueled your economies. Besides oil, you have only one other natural resource. Who are you going to sell sand to?"

The representative of Saudi Arabia slammed his palm on the table. "Enough!" he shouted, glowering at Burns. "I didn't come here to be insulted. Tell me why I'm here and what you want."

Burns pushed himself slowly from his chair, placed his palms on the table, leaned forward, and glowered at the Saudi Ambassador. "Shut. Your. Mouth," he snarled. He remained standing until the Saudi broke eye contact and looked down at the table.

Burns took a calming breath and sat. He leaned back in his chair. Not one of the other attendees came to the defense of the

Saudi Ambassador or said a word about his tone of voice. But, a few complexions blanched, and sweat beads appeared on some foreheads.

Burns addressed the representative from China. "China, you on the other hand, would love to get your hands on the discovery. No need to ever import oil again. You'd have a never ending supply of your own to fuel your economy. Think about how much you could reduce your manufacturing costs. Add your low cost of labor, and you'd rule the export markets."

The representative from Iran slowly raised his hand.

"Yes?" Burns said.

"If I may, sir," the Iranian said, "your points have been made, and I believe we all understand them. Why are we here, and what is it you want?"

Burns' eyes flicked from ambassador to ambassador. "Do you all agree with him? Do you *really* understand what we can do to your economies if we release the formula?"

Around the table heads nodded.

"Okay. As long as you all understand that, I'll tell you what we want."

Burns looked at the representative from China. "Would your government be happy to buy oil at a guaranteed constant price of 25 U.S. dollars per barrel?"

"Of course but how can you—"

Burns held up his hand. "Hold on."

Burns addressed the Iranian and Saudi representatives. "Hezbollah is the client of Iran and Hamas is the client of Saudi Arabia. You fund them. That will stop immediately."

The Iranian and Saudi representatives shouted at the same time. "That's not true That's—"

"Shut your mouths!" Burns screamed. "This is not the time or place for your bullshit. There are no audiences for you to play to. You both know what I said is true."

Both representatives' mouths twisted in snarls, their hands clenched, seething. To their credit, they did not say another word.

"For years, you've both used Israel as the boogeyman, whipping up anti-Zionist fever. Telling your own people, as well as your clients, all the trouble in the Middle East is Israel's fault. You tell them, 'Destroy Israel and all your problems will be over.' Well beginning today, that stops. You will tell each of your clients they are to leave Israel in peace, never to attempt to harm Israel again.

"And you," Burns said, pointing to the Russian. "You will withdraw your support for the Assad regime in Syria. And all three of you will immediately commit ground troops and an air campaign to wiping out ISIS in Syria and Iraqi."

"Are you finished?" the Russian representative asked.

"No, but if you have something to say, please, go ahead," Burns replied.

His voice seething, he gestured to the others around the table. "Does your puny little country think you can blackmail Russia and these other countries?"

Burns smirked. "Actually, we do," he said to the Russian. "Because when you report back to your leaders, they'll think long and hard about it. Will it be worth living with the economic disaster you'll face if they don't do what we ask? We'll make our discovery available to every country you export oil to. More than sixty percent of your country's revenue comes from oil, revenue we are prepared to wipe out with our low cost oil. Think Mr. Putin can still maintain control of the country if that happens?"

Burns paused for effect before addressing the Iranian and Saudi. "How long do you think you'll be able to hold down your people when we do the same to you?"

He formed his finger and thumb into a mock gun and pretended to shoot each in the head.

"I didn't forget the Venezuelans. Yours is a different kind of blackmail. You're being asked to continue selling your oil at a fair price and convince your Latin American counterparts to do the same.

China and the rest of the world get it for a guaranteed twenty-five U.S. dollars a barrel.

Burns paused. He was about to deliver the main ultimatum, the reason his government called the meeting in the first place.

"We know Exxon/Mobil can't speak for the American government. However, you represent the American Fuel and Petrochemical Manufacturers. You're a powerful lobby, and your industry is a significant portion of the U.S. economy. It will be your job to convince the United States government of this next demand, which is, bluntly, Israel's main objective.

"If the Russians, Iranians, and Gulf States don't do as we ask and eliminate the terrorist threats to Israel, we expect the U.S. government and the Chinese government to take military action against those terrorists... and Russia, Iran, and the Gulf States if they interfere."

Expressions of shock appeared on everyone's faces. For the first time, the representative from Exxon raised his hand. "I want to make sure I'm perfectly clear on this. If Russia, Iran, and the Gulf States don't eliminate the terrorism they sponsor against Israel, you expect my government and the Chinese to do it, even if it means war with Russia and the others? Do I understand you correctly?"

"Yup, that about sums it up. But put our demand in this context. In Israel, we have a saying, 'never again.' And we've grown weary of seeing Israeli blood spilled in senseless wars and terrorist attacks. So now we're willing to make the world pay a price for standing by, as these irrational acts of hatred against Israel and threats to wipe us off the face of the earth continue.

"If what we ask isn't done, we'll make the formula available to the world. This will, without doubt, destroy your economies and also plunge the entire world into a long, deep depression. So think about what's in your self-interest as you bring these demands back to your respective governments."

Burns stood and motioned his uncle to follow him as he walked from the room. They didn't speak until they were outside on First Avenue, walking away from the United Nations Building.

Standing on a corner, waiting for the light to change to cross the street, Shernicoff said, "Do you think they'll do what we asked?"

Burns paused a heartbeat before answering. "I hope so. I'd love to lose my job."

www.ingramcontent.com/pod-product-compliance
Lightning Source LLC
Chambersburg PA
CBHW030019180626
46810CB00001B/119